NEARER HOME

Also by Joy Castro

Hell or High Water

Island of Bones: Essays

The Truth Book: A Memoir

NEARER HOME

Joy Castro

Thomas Dunne Books
St. Martin's Press
New York

THOMAS DUNNE BOOKS.
An imprint of St. Martin's Press.

NEARER HOME. Copyright © 2013 by Joy Castro. All rights reserved. Printed in the United States of America. For information, address St. Martin's Press, 175 Fifth Avenue, New York, N.Y. 10010.

www.thomasdunnebooks.com
www.stmartins.com

Library of Congress Cataloging-in-Publication Data

Castro, Joy.
   Nearer home : a Nola Cespedes Mystery / Joy Castro.
      p. cm.
   ISBN 978-1-250-00458-1 (hardcover)
   ISBN 978-1-4668-3706-5 (e-book)
   1. Women journalists—Fiction.   2. New Orleans (La.)—Fiction.   I. Title.
   PS3603.A888N43 2013
   813'.6—dc23

                                                                    2013009120

St. Martin's Press books may be purchased for educational, business, or promotional use. For information on bulk purchases, please contact Macmillan Corporate and Premium Sales Department at 1-800-221-7945 extension 5442 or write specialmarkets @macmillan.com.

First Edition: July 2013

10 9 8 7 6 5 4 3 2 1

For James,
both halves of many a thing

They cannot scare me with their empty spaces
Between stars—on stars where no human race is.
I have it in me so much nearer home
To scare myself with my own desert places.

—Robert Frost, "Desert Places"

Thursday

Prologue

An act of will: to sit utterly still on the park bench. Waiting. Gazing at the lake in the gray air of dawn. Listening to each small sound: the snap of a twig, a black duck flapping its wings on the water. Few cars droned past on the streets at this hour, and those streets were far away.

An act of discipline, of concentration: to sit motionless, rehearsing each move in the mind. The rapid pursuit, coming up behind the woman as she ran, unaware, and the quick and vicious takedown. Dragging her underneath the cypress tree's low-hanging limbs. The spinning head snap that would end it all. Watching as the flush of struggle faded from her skin. Laying decoys for the professionals who'd arrive too late.

Swift footsteps came pounding around the bend, their rhythm fast, precise, determined.

An act of consummate self-control: to glance once, just once, to see and recognize her face. She was running alone. Right on schedule. Her running shoes smacked the asphalt path, her eyes swept ahead of her like searchlights, and earbuds clogged her ears.

To sit motionless as she passed. To leap up in a sudden burst of speed and pursue, closing in soundlessly on her slim muscled legs, her dark ponytail.

An act of precision: to shoot an arm out around the woman's throat, to wrap a leg around her leg. Then the hard jolt sideways, taking her down, hitting the dirt and pine needles at the side of the path, feeling the warm length of her startled, struggling body. Pushing her head forward, cutting off her blood and air as she flailed and kicked and flung her elbows back and grabbled with weakening fingers—ten seconds, twenty, thirty—until she gave way completely. Then it was easy to drag her to the hidden place at the water's edge where wide green elephant's ears grew in thick profusion and the small cove was shadowed by the low sweeping arms of the cypress. An easy thing to spread her on the dew-damp earth.

She lay limp and warm and breathing, unconscious, while her sweat-wicking purple T-shirt, sports bra, and high-performance running shorts were torn away.

Ducks glided by on the lake. The sun crept higher in the sky. From the golf course across the water, faint voices of greenkeepers began to echo. Rusty gray squirrels chided and clucked from the branches.

And then the woman stirred, reviving, her black thong still clinging to one ankle, her sweat-slicked skin shining in the dim light. Soon she would begin to scream.

A broken neck seemed too impersonal after all they'd experienced together, too clinical and quick. Strangling would be more intimate.

But the woman didn't want to die. She fought back hard with her lean strength, her wide dark eyes bulging and terrified and hard to look into. It took awhile, and when it was done, her face was bloated. A shame. She'd been pretty.

Afterward, draping the rosaries across her pale breasts. Spattering blood over her abdomen and thighs. The iridescent feathers strewn in a black halo around her. The stripped, headless bodies of two grackles flung out onto the lake, where they floated and drifted and began to sink peacefully beneath the water's silvery skin.

It was humid and quiet and not yet quite light when a figure in innocuous navy blue running shorts and a T-shirt jogged away from the lake, crouching once to place something in the grass, crouching again farther away, and finally sprinting between live oaks to a side street.

Birds sang.

An engine purred. A black SUV slid into morning traffic.

New Orleans was waking up.

1

As long as I can be with you, it's a lovely day. Ella Fitzgerald's voice, smooth as poured cream, was lilting in my head when I woke up. It's April. It's soft outside.

Fitzgerald's duets with Louis Armstrong are a favorite of Bento's, and they were playing on his phonograph when, with the key I'd reluctantly accepted, I let myself into his little Creole cottage in Mid-City last night. The love songs of the 1950s, laced with the warm crackle of vinyl.

Bento always grips the black discs delicately in his large brown hands, spinning them, inspecting them, blowing off a speck of dust before settling them down on the silver spoke. Sweet simple duets, a man and a woman singing about autumn leaves, moonlight, dancing cheek to cheek—all the lovely, lulling bullshit Bento actually believes, which is why I'm finding it harder and harder to go there in the evenings, to sit at his wooden table sipping Spanish tempranillo, to watch his hard calves as he stands at the stove, snapping off little sprigs from the herb pots on the sill and dropping them into the paella pan. Dark curls cluster at the nape of his neck. His shoulders are broad, his torso long.

Despite his rugged charms, it's become more and more difficult to dance merengue after dinner, until he slowly steers me
down the hall to his bed, where he does the warm, wordless
things he knows how to do so well. To wake up bleary at two
or three A.M., to tug on my clothes despite his murmured *Stay,
querida*, and drive home through the black streets of the city. To
wake at five-thirty for my run, those damn romantic tunes still
wafting through my mind with their promises of some lazy,
lovely future where men love women and women love them back.
Simple, golden, natural. A future that Bento's trying to conjure
with his saffron and whiskey and snifters of 43 and low delicious voice. A future where I don't get up and run home to my
own place. A future increasingly at odds with what I see on the
crime beat each day and what I carry in my head.

I know I should be grateful. Good looks, good job, and good
ethics. He's a coastal geomorphologist at the University of New
Orleans—tenured, no less, which is nothing to sneeze at since
the recession hit last year. He works on restoring Louisiana's
marshlands—the buffer zone between the Gulf and the city—
trying to prevent future catastrophes like Katrina. He cooks,
he's funny, and he knows a thing or two in the bedroom. Plenty
of women would snap Bento up. Yet he wants me.

Problem is, I may not be cut out for the love of a good man.

I don't do relationships. Never have. Until now. Never saw one
growing up. My father took off before I was born—I don't even
know the man's name, despite years of asking—and my mother
raised me on her own in the Desire Projects. She called me Nola,
after the city's acronym, and gave me Céspedes, her own last
name. In the projects, single mothers were as common as the
other kind, and plenty of kids didn't know their fathers. When
it comes to lasting relationships, I don't have a lot of models.

Which is why I've got Daddy Yankee blasting in my earbuds as I run through Audubon Park in the half light of dawn, pounding my feet into the path, obliterating the strains of old-style romance with its thumping reggaeton. The morning breeze cools my face. Moonlight in Vermont? No, thank you. *Dame la gasolina.*

It's been a year since I met Bento, a year since I broke a big story on sex offenders and got moved to the crime beat at the *Times-Picayune,* a year since I entered therapy for post-traumatic stress disorder. A year since I shot the man who raped me when I was eight.

Vengeance isn't all it's cracked up to be, even when the guy's been starring in your nightmares for two decades. Even when he's been abducting, raping, and murdering women from the streets of New Orleans. The beautiful, searing, righteous high of vengeance can only last so long. Then you've got the fallout. The horror, plain and simple, of taking another human life. The guilt, because the public thinks—as you've led them to believe—that you're a brave, heroic girl who killed a sexual predator in self-defense, when in truth his death was the pure product of vendetta. The new, uncontrollable trembling in your wrists when you pick up your gun.

The bad dreams of a different ilk, where you're the monster now.

Shiduri Collins has helped. I've told her everything in her peaceful office on a tree-lined street, including the fact that I think I started planning Blake Lanusse's death from the moment I opened his case file—that the interviews were little more than a ruse, a way to get him alone in his French Quarter condo, to see for myself if he'd changed. Dr. Collins is the only one who knows about my premeditation. When I told her, she only said softly, "I'd like to have put a bullet in my uncle's head." When I confessed the full, serene, blossoming joy I'd felt when I learned that Blake Lanusse hadn't changed at all—had deteriorated, in fact, upping the ante from rape to murder—and that no one would miss him, except perhaps his duped, overstuffed wife, Lily, *pobrecita*, which gave me the moral greenlight to take him off the streets forever, Dr. Collins only smiled her soft, ambiguous smile. "There are other ways, Nola," she said. Ways to deal, she meant. Healthy ways. Legal ways. But the shine in her eyes looked like pleasure.

Shiduri Collins is the therapist I interviewed for the *Times-Pic* feature on sex offenders—my big break, the story that flicked all these dominoes tumbling. For the last year now, she's been helping me sift through the debris of my rape at eight years old and the messy "mechanisms" I've been using to "cope" ever since: the drinking, the workaholism, the no-strings sex with random strangers. Dr. Collins works with me on deep relaxation breathing and EMDR. I sit in her office and count backward with my eyes closed, loosening each part of my body from my toes on up, melting into her soft little couch. I visualize myself in hammocks on warm beaches. I write accusation letters that I read aloud to her and then tear up. I hit the little couch with a foam bat, feeling stupid. If I could only learn to meditate, she'd be thrilled.

A lot can change in a year. I've gone from being a frustrated fluff reporter, covering fashion and charity balls and gallery openings, to the City Desk at the *Picayune*, reporting rapes and murders. Drug busts, when the NOPD can manage them. I love it, and my editor, Bailey, loves my work. Crime is my métier.

Thanks to the sluggish post-Katrina real estate market, I've moved into my friend Soline's elegant condo on St. Charles, which wouldn't sell when she bought a new place with her husband, Rob. I live there now "as a favor," she keeps insisting, but I'm paying only half her mortgage, after vaulting several social classes for the price of a one-day U-Haul rental. I left behind my good friend and roommate, Uri, in our creaky, comfy old apartment over Fair Grinds. I miss him. I miss his humor, his kindness, his brown dog Roux. I miss the way he bails me out of my own messes. Soline's apartment is pretty like a magazine, but it's lonely in the evenings.

Other things have changed, too. My mother, in an inspiring late-life renaissance, has come out of the closet in every respect, moving in with her girlfriend Ledia, joining a seniors' water-volleyball team, of all things, and getting loud at immigration rallies. This transformation for my shy, quiet mother, who lived in the projects for years, muted by her broken English, her poverty, and her fear, is little short of a miracle—though not one the Pope would approve.

Running faster to keep up with a quicker beat, I round the bend under the live oak trees. Spanish moss dangles down in gouts of gray. Up ahead, the lake glimmers.

My friends' lives have changed, too. Calinda, who always loved the single life, hit thirty this year. Baby fever blindsided her. Having already dated all of this city's eligible bachelors and most of the ineligible ones, Calinda abruptly gave up on what she now calls "the propaganda of the nuclear family" and has been browsing local sperm banks. A crack public defender, she's still working at the DA's—and still complaining about it. But I've noticed she hasn't been applying to any cushy private firms like she always used to say she would. Maybe grit's addictive.

Fabi, our Chicana princess, is still ambivalently stringing along her Italian stockbroker-and-restaurateur Carlo, who keeps pulling out the fat pear diamond and having it rebuffed. She still teaches high school as an act of charity and dreams of becoming Mother Teresa, as soon as she can relinquish designer clothes. Already as waifish as a ballerina, she's become a vegan—for environmental reasons, she says—and may soon disappear altogether. She calls it planetary awareness. I call it a problem.

Soline, whose shop Sinegal is flourishing on Magazine Street, remains ensconced in newlywed bliss. She's working on plans to open her first branch, Sinegal Miami, and keeps hinting around about a girls' trip to South Beach, which I cannot afford, for the ribbon-cutting.

My weekly visits with Marisol, my Little Sister through Big Brothers Big Sisters, have mushroomed from two hours each Saturday afternoon to four, and sometimes she stays for dinner. We've explored the city, done homework, and are currently trying to skateboard—at Marisol's instigation, and to her great amusement. Wobbling and weaving down the sidewalks together, I've been unlocking, a little at a time, my memories of what it should have been like to be twelve, thirteen. To really be a kid.

And romance. I won't call it love. Bento. That's a change, too.

I don't know what most bachelor bedrooms look like in New Orleans. My previous escapades rarely took me that far. But I'd lay money they don't look like Bento's.

He shipped everything over from Spain when he came here. On the walls over his bed, old Moorish mirrors face each other—which makes for a pleasantly pornographic view, depending on the occasion. The intricately carved wooden frames, peaked at the top, make it strangely mosquelike, as if the Kama Sutra were framed by something holy.

The bed itself is low and plush, a mattress and box spring flush to the floor, clad in simple white linens. The mattress is one of those Tempur-Pedic memory-foam things that welcomes you down. You sink, and it cradles you. You wonder why you ever left the womb.

At the foot of the bed on a carved wooden trunk sits a beautiful old backgammon board, inlaid with marble and mother-of-pearl. In candlelight, it glows. One set of pieces is turquoise, the other green jade. The small disks are cool and smooth in your fingers. They click against each other with the pleasing heaviness of river stones.

The first time I went to Bento's house—the first time we drank wine on his couch, night fell, and he took my hand and led me to his bedroom—I was surprised. He didn't tear my clothes off, didn't make a move. He sank to the mattress, gathered the dice into the cup, and shook it, smiling up at me.

I stood there. I didn't know how to play.

I drop to a walk, wiping my hand over my forehead. Four miles at a quick clip is enough. A man bicycles past. Sweating and breathing hard, I switch off Daddy Yankee and cross my arms up over my head, opening my lungs, stretching my spine.

Ducks swim and flap on the lake. It's still so early, so quiet. Audubon Park is nearly empty. At dawn, before the people come, it feels a little like Eden. It's where I run now. My haven. It used to be a plantation, of course, like all the land in New Orleans. A sullied Eden.

I step off the path into the green grass by the water, breathing deeply, and all the fertile smells of spring rush into me. Words like *peat* and *loam* and *fecund* come to mind. The sun's not fully up yet, and the wind is cool. The lake lies silver and smooth beside me, swathes of green algae veiling its surface. Far over to my right, across St. Charles Avenue and its light traffic, are the redbrick buildings of Loyola University. As I keep walking, the creamy stone campus of Tulane appears, still fast asleep. Tulane, my alma mater.

Beneath my steps, spears of green grass push thickly up, and the tune seeps back into my head. *As long as I can be with you, it's a lovely day.* So much for ridding my mind of romance. I walk, humming.

Up ahead, I spot something. A little distance off the path lies a small, shining, black thing. An odd thing, an odd shape. I approach and crouch down.

It's a severed head. The head of a crow or grackle or blackbird, its beak pressed tightly shut, its feathers iridescent, its small eyelid closed. There's no stench, no sweet rotting smell of carcass. It's fresh. A tiny clean white stem, its spine, protrudes slightly from the black feathered neck.

Among the fragile green blades of grass, the head lies there like an icon of violence, so small I could hold it in my hand. But I don't. I photograph it with my cell phone. Odd: just lying there, like something from vodou.

Its beak points in the direction I've been walking.

I stand and move on, heading across a span of grass toward the water's edge where the pine and cypress trees thicken. The soft wind blows my T-shirt against my spine.

Another small black thing. I move close, chilled and curious. It's a second head—a grackle's, almost certainly—fresh, lying with its eyes closed and its closed beak again pointing like a slim black arrow toward the water.

And suddenly there's something too coincidental about them,

too creepy. Too human. No other animal does this. A shiver spins across my shoulder blades, and I feel my small aloneness there in the green bowl the land makes, alone in my jog bra and shorts, my little phone and lip balm and keys zipped into my pocket. Alone in the grassy field with tender new shoots springing up and severed heads scrying a path forward toward the lake's lonely edge.

Abruptly it runs through me: a cold quickening down my spine and through my limbs and gut. The sick, sure tingle of a crime scene. My legs begin to run of their own accord, carrying me clumsily at first and then swiftly toward the lake in the dim gray morning air, and I spot them, the running shoes upturned with their reflective stripes shimmering in the gloom, the pale ankles, and now I'm moving faster, desperate, *Please let her be alive.* I know it's a woman, and as I get closer I see that it is, that her clothes are torn away and her limbs are limp in the dirt between the knobby roots of the cypress, the green leaves of elephant's ears smashed and splayed around her. Her head tilts back off the bank, the ends of her loose hair snaking lazily into the water. There's something familiar about her face, and I'm crouching down next to her, muttering *Please* as my fingers search the flesh of her still-warm throat for a pulse but find nothing, nothing, nothing.

2

When the police arrive, a big, solid cop from Homicide walks me gently away from the body. We settle on a bench near the fountain in which a bronze topless maiden dances, holding a bird on her arm. The goddess of flight? It's very droll, under the circumstances.

The cop is middle-aged with shorn hair the color of salt. His eyes are blue, his face lined and tan. Winterson, he says his name is. Detective Tom Winterson.

The other police officers are marking off the scene, running yellow tape not only around the cypress tree but all the way to the asphalt path, which means they must have found scuff marks. She must have been running on the asphalt and then been dragged. The EMTs roll the body past on its gurney, and an officer squats to bag the crows' heads. On St. Charles Avenue, squad cars form a wall of flashing red and blue. Early commuter traffic slows, squeezing by.

"Sure you're feeling okay?" asks Detective Winterson. His eyes scan my face. "We can have one of the EMTs check you."

For shock, he means. I hold out my hands in front of me, and we both gaze at them. They hang quietly in the air, brown and ringless. Steady. "Yeah, I'm okay."

When I spell my name for him, he writes it, then frowns down at the letters. "Now, why does that look familiar?"

I tell him I'm a staff writer for the *Times-Picayune,* and he rolls his eyes.

"Great," he says. "Just my luck. So I guess there's no way of keeping the details off the front page."

I grin. "Good luck with that." Then I think of the dead woman. The grin falls from my face.

Detective Winterson's questions take only a few minutes, and I don't have a lot to say. He nods and listens and writes. I heard nothing unusual, saw no possible assailants, and believed I knew the victim: Dr. Judith Taffner, a journalism professor from whom I'd taken two required courses at Tulane. Her face was bloated, but I'm pretty sure it's her; I had spent two semesters studying her every move.

I leave out the fact that I'd clashed with her repeatedly—that her air of smug privilege, her certainty, her crisp linen blouses, and her perfect hair had irked me. That I'd challenged her in class whenever possible, and she, in turn, had used my fledgling writing assignments as bad examples, putting them up on the overhead, circling and striking through my clumsy choices. She had given me grief about my tardiness, her eyes flicking disdainfully over my cutoffs and Walmart T-shirts, my rubber flip-flops, and my messy long curls. Fresh from graduate school, she wasn't that much older than her students. She must have been nervous. I could have been nicer. But at the time—eighteen, on scholarship, and pissed off at everything rich and creamy in the new world I'd entered—I couldn't have cared less. I just hated her.

I leave all that out of my account and stick to the facts of here and now. Dr. Taffner's throat had still been warm when I'd reached for her pulse.

Detective Winterson jots my replies into a small notebook, and finally we finish and rise. He reaches into the breast pocket of his gray suit jacket. With his index and middle fingers, he proffers one of his business cards, in case I recall anything else.

I take it. "Am I free to go, then?"

He nods. "Sure you're all right? One of my officers can drive you home."

"I'm fine." I shake his hand firmly to prove it, and we part, he to his crime scene, me toward St. Charles at a deliberately natural, easy, inconspicuous pace.

Home's not where I'm going.

Hundreds of people are murdered each year in New Orleans, but most are young black men. Sometimes their deaths still make the front page; sometimes not. Dr. Taffner's death isn't just another murder story. It's a piece about how New Orleans isn't safe even for professional white women jogging in Audubon Park uptown. It's a profile of someone who did everything right— who had every advantage, followed all the rules—but still was killed. It shatters the illusion of safety, the myth that class or race or staying in the right neighborhoods will protect anyone, and it's a slap in the face of the fragile post-Katrina rebound and the record-breaking influx of tourist dollars.

It's an above-the-fold headline. And all I have to do is scoop it.

Squeezing my way between the bumpers of squad cars, I wait until a rubbernecking driver lets me cross the street.

On the opposite curb, on the groomed green lawn at the edge of Tulane University, I turn back to look at the park. The day is still young, the air fresh. Sweat has dried on my skin. I stand there, squinting at the crime scene. Detective Winterson squats near the cypress tree, intent, and the other officers are all busy bagging up evidence or talking to one another. No one is looking my way.

I turn back toward the campus where I'd spent four unsettling years. Where I'd been Dr. Taffner's student. I have the sudden, strange compulsion—grief?—to go to the place where I knew her best. Tulane is still quiet, hushed before classes start. The stone buildings breathe out their magisterial calm. Green lawns unspool as smooth as a landscaper's dream. There's not a soul in sight.

I begin running into the heart of it, toward Newcomb Hall.

Backgammon, Bento says, is the game that's most like life. It includes chance: what the dice give you. Then there's skill: what you do with what's been doled out.

The given day, and how you play it.

Chess, he says, is too controlled for him, too cerebral, too much like battle. In chess, the goal is to control the board, dominate it. The goal is territory. Ownership.

In backgammon, all the pieces are identical. No one is a king, no one a queen. You race to get your pieces off the board—to divest yourself, piece by piece, from the game. You race toward emptiness. Leaving completely is how you win.

It's very Zen, he says.

According to my iPhone, it's 6:50 A.M. when I arrive at Newcomb, and the building's windows are still unlit. The main doors are still locked, but someone—probably a tired, bored work-study student on security rounds—has failed to push a steel service door completely shut, and I slip inside. The wide corridor is quiet and eerie, and my footsteps on the buffed wood floors are the only sound as I pass empty classrooms and lecture halls. The secretaries won't arrive for at least another hour, and two or three more will pass before any professors show their faces. The privilege of academe.

I run up the stairs to the third floor and move quickly through the warren of narrow hallways, reading the signs on the office doors, passing bulletin boards leaved thick with bright flyers. Though it's been years, I find Dr. Taffner's office soon enough, tucked into its corner of the building.

My B&E skills aren't much to write home about, but some-times growing up in the projects pays off. Within thirty seconds, using my driver's license and a straightened paper clip from the unswept floor, I let myself inside.

I pause just inside her door, listening, but there's still no sound. No footsteps come to see what I'm up to. I ease the door shut behind me.

Two large windows let the morning sun pour in, hazing the room in gold. Potted plants line the deep stone windowsills, and real framed art hangs on the walls. This is the room where Judith Taffner badgered and hectored me. This is the place I think of—however inaccurately—as her home. The home of her mind.

I look around, remembering. She'd still liked Paris, apparently. Prints of the Eiffel Tower, bridges over a river. A red kilim lies on the wooden floor, and the same two leather chairs wait for students to visit during office hours. I remember sitting there, sullen, as she informed me that not every single story of street crime in New Orleans begged for my analysis of class injustice. "Sure, it does," I'd said, wishing I had gum to snap.

Everything is familiar, shaded by the passage of years and my memories of sophomoric resentment. Only the computer has changed. On her desk, a new laptop stands open. I pluck a tissue from her box, wrap my finger in it, and press her computer on.

It opens straight to her desktop—no password protection. Academics can be so trusting.

Using the tissue over my thumb and fingers as a makeshift mitt, I open her desk drawers, rummaging until I find a USB flash drive.

The police or the university would notice a missing laptop. A missing flash drive, not so much.

I insert the drive and sit down in her ergonomic desk chair, skimming her desktop and then her documents. Mostly routine stuff. Syllabi labeled by course and semester, lecture notes, handouts, exams, and a thousand letters of recommendation written for students and colleagues. Nothing unusual, nothing interesting—except, possibly, a couple of dozen files whose icons squat on the screen, which means they're probably current. I drag them all, including a document called "Bad Shoot," to the flash drive and watch as the little bar fills up with green while they load.

Interesting. *Bad shoot* means the unjustified shooting of a civilian by a police officer, an all-too-common fuck-up in the psychotic, jittery, adrenaline-fueled days right after Katrina when the Superdome was melting down, looters ran rampant, and scared cops ran on no sleep and the throbbing undertow of racism. Four years after the fact, the investigations into the shootings on Danziger Bridge and elsewhere keep dragging on.

Pocketing the thumb drive, I shut Dr. Taffner's computer down. A quick search of her desk produces a pack of Camel

Lights, a brass lighter, and a first-edition hardcover of Hunter S. Thompson's 1966 *Hell's Angels*, with the flyleaf inscribed, "To Jude, from Cory." Tucked inside the book is a receipt from The Columns, a beautiful old historic hotel on St. Charles. I know the place. My ex-roommate Uri tends bar there at the Vic, but I've never been inside the hotel part.

The receipt is for a single night in a suite. It's only a month old, and it's charged to Dr. Taffner's credit card.

I take the receipt and the thumb drive, drop the paper clip in the full trash can, and use the tissue to pull the door shut behind me, feeling the click of the lock.

The corridors are still silent, and I slip quickly down the stairs and jog along the main hall on the first floor.

Rounding the corner, I almost plow into a custodian, a short brown man in his early fifties with suspicion baked into his eyes. He holds a bottle of Windex in his hand, aimed at me. He looks me up and down, taking in my running shoes, shorts, and jog bra, my sloppily pulled-back tangle of dark curls. He glances at the flash drive and slip of paper in my hand.

"You a student?" With his free hand, he begins to fumble with the walkie-talkie on his belt.

"Alum!" I say brightly, flashing my widest smile. "Class of '03! And how are *you* on this beautiful morning?" I veer around him, push through the big wooden door, and hit my stride toward home.

In the comfortable, shabby Mid-City apartment I shared with Uri for two years, the paint was peeling off its green shutters, and the water pipes shrieked and clanged when you filled the old claw-foot tub. I miss that place like family.

Uri fell hard for a cardiology intern at the LSU med center: a solid, good-looking guy named Brian who, as far as I can determine, has no sense of humor at all, much less a sense of irony, which makes his relationship with Uri hard to fathom. But he was steady, serious, and obviously besotted. A mere three months into their relationship, Uri started hinting around that they wanted to live together. It had been Uri's place before I'd moved in; I was the one who should go. Happy as I was for my friend, I felt like a Dickensian orphan, cast out into the cold.

When Soline learned, during one of our weekly Girls' Nights, that I had to move out, she looked at me thoughtfully over her duck maque choux. Her eyes narrowed. She pursed her lips, leaned back, and crossed her long legs. Blue fabric fluttered around her knees.

"Just exactly what are you paying over there?" she asked.

"My half of the rent? Five hundred. Plus utilities."

"Five hundred," she repeated, nodding, her entrepreneurial mind running the numbers. Then she made her offer.

"No way, Soline," I said. "You can't tell me five hundred a month covers even half the mortgage on that place." Soline's condo, immaculate and gorgeous, is on the third floor of a fully updated historic building on St. Charles, perhaps the city's most desirable location. Her kitchen has counters of white marble. The master bath has a tub you could throw parties in.

She sipped her cabernet and nodded. "No, that's true. But right now, me and Rob are carrying the whole payment, on top of our new place, and it's just sitting empty. I'd feel good knowing you were there."

I opened my mouth to protest, and she put her long, cool hand on my arm. She knew me too well. "It's not charity," she said, her dark eyes locked on mine. "You'd be doing me a solid. Win-win."

A month later, I moved in, and for the last four months, it's been home. Sort of. There's still nothing familiar about it. I feel like a squatter in a museum, a hobo who stumbled into someone else's life.

My pace slows to a jog. On the corner of the block, the elegant gray-green stucco building looms up, surrounded by towering magnolia trees, their pale blossoms splayed fatly open. I mount the slate steps and swipe my keycard, and the steel pedestrian gate glides open silently, as if pulled by unseen, obsequious hands. Once I'm through, it slides shut behind me, and the lock clasps with a firm, airlock click that sounds like a high-tech lair in spy movies. It's the sound of security, of money.

The slate-paved courtyard is pretty. I pass the fountain, the palms, the thicket of blossoming pink oleander. Soline's key lets me into the building, and my feet fit the declivities in the marble slabs as I climb the stairs to the third floor.

At two thousand square feet, Soline's apartment is triple the space I've ever inhabited before. I walk in and drop my keys on a lacquered French provincial table that probably cost more than my Pontiac. The rooms are spacious and uncluttered. Pristine white walls are saved from blandness by ceilings that Soline painted aqua, the way some folks paint the ceilings of their porches blue to make the light feel cool. The upholstery, whether silk or linen or velvet, is white. Thick white rugs cushion the hardwood floor. In the kitchen, a chandelier hangs over the sink. Soline lived here for four years with Puppy, her bichon frise, but there's no trace of dog, no gouges clawed in the pale oak floors, no fur clumps cowering at the backs of closets, no faint canine smell. Like Soline herself, the whole apartment is elegant, clean, plush, and unstudied—which generally makes me feel like the unwashed masses when I sit cross-legged on her sofa, eating generic cornflakes for dinner.

The place is nice. Too nice. Each day, I come home from shootings and stabbings and rapes and the clutter of my desk at the *Picayune* to this layout from *Architectural Digest*.

I enter the bedroom, where I sit at Soline's desk, a Louis-the-whatever reproduction, and wake my laptop up. It chimes hello, and I push the flash drive in. While I wait, I call my editor, Bailey, and leave a voice mail message, quickly describing the murder in Audubon Park. "It's mine," I say. "My story. I was first at the scene." Leaving out the damning fact that I knew Dr. Taffner personally, which makes for a conflict of interest, I just tell him I'm on it—"No need to task anyone else"—and hang up.

Then I dial Calinda. When she picks up, I hear Professor Longhair blasting in the background, so she's not at the DA's yet. "Hey, baby!" she says.

"Hey, I'm reporting a new case. Just happened this morning. I want anything you get on it."

Her voice goes stern. "You know I'm not allowed to share information." Then she laughs.

I laugh, too. "So anyway, white female, forties, found dead this morning in Audubon Park. Probable rape and strangulation." I push my running shoes off and strip away my socks.

"You got a name?"

"Judith Taffner. Professor at Tulane. Looks like she was out jogging alone and someone blitz-attacked her." I twist my toes into Soline's thick, soft rug. It feels good on my bare feet.

"What else?"

"Yeah, well, it's kind of freaky."

"All killing's freaky, Nola. Freaky how?"

"TV-show freaky. The attacker decorated the body." I close my eyes, seeing it all again. "Rosaries, dead crows, feathers. There was a pentacle drawn in blood on the vic's abdomen. And some numbers inside it. Two and twenty-one, with a colon between them."

"Ew. Okay, yeah. That's freaky. What do you think the numbers mean?"

"I don't know. A Bible verse, maybe?" I imagine some sergeant down at HQ, eating his muffuletta and flipping slowly through the thin, crinkly pages of a Bible, checking the second chapter and twenty-first verse of every biblical book to see if there's a connection. Genesis. Exodus. Overtime. "But listen to this," I say. "It gets weirder. She wasn't cut. So either he cut himself and used his own blood to fingerpaint, or he brought blood to the kill site. In which case, the question is—"

"Whose blood?" she finishes. "That's weird, Nola." There's a pause as she thinks it through. "Sadistic sexual killing, markers of ritual. And he might have a captive somewhere and is using her blood to play with the cops. Fun with DNA."

"Exactly," I say. "Which seems really strange to me."

"Thank you, Dr. Obvious."

"No, listen," I say. I look out the window into the green leaves of a magnolia tree, close enough to reach out and touch. A bee circles one fat white bloom. "If you're into ritual, you need privacy, time. You want to get it right. So why choose a public space, where you could get interrupted? Why not break into her house while she's sleeping, or abduct her and take her to someplace private, some environment you can control?"

"Ooh," says Calinda. "And I thought my job made *me* cold."

"I'm just saying."

"No, you're right, you're right." Calinda pauses, and I hear Professor Longhair singing about how his woman's mind done gone. "But now wait a minute." A smile seeps into her voice. "How'd you already get all these details, if it just happened this morning? You sleeping at HQ these days?"

A second passes. "No," I say slowly. "I was first at the scene." When I speak the words to my friend, it all suddenly hits me. "I found her. She was my professor."

"Oh, my God," she breathes. "Oh, Nola, I'm sorry." The volume on her stereo turns way down. "But now wait a fucking second. You were there in Audubon Park? What time?"

"About six this mornig."

"Jogging," she says flatly. "Alone. Where she was."

My silence answers her.

"Nola."

I stare at my laptop, at my brown toes curling into the white carpet, at the deep green magnolia leaves outside.

"Nola," she says again, concern and frustration thick in her tone.

"I'm fine, I'm fine. Listen, I've got to run, so feed me anything you hear, okay?" I hang up before she can answer, and when her name flashes on my phone seconds later, I push *Ignore*.

Suddenly my eyes won't focus on the computer screen, and I stumble to my feet. Time to shower, dress, go to work.

Unsteady, I weave into Soline's closet, where my altar to *La Virgen* and my ancestors stands with its candles and little saucers of rum and Diet Coke on top of Soline's built-in bureau. Mardi Gras beads and my rosary hang from Mary's prayer-clasped hands, and curling black-and-white photos of my mother as a young girl in Cuba are propped against the statue's golden robe. I think of the dead woman, her nude body left in the dirt. *Queen of Heaven, pray for us.*

Acres of Soline's cool short linen frocks, white and blue, still hang from the poles. She said I could borrow anything, but what looks gorgeous on a coltish five-foot-nine black woman doesn't necessarily suit a five-foot-five Latina with a traditional Cuban backseat. I reach instead for my own charcoal slacks—stretch weave, *verdad*—and a red blouse.

But my hands, as they stretch toward the hangers, are trembling.

3

After I've showered and dressed, I stand in front of Soline's elegant little desk, leaning down toward my laptop, chewing an under-ripe banana and typing *Judith Taffner* into the white pages online. Her home is only a five-minute drive from here, on Nashville Avenue.

I toss my keys and notebook into my handbag and head downstairs and around the back of the building to the private parking lot, where a Mercedes the color of new steel and a sky-blue Jag flank my poor old Pontiac Sunfire, its original black finish baked to a tired ash, the paint across its hood starting to crackle. A year doesn't change *everything*. I get in, gun the engine, and throw it into reverse, twisting the wheel. The wide steel gate slides smoothly aside, and I glide out into traffic.

The main streets are noisy, crowded with morning commuters, but Nashville Avenue is quiet, lined with small houses of varying styles and suffering varying degrees of neglect. Judith Taffner's home, a cocoa-colored shotgun house with white trim and white shutters, has been energetically gentrified. White roses and gardenia bushes press against an honest-to-god white picket fence.

There's a cop car parked out front.

I cut my engine and walk over. As I approach, the officer in the front seat looks up from writing, and his bright blue eyes lock on me. He's young, slender, with a crew cut so blond it's translucent. I glance at his name tag: Doucet.

I tilt my press pass toward him. "Anything new on the case?"

Doucet shakes his head and jerks his chin toward the house. "Worst part of the job." Telling the family, he means. So where's the female officer? Usually they send one along to soften the blow.

I guess the NOPD's stretched thin this morning. Again.

"Who's she survived by?"

"Husband and kid. Little girl. Cute." He sighs and rubs his pale jaw. How can a man have stubble by eight A.M.? He must have been out all night. Which makes this overtime. Or maybe he was moonlighting, working security somewhere to make ends meet. A lot of cops do.

I head for the little brick path between the bushes.

"Hey," he calls. "You could give them a minute."

"I could," I say, hesitating. Just then, a white WDSU TV news van rounds the corner. I head for the door.

When I knock, the man who opens the door wears a numb expression and is carrying a kid on his hip. He has the earnest brown eyes and square spectacles of a scholar but the bulked, firm build of a middle-weight prizefighter, and he's still in flannel pajama pants and a white T-shirt, as though time stopped when the cop knocked at his door. The girl wears pink footy pajamas, her hair tousled by sleep.

"Mr. Taffner, I'm Nola Céspedes, from the *Times-Picayune*. I'm so sorry for your loss."

Judith Taffner's bereaved husband glances down at my press pass.

He looks up at me, emotions flickering across his face. Pain. Sorrow. Disgust.

"No." He starts to shut the door, but my sandaled foot keeps it wedged open.

I gesture toward the TV news van, struggling to parallel-park. "I was a student of Dr. Taffner's at Tulane. She taught me, mentored me. I can promise a fair and balanced story that treats her with respect." I leave out the fact that respect, fairness, and balance were no part of my relationship with her ten years ago.

He looks at me. Glances at the TV news van.

"Better me than them," I say quickly.

He opens the door wider and runs a hand over his daughter's hair. "Yes, all right. Come in."

In the Taffner living room, four large gilt-edged mirrors reflect white love seats, a hearth, and low tables. Gold-framed Audubon prints of kingfishers and flamingoes adorn the cream-colored walls, and fresh peonies nod from immaculate crystal bowls. It's elegant, correct, gracious—everything I'd predict from Dr. Taffner. The only evidence that a child lives here is a stuffed bear splayed on an ottoman. And it's a pretty elegant bear, truth be told. No worn raggedy bits.

"Luke Jourdan," says the man, extending a hand.

I lift an eyebrow. "Jourdan?"

"Jude didn't take my name." He waves at one love seat and sinks into the other, shifting the little girl to his lap.

I sit down and pull my notebook out, fuss with my pen, hiding the surprise I feel that Dr. Taffner was someone named

Jude. *Judith* had seemed to fit her uptight, fussy demeanor. The name *Jude* suggests a person at once both cooler and warmer, more real than the one I'd known.

I start with something light, easy. Nothing to do with murder. "Why didn't your wife take your name?"

He shrugs. "She's an academic. She already had publications in her maiden name. She was pretty far along in her career when we met."

Hard knocks pelt the door, and he startles. The TV news guys.

I shake my head. "Just ignore them."

"Really?"

"Really. They're used to it. So how did you two meet?"

A faint smile lights his eyes. "At Whole Foods. She was standing in the produce aisle, holding a bunch of chard. I told her not to get it, that it was past its prime. And she said, 'Do you cook?' And I said, 'Yeah, I love to cook.' And she got this huge smile, and she said, 'Well, what should I get, then?' So we walked through the vegetables together, picking stuff out, and then we pushed our carts together for the rest of the way, talking, and then after we checked out we sat at the coffee bar, talking some more."

He's comfortable telling the story, as if he's told it often—as if it's endearing, a winning anecdote among the kind of people they socialize with. Cocktail-party chitchat.

For someone who's just lost a spouse, he's strangely coherent, calm, collected.

Or maybe he's just on automatic pilot.

The little girl squirms in his lap and slides down to the floor. She stands there, looking at me with interest for a moment, then pads out of the room. Luke watches her go, his gaze soft.

"I was just amazed by my luck," he says. "Here she was, this beautiful, smart woman, completely together, completely on track with her life. Me, I was just working the cold line at this Italian dive on Esplanade. But she liked me." He looks at me and shrugs, as if the amazement still lingers. "A few months later, we were married."

"Mr. Jourdan, how old was your wife?"

"Jude's forty-four." I note his use of the present tense. Classic denial.

I mimic it, keep him in the dream, keep the answers coming. "And you've been married how long?"

"Almost five years."

There in the produce aisle at Whole Foods, Judith Taffner had been thirty-nine years old.

Squinting at her husband's open, sincere face, I can almost see what she saw: a handsome, kind, well-built man—one of those determinedly nonsexist, nonracist, pro-environment, Emo-souled white guys with impeccable progressive politics. A man who cooked, no less. A man she could manage.

I'm no one to tell him he looks like Judith Taffner's last-ditch attempt at the storybook ending.

Their daughter wanders back in, her thumb in her mouth and a stuffed gray seal under her arm. She walks over and puts it in my lap.

"Thank you," I say. "What's your name?"

She doesn't speak.

"Chloe," her father says.

"Thank you, Chloe. And how old are you?"

She looks at her hand with great seriousness as three fingers unfurl. She shows them to me.

"Wow. Three years old. You're a really big girl."

She nods.

I pick up the seal and look into its plastic brown eyes. "And who is this?"

The thumb slips out. "Sergio." She says it the American way: *Surge-ee-o.*

"And what's Sergio up to today?"

"His mama died." She puts her thumb back in her mouth and climbs back up into her father's lap.

Luke's eyes close briefly.

"I'm sorry," I say softly. "It's sad to lose a mama." She nods and presses her face to her father's chest, one green eye still watching me. Soft strands of her hair, the browned gold of iced tea on a sunporch, fall against his white T-shirt.

Something in me winces. Even in this strained and horrible moment, probably the worst moment of his life, he holds Chloe easily against him, like she belongs there. My hands tighten on my notebook. Growing up fatherless, I never knew the sleepy contentment of a father's certain care. At home with my single mother in the Desire Projects or at school in the Quarter, men were peripheral—or worse. Paternal affection is outside my realm, and it stirs something uncomfortable inside me.

Focus, Nola. "So tell me about your wife's job," I say.

"She loves her work," he says. "She lives for it. She loves Tulane, her students, her colleagues. She's very good at what she does. Very conscientious."

That's one way to put it. "In her teaching or her research?"

"Both," he says, "though her research agenda geared down when Chloe was born. She was ramping it back up, though. Working on some articles. She was planning to go up for full."

I note his slide into past tense. "Full?"

"Full professor. The highest rank. She already had tenure

when we met. She didn't have to start writing investigative pieces again; the department was happy with her, and she could have just kept doing conference papers and articles for professional journals. But she wanted to do it. Get back in the game, she said."

I'm nodding and writing. "And her background? Where was she from originally?"

"She grew up in Virginia. Horse country. Her family's still there, on a farm outside Richmond—" He breaks off, staring out the window. "Oh, God," he says. "I have to call them."

I let a few seconds pass. "Did her family have horses?"

"Yes. She rode. Used to show. Hunter-jumper. She was good." I could see that: Dr. Taffner's slim, tight frame on horseback. Controlled, controlling. "She went to UVA and then to Ann Arbor for graduate school. She interned with the *Detroit News* in the summers, and then came here when she got her doctorate."

"Straight out of grad school. Your wife was quite a success."

"Yes. Very much so. She worked long hours, was respected by her peers, gave papers at conferences around the country."

"What did she do for fun?"

He looks blank.

"Hobbies? Sports?"

"She goes running every morning," he says, and his voice cracks briefly before he regains control. "But I think she does it mainly for exercise, not fun. We spend a lot of time with Chloe, of course. Between that and work, there's not much time for other pursuits." He squeezes Chloe. "Do you have kids?"

People don't usually ask the reporter questions. "No." My answer seems too bald, hanging in the air between us, and I feel compelled to soften it. "Not yet."

"Well, they pretty much take over your life." He smiles.

"Did your wife go running at the same time every day?"

"Yes. Jude's very keen on sticking to her schedule. With a full-time job and a young child, you pretty much have to be." Which unfortunately made her an ideal victim: easy to track, easy to prepare for.

"And your job, Mr. Jourdan? What do you do?"

His face lights, and he describes his teaching job at a charter school in Tremé. Seventh-grade English. To me, it sounds thankless, but he seems enthused, happy to be talking about something other than his murdered wife. His students are rehearsing *Measure for Measure* for the school's annual festival.

"*Measure for Measure*? Isn't that a little heavy?" The knocking hits the door again, louder this time. Hammering. He glances at it, and I shake my head again.

"My kids are used to heavy," he says. "And kids are smarter than you'd think. They get it. They're doing great with it."

"So you and your wife are both educators."

"Yes. We talked about teaching a lot." He rubs his hand through his hair. Bashful. "Jude said my approach was too touchy-feely."

Nothing touchy-feely about Dr. Taffner. I remember her sharp lectures, her crisp collars, the cutting comments she'd make after class about my work, my appearance, my chances in a ruthless field.

"I wasn't a teacher when I met her, of course," he continues. "She helped me get motivated, helped me focus." He nods. "I was just doing restaurant work, playing sax in a band . . ." He shakes his head. "But that was never going to go anywhere. Jude's really the one who got me on track."

Dear Lord. Now it all comes clear. He'd been her project.

"Did your wife have any vices?"

I'm thinking of the Camel Lights, the hotel receipt.

"Vices?"

"Did she smoke? Drink? Gamble? Have any kind of secret indulgence?"

"Oh, God, no." He shakes his head. But then he pauses. Something happens behind his eyes, but I can't tell what it is. When he speaks again, his face is closed, his voice slow, deliberate. "She doesn't have any vices. No."

Chloe shifts to face me. "Mama and Daddy are taking me to Jazz Fest."

I put on my best nice-to-kids face and uncross my legs to lean toward her. "Are they?"

"Yes. We're going to the children's tent."

"Are you now?"

"Uh-huh!" She nods vigorously.

Luke's face is pained. "I don't know, honey. We'll have to see."

Chloe's lips puff into a disappointed pout. " 'We'll see' means that we won't go."

Smart kid. I turn to Luke. Suddenly, words come out of my mouth before I think. "You should take her."

Luke glances at me, surprised. I'm a little surprised myself. What do I care if the kid goes to Jazz Fest?

"She's going to have a lot to deal with," I say. "A lot of change. If you can keep one thing stable and steady—keep one promise—it will help her cope."

He looks at me and then nods slowly. "I thought you didn't have kids."

"I don't." But I think of Marisol, of her five little sisters and brothers. I play with them on the floor of their Metairie apartment when I go to pick her up, and I've babysat occasionally so her exhausted parents can go get a beer and a taco in peace. I think of my patient, gentle mother raising me in the projects.

Luke Jourdan is looking into my eyes, and there's a strange, long moment that feels like connection. He's not a bad-looking guy.

I shake it off, rising to my feet and handing Sergio the seal back to Chloe. "Did Dr. Taffner have an office, a study, here in the house?"

He nods. "Sure. She had to. She worked at home a lot."

"May I see it? Seeing a person's space can give me a fuller sense of who they were," I explain. "It'll help with the story. You know: the illustrative detail."

He nods slowly and then rises. Chloe clings to his side like a soft little barnacle.

Luke leads the way down the hall to a small room furnished with bookshelves and a Mission-style oak desk. I pause, looking around.

"Daddy," Chloe murmurs, pulling his T-shirt. "I've got to go."

Perfect timing. I should pay that kid.

He carries her out of the room, and I begin to riffle through the stacks of paper on Jude Taffner's desk. It won't be long before they'll be back, so it helps that she was tidy. There's nothing of interest on the desk, on the bookshelves, or on the broad windowsill, which holds only a potted fern.

Quickly, quietly, I slide her top drawer open. Staples, paper clips, a couple of expensive fountain pens in a wooden box. The second drawer holds clean envelopes, stamps, and a leather address book. It's all about as professional and unhelpful as her classroom demeanor used to be.

In the lowest, largest drawer, on top of several file folders, lies a paper-clipped sheaf of papers. Bills of sale. Squatting, I pull them out. They're for horses. I flip through them. Thorough-breds. All sold in the state of Louisiana.

Footsteps approach down the hall, and a weird impulse makes me shove the bills of sale into my purse.

Call it a hunch.

By the time Luke Jourdan appears in the doorway, I'm standing up, studying the spines of her books.

I'm all smiles and handshakes as I maneuver my way around him and Chloe toward their front door. "Mr. Jourdan, thank you so much for your time." He trails behind me, looking bewildered by my sudden change of gears. "I'll do my best to make sure the story represents your wife in the best possible light." I pull out one of my business cards and hand it to him. "If you think of anything else—anything—don't hesitate to call."

As soon as the door opens, TV reporters surge forward, wailing their questions, microphones waving, and I thread my way through them, leaving Luke Jourdan to his own devices.

4

It's almost nine A.M. when I leave the Taffner house and swing over to NOPD headquarters on South Broad to get a copy of the police report on the case. I stand there in the lobby, reading, shifting from one high heel to the other. No surprises. No one's in custody, and the PD knows no more than they did when Detective Winterson told me I was free to go. Forensics won't be back for a while yet.

I drive to the big white block of the *Times-Picayune* office building, its tower rising like some Soviet-era dream, and park in the shade of the highway overpass. Inside, I ride the escalators up to the third floor. In the hushed bustle of the vast gray newsroom, I sit at my desk, thinking.

Something feels wrong. Luke Jourdan had been shocked. But not shocked enough. Grief-stricken, but distracted.

Reporters walk past—mostly men, mostly white, with their sleeves rolled up and their ties loosened. They shoot me quick greetings and gibes as they pass, and I snap back while I type my interview notes and begin shaping the story. I have to provide what the local TV news can't—or won't: depth, texture, a stab at analysis. TULANE PROFESSOR MURDERED IN AUDUBON PARK is the obvious headline, and since I saw the feathers and rosaries and pentacle-in-blood for myself, the cops can't suppress those details. I end the story with the standard warning: "Until the culprit is apprehended, joggers in Audubon and other city parks are reminded to run during daylight hours, with a partner, and in populated areas. Everyone is urged to use particular caution."

I file the story and then start to work on one from yesterday. A body was found burned beyond recognition near one of the tent cities under I-10, and the victim is presumed to be a homeless man who got in an altercation and was then set aflame by someone who wanted to destroy evidence. The coroner's office had called in a forensic anthropologist and was awaiting dental records. I finish typing it up and file it. Sad, but run-of-the-mill. It wouldn't get nearly the public attention that Judith Taffner's murder would. A middle-class professional, a wife and mother, doing the same thing thousands of women do each morning? *That* would grab the attention of New Orleans.

I call Fabi. "Hey," I say when she answers. "Can you break away for lunch?"

"Nola. Friend." Her patient tone is the one she reserves for her reality-challenged students. "As you may recall, I teach high school. I do not 'break away' for anything. I only took your call because I'm on—"

"Just messing with you."

I hear her sigh.

"So can you have dinner with me tonight?"

Her voice lights up. "Now *that* I can do."

I suggest Jacques-Imo's over on Oak Street, my favorite place for gumbo.

She declines. "How about Juan's Flying Burritos?"

"Seriously?" I love Juan's, but affordable Mexican food is not how Fabi rolls.

She says yes, the one on Magazine.

After grabbing a pale, tired salad from the *Picayune*'s cafeteria and eating it at my desk while I scan headlines from BBC, *The New York Times*, CNN, *The Wall Street Journal*, and Al-Jazeera, I close up shop for the day, locking my desk drawers and shutting my computer down. I have a sudden, strong urge to visit my old mentor and friend, Tómas Guillory. He taught me at Tulane before he retired, and he knew Judith Taffner. I want to tell him in person.

When I pull up beside his little hot-pink Creole cottage in the Faubourg Marigny, just downriver from the French Quarter, it's two o'clock, and the air is thick and bright. When I was growing up, the Marigny was dodgy, but gentrification set in. Now Frenchmen Street boasts what might be the best live-music scene in the city. It's where Soline's husband founded his club.

During Katrina, the Marigny saw some flooding but was spared the worst of it, since many of the older structures are raised on pilings, like Professor Guillory's nineteenth-century cottage. He came home to dry floors. He was lucky.

His small front yard is stuffed with green palm trees, their fronds glinting in the sun. A brick path leads to creaky wooden steps. On the porch, I ring the doorbell, a little rusted knob that you twist. It trills like an antique bell.

Professor Guillory opens the door in a white guayabera and khakis, his skin the color of wet sand, his body thin and fragile now with age. Besides my mother, he's the only Cuban I know.

His face lights when he sees me. "Come in, child!" he says,

ushering me inside. Across the wood floor, beyond the woven cane chairs, French doors spill into a back garden full of hibiscus and gardenia and more palms. In his living room, fading photographs of the Malecón hang on the walls. An antique iron cross, crafted here in New Orleans by early Congolese blacksmiths, rests in the white stone fireplace. Professor Guillory squeezes my arm. "What brings you here?"

I open my mouth, but he interrupts me.

"No, wait," he says. "Iced tea?" He checks his watch, winks. "Something stronger?"

I love Professor Guillory. "Tea would be great."

"Come on back, then," he says, and I follow him to the kitchen. "Have a seat."

I pull a rattan stool out from under the counter and make myself comfortable while he fusses with a pitcher and some leaves of mint. The glass he hands me is refreshing. Cold and wet, but not sweet.

"So to what do I owe the pleasure?" he says.

My voice is gentle. "You should maybe sit down."

A frown wings across his brow. "Uh-oh," he says, levering himself onto a stool.

"Yes." And I tell him about Dr. Taffner. How she died, how I found her. The files I pulled from her computer at work, and the bills of sale I took from her desk at home.

At the first news of her death, he makes a sound like someone punched him, a soft, sad expulsion of breath. At the details— the apparent rape, the blood, the birds' heads, the rosaries—he shakes his head, eyes closed. Then he just listens. When I finish, he sits, chewing a sprig of mint, looking through me, his eyes glazed with thought and distance. He thinks. I wait.

He swallows. "Seems to me," he says, "it's just an unfortunate coincidence. A tragedy. Pretty woman, wrong place, wrong time. This city's full of killers." His eyes sharpen into focus. "On the other hand, she's got stories under investigation. And those bills of sale—those could mean something." He pauses, expectant. "And what about her computer files?"

"I haven't read them yet."

"Why haven't you?"

Good question. Reading the files would be the next logical step. Why haven't I? Maybe because I've been interviewing the bereaved widower. Maybe because I had a couple of stories to write myself. Maybe because I'm a little more shaken up by the sight of Judith Taffner's nude, blood-painted body than I want to acknowledge.

Or maybe it's my own closeness to the crime that's got me rattled. I hear Calinda's incredulous voice in my head: *Jogging. Alone. Where she was.*

"Yeah," I say. "That's next. I'll read the files."

He looks at me closely for a moment, then changes the subject. "Judith Taffner was a fine professor," he says. "Always did more than her share. Always professional, always collegial, always kept her ego in check—which you can't say"—his eyes roll— "about all academics." He sips his tea, reflecting. "She was a good teacher. Strict, demanding, but her students—the ones who liked her, that is—were devoted to her. They said she taught them how to be professionals, how to be objective, how to demand more from themselves than they'd thought possible." He smiles. "Not a warm person, though. A bit tense, shall we say."

"Uptight's more like it."

"Very well, then. Choose your adjective."

"She could be mean."

He looks at me, nods. "I can see that," he says. His face shifts in recollection, amused. "On the other hand, you weren't always an easy character to be nice to."

I laugh. "Fair enough." In college, I had a chip on my shoulder the size of the Cabildo. I was angry and stubborn and quick to see slights. "Still. She seemed to have it in for me."

"Sometimes that happens," he says, shrugging. "A particular student gets under your skin. Something about them—you feel challenged, irritated. They push all your buttons. They question your authority. If you're not comfortable with yourself and confident in your training, you'll go on the defensive."

"Or offensive, in her case."

He smiles. "Hard to say."

"She didn't like me."

"She didn't have to." He shakes his head. "Professors aren't there to be your friend. You know that."

"Fair enough," I say again.

"And she was young. Probably insecure. Oh, she came off tough enough, but that was all façade. She hadn't really done time in the trenches, like those of us who'd been actual reporters for years. For her, it was all theory. Book-learning. She didn't have on-the-ground experience. Honestly, at first I wondered why we hired her. She looked good on paper, but she hadn't earned her chops out in the field. And she was surely aware of that. That skepticism about her. That would make her feel nervous if someone questioned her." He laughs. "And you were a pretty aggressive young lady, if I'm remembering right."

I grin. "Yeah. Okay. I maybe gave her a hard time once in a while." I remember with a certain amount of pleasure Dr. Taffner's outraged face in class, her neat, sleek bun and careful skirt suits, the crisp way she'd tap her pen on the overhead, pointing to one of my errors, and the little unnerved gasp she'd give when I'd call her out in class.

But then the image fades away. I see instead her damaged body among the cypress roots, her swollen face, her brown hair drifting like seaweed. A little tremor runs through my hands, and I clasp them together in my lap. "Someone needs to solve this," I say. "I want to find him. She can't turn into just one more damn murder statistic."

Professor Guillory's voice is stern. "That's dangerous territory, Nola. You've made enough trouble for yourself." His eyes fall to the white scar that rings my arm like a bracelet.

I fold my arms, hiding it away. "I don't make the trouble."

"You're there to report. Leave the detective work to the police."

"Oh, and we all know how well that works around here."

His chuckle is wry but dries up quickly. "They're not always the finest. But let them do their job. Stick to yours. You're a writer."

"I investigate. You should know that. You taught me."

He sighs. He reaches over and gently unfolds my arms. He lays his lean hand on the scar. His touch is warm and smooth and feels like guilt. "People care about you, Nola. I'm an old man. These crimes you get involved in. Killings. Violence. I want to see you reach thirty."

His words fill the air with something heavy, a thick fog of emotion, an obligation that feels almost familial. I clear my throat, but my voice still comes out soft and strangled. "I know that." I feel like I'm talking with my mother, reassuring her. "I'll be careful."

He looks at me as if he's adding up numbers. As if he doesn't like the sum.

"You do that," he says softly. "You do that."

After I leave Professor Guillory's little house, I drive to Audubon Park. I park my Pontiac in a spot on St. Charles and walk to the fountain where Detective Winterson had sat on a bench with me and taken my statement. Yellow crime-scene tape still rings the kill site, and a woman in blue gloves is fine-combing the ground.

I sit on the stone ledge that rings the fountain. The stone is warm against my legs. I sit and stare at the lake and the yellow crime-scene tape, at the oaks and the pines and the park benches and the joggers who go by, the mothers with their toddlers, the squirrels and the Spanish moss.

Someone came here in the dark. Someone waited for a woman. My teacher. Someone terrified her, and hurt her, and then snuffed away her life.

I know I should put her thumb drive in my laptop and see what she wrote about. If she were here, that's what she'd do. No fuss, no delay, no dillydallying.

But I sit and stare as the crouching woman in her lab coat inches her way across the dirt. I close my eyes. The sun bathes my face. I sit in Audubon Park and think for a long time.

5

When I arrive at Juan's Flying Burritos, dusk is falling, and Fabi's already waiting in one of the booths.

In a rose linen suit that shows off her collarbones, her dark hair parted low on the side and caught back in a smooth chignon, she looks out of place sipping iced tea from a Mason jar. The décor of Juan's Flying Burritos is deliberately ramshackle, makeshift, with the unifying motif of small winged burros spray-painted on everything, including the bottle chandeliers. I slide in across from Fabi and wave my hand around, eyebrows raised.

"I know, I know," she says. "But it's the only place in town where I can get a meal that tastes good now."

Oh, right. The vegan thing. "You're still on that?"

Fabi looks horrified. "This is not a phase, Nola. This is a choice for the health of the planet." She treats me to a mini-lecture about using water and land responsibly and ending cruelty to animals.

"But what about *your* health?" Fabi is, if it's possible, even thinner than before. The bones of her wrists prod her golden skin.

"I'm healthy, Nola. My cholesterol levels are superb, my heart is in great shape—"

"Yeah, okay, okay." I open the menu. "You're a triathlete." When the waitress comes, Fabi orders a vegan burrito with everything, and I order the plate with the maximum number of dead things on it. Fabi wrinkles her nose.

"Seriously," she says when the waitress is gone. "This is something we all need to consider for the future of the earth." Her chin lifts. Lord help us.

One thing about being a teacher: Fabi can sure lecture. She goes on for a while. I nod politely.

Our food arrives. The waitress plunks our plates down hard on the table and turns away without asking if there's anything we need. Commander's Palace, this ain't.

I cut into my food as Fabi presses her slim fist to the table. "What's the use of progressive political stances—of arguing about race, class, and gender," she says, "if the planet is destroyed by global warming?"

"Look," I say, forking up a big bite of *carne asada,* "I'm not *pro*-planetary destruction."

"Your actions are more important than your words."

"What do your folks think about it?"

Fabi's parents are part of the country-club set in Mandeville, on the north shore of Lake Pontchartrain. They're the token Chicanos—the rich, cultivated, acceptable kind. When you dine with bankers and businessmen, filet mignon and lobster—and mounds of crawfish, to show your local soul—are de rigueur.

Fabi's Gandhi-smile of purity broadens into something less noble, and her eyes gleam. "They hate it," she says. We both laugh.

"How's work?" I ask.

"Great! Love the kids. We're doing Buddhism now. They're really into it." Fabi teaches world religions and literature at Cabrini High, a private Catholic school on Esplanade.

"Cool. Relinquishing desire. The Middle Path."

She nods. "Yeah, things are great in the classroom." She chases a chunk of sweet potato around her plate. "But faculty meetings are getting weird. With the recession, alumni aren't donating like they usually do, and we're starting to feel the pinch. The headmistress is always talking about tightening our belts and what we have to cut. Field trips. Art supplies. Merit raises."

"Grim," I say.

"Yes. The teachers' lounge is not a happy place right now. And we're starting to hear from parents about the curriculum, which is weird. 'Is this necessary?' 'Is that necessary?' They're getting really specific about what we cover in class. 'Do you have to teach other religions? Can't you just do Christianity?' I mean, we haven't heard that before. It's like the economy is giving people an excuse to push their political views."

"What about the arts? In public schools, those are the first to get cut."

"No, our parents are pretty committed to a traditional sense of culture. We won't cut art, or music, or French, or Latin. The art-supply budget has already been chopped, like I said. But we won't cut art as a course." She pauses and takes a long drink of cold tea. "Not yet, anyway."

"Maybe this'll all end soon," I say, meaning the economic downturn. "Maybe it's just a blip."

"Maybe. Let's hope so."

"So, all right," I say, "I've got a rich-people question for you." Things have certainly gotten easier between my friends and me since I came out of the closet about my background in the Desire

Projects. With my tentative new candor and their answering kindness, the class tensions that used to attend our shopping sprees and fancy evenings out—where I pretended that nothing pleased me enough to purchase, or that I loved side salads with a glass of water for dinner—have largely melted away.

Fabi smiles. "Sure," she says. "Fire away."

I pull the sheaf of horse receipts from my handbag. "A woman jogger was murdered in Audubon Park this morning. A journalism professor from Tulane. A former professor of mine, in fact."

Her hand goes to her mouth. "Oh, my God, Nola. I'm so sorry." Fabi went to Loyola, right next door to Tulane. She used to run in Audubon Park, too. "Were you close?"

"Um, no."

"Still. I'm so—"

"Yeah. Thanks. My question is, why would she have these"—I push the bills of sale across the table—"in her desk? Her name's not on any of them."

Fabi nods and begins reading the first one carefully. Then the second and the third. She leafs quickly through the rest and looks up.

"These are all bills of sale for horses."

"Yeah. I got that much. But I'm hoping you can help me understand why she might have had them. Didn't one of your brothers ride?"

"Miguel. Yes. He did some showing back when we were in high school." She taps the stack of paper. "What I can tell you is that these are all Thoroughbreds. Pedigreed, valuable. Racehorses, or horses for showing, at the very least. And the same name keeps appearing as the seller. Elaine Claiborne."

"Yeah, I saw that. Does it mean anything to you?"

She thinks.

"No, the name doesn't ring a bell, but other than my brother's lessons, which ended years ago, my family's not really connected with the horse world."

"Dr. Taffner's family was. But they're in Virginia. Could there be some kind of link?"

She purses her lips. "Maybe. The horse world is national—international, even—and it's a small world. People know people." She sifts through the bills of sale again. "But these buyers all have Louisiana addresses, and the seller, this Elaine Claiborne, has her farm just across the lake in Mandeville—Hmm," she interrupts herself, "you'd think I'd know her."

"Why?"

"The address isn't far from where my parents live. On the lake." She looks down at the papers again. "But no. This doesn't ring a bell."

"What about these prices for the animals? Seventy thousand, a hundred and twenty thousand. There's one that's three hundred thousand dollars. Is that normal?"

"I think so." Fabi delicately forks up a chunk of spiced eggplant, a pale substitute for the chorizo I'm chewing. "I think it's fairly typical if the horses have a good record at early trials or a lot of promise based on their bloodlines. If horses race well, they can bring home significant purses. After their racing years, the stallions can make a fortune in stud fees, and the mares are valuable because they produce."

"You could get a couple of Porsches for that much, and never have to shovel up after them."

"Nola," she chides. "Just because we can't see the emissions doesn't mean—" and off she goes, channeling Al Gore.

There's not much more to say about the horse sales, or even about Judith Taffner, really, so we talk about work, her Carlo, my Bento, her resistance to her mother, who pushes constantly for a wedding, and my own resistance to anything with the whiff of commitment.

But I don't tell Fabi about my troubles in the bedroom. That's too personal. And too fucked up. It's what I pay Shiduri Collins for.

6

Home at Soline's condo by nine, I'm restless, brimming with nervous energy, but there'll be no running in Audubon Park alone after nightfall, much less trawling the soccer fields to find some guy to work the edge off with. I promised Shiduri I wouldn't.

And Bento, I guess, would be none too pleased if he found out. Which he wouldn't. I'm good at hiding things. Lots of practice.

He deserves better. He loves me, and he's kind. The soul of kindness. He teaches me things, takes me places I've never been.

When I told him I was afraid to fly, that I'd never flown in a plane before—that I was afraid I wouldn't be able to handle the trip to Miami for the opening of the new Sinegal—I thought he'd laugh at me. Fear doesn't fit with my tough-girl image. And Bento flies all over the world as a matter of course, giving invited talks about coastal reclamation and wetlands preservation at universities and think-tanks.

But he didn't laugh. Instead, a smile broke over his face.

"I take you up," he said. "You will see there is no reason to be afraid. All beautiful. Nothing bad."

"Wait a minute," I said. "You'll take me up? You know how to *fly*?"

He nodded and spread his hands on his knees. We were sitting on his front steps, drinking margaritas. "Is nothing," he said. "Easier than car."

"But excuse me? When did you learn *to fly*?"

"Sometimes locations are very remote. Or sometimes aerial views are best. If you can fly a small plane, is better. So I learned. Back in Spain, when I was young."

"Why didn't you tell me you knew how to fly?"

He shrugged and grinned. "I am—*¿cómo se dice?*—international man of mystery."

I shook my head. "What *don't* you do?"

What he didn't do, it turned out, was make empty promises. The following weekend, he rented a little Cessna Skyhawk. I swallowed a Dramamine with vodka from the Evian bottle in my bag, my pulse rabbiting around in my throat, and we took off from the Louis Armstrong International Airport and soared south over farmland and pastureland until we were hovering above the miles of green and silver marsh that lie between New Orleans and the coast.

"Beautiful, no?" Bento said, his hand deft and easy on the plane's black yoke.

And it was. The wetlands stretched like a shimmering sea below us, the grasses waving, the water glinting with light. Bento made the little plane glide and dip, and my belly relaxed into the thrill of it. I even rested my hands on the yoke for a while—even, at his urging, guided the Cessna through the smooth air for a few heart-stopping seconds. Above us and ahead of us was nothing but blue. The sun shone. The engine and Bento's occasional explanations were the only noise.

He was right. Flying wasn't scary. It was beautiful.

We hit the coast, and the deep blue horizon of the Gulf lay sprawled before us, oil rigs spotting it like small black toys. Bento flew out toward them, launching into a lecture about the threat of oil spills and fuming about how President Bush rescinded, last July, the ban on offshore drilling. "One stroke of the pen," he said, "and over. Done. Twenty-seven years, the Outer Continental Shelf is protected, including your Gulf. No more. Is too much power for a man in bed with oil." Talking with his hands, the way he does when he gets passionate about something, he bemoaned the impact a spill would have on the coast, the wetlands, the sea creatures, the birds. "We should be conserving," he said. "Not going deeper for more." With some indignation, he reminded me of the scientific consensus on climate change and how we're careening toward an ecological tipping point by 2025, with mass extinctions and devastation to follow.

I wanted to say, *Shut up. Stop lecturing. I'm not one of your students, and you're depressing the hell out of me.* I wanted to say, *Hey, buddy, keep both hands on the yoke.* But that would have been my fear talking. So I let him ramble. I focused on thinking about the blue sky ahead and not the dark water below, on the beauty of the moment and not the future that loomed. Swigs from the Evian bottle helped.

But thinking about Bento, much less the fate of the world, won't get the Taffner story written.

I change into cutoffs and a Radiators T-shirt, pour a shot of Belvedere from Soline's well-stocked bar, sit cross-legged on her white linen sofa, and turn my laptop on, sliding Judith Taffner's flash drive into its port.

Her icons wink to life on my screen. I sigh and start wading through the dozens of files. Drafts of articles for professional conferences. Yawn. A report on the state of journalism in the academy today. A seven-page, single-spaced memo on department assessment.

And then I click on the file labeled "Bad Shoot."

As its title suggests, it's an investigative crime story about the NOPD. Jonas Applewhite had been a retired airplane mechanic who lived in the Upper Ninth Ward—and whose only crimes, according to Judith Taffner, were being black and having the bad sense to come down off his porch when a patrol car cruised his street.

There were no eyewitnesses. The case was closed. Only his elderly wife, Mahonia, who'd been at a friend's house three blocks away when the shooting occurred, continued to insist that her husband had never owned a gun. He'd hated guns, she said—wouldn't have one in the house. His father had been shot down outside a bar in the Ninth Ward one night for his gambling winnings, ending any allure of firearms for young Jonas. "His whole life was about getting away from that world," his wife said. "No way would he have brought a gun into our house."

Despite Jonas Applewhite's loathing of guns, New Orleans' finest had mysteriously managed to find a stolen pistol at the scene, which they claimed he'd aimed at them as he'd come down off his porch that afternoon. The two officers, Tony Cinelli and Darryl Doucet, whom the piece described at length, swore they'd found it there, but Mahonia Applewhite felt sure it was planted. Maybe her husband had been carrying a tool—he was always fixing something—but not a gun.

Doucet. The guy in the squad car outside Jude Taffner's house. The guy who broke the news to her husband and kid.

She had interviewed the two patrol officers in question, so they knew who she was.

The article described them in leisurely detail, almost gushing. Tony Cinelli was "a hulking bronze statue, well over six feet tall, with a torso that proclaimed his gym membership," while Darryl Doucet was "in his late twenties, a wiry man, slender and fierce, with pale skin, cropped pale hair, and eyes the shocking blue of cornflowers."

Eyes the blue of cornflowers, indeed. The florid style surprises me, since Taffner always seemed so disciplined, controlled. It sounds like the prose of a woman in heat.

But it's a draft. Maybe she'd have tightened it up, if she'd gotten the chance.

With the Danziger Bridge case smoldering and the *Times-Picayune* constantly on their back like roux on rice, the New Orleans Police Department has enough bad PR to last until the next hurricane. They don't need another bad-shoot story to break, and Judith Taffner, from the look of things, had been just about to descend from her ivory tower to break one.

I stand, stretch, and refill my glass, disturbed by the memory of Darryl Doucet parked out in front of Taffner's little shotgun house. Would the police really cover up one murder by committing another? Would they stage it as a creepy ritualistic sex crime? They clearly had motive, and the NOPD always has opportunity. The sinister thing about a blue uniform is that a cop can be anywhere, anytime, and no one will question his presence. Folks in the Ninth would hardly trust or welcome a police officer, but a white woman jogging in a park uptown would anticipate only protection.

The vodka's warm and mellow in my throat as I sit back down and open the file called "Senator." I first see a bulleted list of notes:

- Dem donors
- bribe? purpose?
- JS.

Then the page becomes regular text, and I begin reading.

It's a profile of Senator Caleb Claiborne, a long-time conservative congressman known for his love of big donations and Big Oil.

Claiborne. Like the last name of the seller on the bills of sale. I sit up straight, my eyes moving faster down the screen.

Incorporating quotations from an interview that Judith Taffner must have conducted, the story covers his planned run for reelection in 2010, his charitable support of New Orleans art museums, and his two charming daughters, both married to investment bankers in Connecticut. It reads like a *New Yorker* profile—smart, well written, and going nowhere slowly. It's rough around the edges, but it could be polished up. Maybe a Louisiana magazine would want it. But it's just a well-researched profile. There's no hook, no angle—until I get to the part about his lovely wife Lainie and their horse farm on the north shore of Lake Pontchartrain. Elaine Claiborne. The seller.

But what do horses have to do with a senator's bid for reelection? I scroll back to the beginning and scan Jude Taffner's cryptic list of notes again.

- Dem donors
- bribe? purpose?
- JS.

I click the file closed and sit there, thinking.

Both stories—"Bad Shoot" and "Senator"—look juicy, and both could use more investigation. Both could have major political fallout.

Now both are mine.

Mentally jazzed and physically fading, I swallow the last of the vodka, stretch my legs, and click—more from a sense of obligation than anything else—on the last file, "JOUR 101 Grading Rubric." Who cares? I already know how Dr. Taffner graded. She looked at you, hated you, and gave you a C.

But the file I open has nothing to do with grades. It's Taffner's personal diary, hidden in plain sight.

And where could it have been safer? Who would dare to enter a tenured professor's office and mess with her computer, especially to read something as dull as a grading rubric? Camouflaged on her desktop at work, it was perfectly concealed.

And the inner world of Jude Taffner, as it turns out, is hidden for a reason. So much for storybook endings.

C & L driving me crazy. That damn saxophone blaring through the house while I'm trying to write, & C clamoring always for attention, attention, attention. How am I supposed to get *work* done? She won't pick up her room, won't put away her bath toys. And L says he'll clean the kitchen and then leaves the damn counter unwiped. "But I washed the dishes," he says. "Like you asked." Like he deserves a fucking medal for it. Like I should have to ask.

It's page one of forty, and there's more—much more—of the same. I scroll down to page twenty-three and stop at a random paragraph.

Insane day at work, as usual. 4 committee meetings, 2 classes—with students checking Facebook while I'm talking. Then another run-in with Gladys, who somehow believes that we exist to fill out office-supply request forms.

I used to love teaching. When did it become all about bureaucracy, reviews, assessment? It feels like we just finished our last damn APR, & now we've got another one coming down the pike. Death by paperwork.

And then office hours w/students who tell you about their *headaches,* for God's sake, & how they didn't get enough sleep to be able to do their "very best" on the assignment, & so, really, they should get the option to rewrite it, with no penalty to their grades.

Do I *ever,* I want to ask, complain about my headaches to you? My insomnia? My 3-yr-old who wakes up in the night w/bad dreams & wants me to read *Olivia* 17 times in a row?

Ouch. The professor I had known—tense, perfectionist, and uptight—had apparently become only more so with the addition of domestic stress.

But then the tone of the diary starts to shift, to lift. Page thirty-seven:

Met CB after work. The light at dusk was beautiful, the air soft. It feels like I'm 20 again, studying abroad in Paris, haloed in rose. We have to be careful. But it's worth it. He's worth it. His lips against the nape of my neck slowly, slowly—His hand cupping the side of my waist. We talk about books, art, music. I feel alive again for the first time in years.

No one can know, & that scares me. But maybe it's part of the electricity, too: the hiding, the sneaking, the quick illicit visits after dark. The way we have to lie and be clever. It all adds a certain frisson. I won't deny it. Like we're spies. Spies in the house of love. Hmm. Haven't thought about Anaïs Nin in years.

I confess, there's been something so *dull* about everyone always nodding in approval at Luke. Acceptable. Oh, so very acceptable. So daylight, so boring. Everything all on the surface, all given the grand social stamp of approval by my friends, my parents, my colleagues. Oh, look how good he is with Chloe. Oh, look how giving he is, how generous, teaching those at-risk kids. While I'm what? Kicking back in cushy tenured bliss with the cream of the crop? Like that's not work? That's their unspoken narrative. That's what everyone thinks. He's so *good,* so *good.* So what does that make me?

Fuck them all and their lazy assumptions.

So Dr. Taffner was stepping out. I remember the hotel receipt for The Columns, right there on St. Charles. Perfect for an affair: convenient, and upscale enough to suit Dr. Taffner's refined tastes. But who's CB? That name inscribed in the Hunter S. Thompson book in her desk in the Tulane office—Cory? Cory B. I scroll down, skimming. She took CB with her to interview Senator Claiborne. Is Cory B another journalism professor—thus the Thompson book—or someone from another department? Or someone completely unconnected with Tulane?

When it comes to the official investigation of Judith Taffner's rape and murder, I know her sex life will be off limits. As it should be. She's the victim here. She's not on trial. Unless this

CB guy is implicated, any affair she had is utterly irrelevant to the investigation of the crimes against her. In general, I'd oppose anything that smacks of investigating the victim's sex life, especially in a rape case. Our courts have too long and ugly a history of making women responsible for the violence against them.

But this isn't general. This is a woman I knew, a woman I resented. A woman whose husband's warm hand I'd shaken this morning. I'd seen his brown eyes soften at the sound of her name.

L's clueless, suspects nothing. Told him I had to work at the office all Sunday to finish a conference paper. Spent it with CB on his sailboat out on Pontchartrain.

The weather was gorgeous. So was CB. His soft blond hair, his bronzed body. Those muscles. All of him. Three times on the deck we made love, in front of God & everyone. I felt 21 again.

Afterward, we swam. And did it again in the water, holding on to the ladder, the waves rocking us.

I can't remember being this happy. Ever. Just writing this brings tears to my eyes.

This summer, I'll file for divorce & joint custody—or let L have her. He's obviously the better parent. And the house is still in my name. He can buy me out. I'll take the cash, start fresh with CB somewhere.

Once he graduates, things will be different. Only a month away now. How strange it will be to sit there in my cap and gown, watching him cross the stage. Our secret. And why not? Male professors have done it for years. Dr. Tolliver did it with me. *To* me, some would say. But love is love. There's no harm in it. What's that Millay line? Our divine commodity, filched before provosts and everyone.

The document ends. I check the date: three days ago. April 20, 2009.

Dr. Taffner was robbing the Tulane cradle.

Friday

7

The next morning at five-thirty, I go for my run. I stick to St. Charles Avenue: two and a half fast, sweaty miles south and east to Foucher Street. Two and a half miles back. In the dim light of dawn, I'm careful to stay constantly in sight of the early commuter traffic. We don't know yet if Judith Taffner was a one-off or the beginning of a spree. I'm taking no chances. If Audubon Park is Eden, I've been effectively expelled.

Cement sidewalks are a little harder on my knees than the soft dirt track of the park, but running along St. Charles isn't bad. The shade beneath the reaching oak trees is cool and green, and the columned manors with their vast, smooth swathes of lawn are soothing to look at, like décor magazines. Surreal.

At this early hour of the morning, the air is cool and humid against my skin as I run, and it smells like magnolias, gardenias, a blanket of Confederate jasmine flung over a fence. Sweet and dreamy. The Garden District is where the city's rich built their fancy Victorian homes and displayed their wealth, English-style, in large, exquisitely landscaped grounds. Back in the 1800s, there were only two manor houses per block. Over time, others sprouted between them—still grand, still lushly adorned with broad green lawns, shade trees, and bright blossoms wafting their intoxicating scents. My feet pound, and I think of all the people living in the Upper Ninth where I grew up, whose smell-scape consists of hot Dumpsters fermenting, dried layers of urine, the stench of a dead animal rotting somewhere. At least, you hope it's just an animal. And then the sirens come.

Sometimes I can't believe my life, my strange luck. Sometimes I can't believe the fucked-up way the world's arranged.

When I run, a hard peace fills me, despite the fact that I don't belong, that I'm just a squatter, that none of these houses could ever be mine for real. A discreet Sotheby's sign behind the iron fence of one plantation-style mansion proves my point. Soline's condo is, for me, just a better class of subsidized housing.

Sometimes after making love, Bento rolls away to pour us each another glass of wine. He pulls the backgammon board onto the bed between us, sets up the pieces on the points.

We lie there lazily, propped on our elbows, playing backgammon in the candlelight, in the glow of ease and release. We sip wine, our laughter soft. The tokens slide in my fingers, smooth and dry, clicking against each other in a solid, satisfying way. We play and drink, our gazes flicking over each other's bodies, until we want to go again.

Sometimes in the dark exhausted bliss afterward, when I lie with my head on his chest and his arm around me and my leg twined over his, the thump of his heart slow and steady under my ear makes a sound like home.

But that's on a good night.

When it's time to run alongside the length of Audubon Park on St. Charles, I watch for suspicious lurkers. A few joggers run in pairs on the asphalt track. I stick to the sidewalk.

Sweat soaked, I get home and let myself into the silent apartment, reveling in the double heads and ample water pressure of Soline's walk-in shower. After a run, everything feels good: hot water on your tired muscles, shampoo scrubbed across your scalp. The heat and freedom of it, the looseness. I throw my head back and gulp hot water straight from the stream that rains down.

Once I'm dressed for work—black blouse, red skirt—I call Senator Claiborne's office for an interview. I give my press credentials, leaving out the fact that my usual beat is crime.

A bland secretarial voice tells me the senator is currently in Washington. "I'm afraid the senator's very busy," she says.

I explain that I want to write a positive profile, a feature in preparation for his 2010 campaign.

Papers rustle. "It's a bit early for that, isn't it?" she says, her voice dubious.

"Lay the groundwork," I say. "Get the word out. Remind the public who the senator is, what he's done."

"Hmm," she says. "Let me see."

Turns out, the senator will be back in town tonight, and she can work me into his schedule on Monday. If I can be at his home office in Mandeville at nine o'clock in the morning, I can have an hour with him.

A full hour with a senator? For a reporter, it's the grail.

I thank her. She demurs. We hang up.

Then I call Luke Jourdan's home landline.

His voice on the answering machine startles me. "Hello. This is Luke and Chloe. Jude passed away unexpectedly on April twenty-third. Please understand if we don't respond to your call for a while."

Though sad, his voice is steady. What's surprising is the fact that he's already changed the message. It seems eerily practical for a husband who's supposedly overwhelmed by shock and grief. Odd. Cool customer.

I leave a brief message—"Hi, Mr. Jourdan. It's Nola Céspedes from the *Times-Picayune*, and I just have a couple of follow-up questions," et cetera—and hang up.

Soline's apartment is quiet and still around me. The refrigerator hums. Cool air shushes through vents in the wall. It's not quite eight o'clock in the morning.

At loose ends, I stand in front of Soline's built-in bookshelves, staring at the smooth spines, my eyes scanning, my mind blank. *The HarperCollins Study Bible,* thick and pale and patterned like parchment, catches my eye, and I pull it out.

Flipping to chapter two, verse twenty-one in each book is quick; plenty of second chapters don't even go that high. With the thin Bible paper slipping and wrinkling beneath my fingers, I find one verse about a prophet who threw salt in a spring, one about eunuchs, and one about a good vine that turned into a wild vine—but no likely candidates for crime-scene decoration. I keep flipping, shifting from foot to foot, until I get to the Bible's last book, everyone's favorite doom-fest, full of apocalypse and Armageddon. And when I read the verse, I know it's the one.

Revelation 2:21: "I gave her time to repent, but she refuses to repent of her fornication."

I decide to go over to Nashville Avenue myself.

When I knock, Luke Jourdan's muffled voice comes through the door's wood. "Who is it?"

I tell him. The door eases open. An inch.

"What do you want?" He looks exhausted. He's freshly shaven, though, and he's wearing a different T-shirt, heathered gray. The smell of soap wafts out. I feel guilty for my doubts. The changed answering-machine message could be just a man staying afloat by staying busy—a strategy I know well.

My voice is gentle. "Sorry to disturb you, Mr. Jourdan. I just had a quick follow-up question."

The door doesn't budge.

"Well?" He eyes me warily.

I switch tactics. "Did you see the story in this morning's paper?"

"Yes." He nods, and the door eases wider open. "It was good. I didn't know what to expect, but you showed Jude at her best." He glances briefly behind him, then back at me. "I clipped it out for Chloe when she's older."

"Oh, good. I'm so glad." I smile back at him, trying to exude warmth and concern. I pursue my best way in. "How's she doing?"

The smooth pale skin across his forehead furrows. "I think she's doing okay, I guess. Given her developmental stage, I mean. She drifts in and out of remembering that Jude's—gone."

"I think that's normal. She'll absorb it a little at a time, as much as her psyche can stand." That's how it happened back in the Desire Projects, anyway. I knew kids who lost their dads, their brothers, their moms. You can't take it in all at once. It comes and goes, until it's real.

The door falls farther open. "It's kind of weird, actually. She cries for a while and wants to be held, but then she'll get down and go play like nothing's happened."

"That's probably healthy."

"I think so," he says, but his voice sounds doubtful. "I looked at some child psych Web sites online, and it seems to be a pretty typical response."

I smile sympathetically again. He's definitely keeping busy as a way to cope.

"So what was your question? Do you want to come in?" He opens the door fully, and I see the rest of his body.

In his hand, hanging down by his thigh, gleams a knife.

I step back, my hands raised in front of me. "Whoa, there."

He looks at me, down at the knife in his hand. Back at me. "Oh," he says, lifting the knife in the air. "Oh." He looks surprised, as if he'd forgotten he was holding it. "I was chopping vegetables. I was in the kitchen when you knocked."

"Really."

"Yeah." His smile is weak. "It's what I do. I cook."

I guess I look unconvinced.

"Seriously," he says. "Come on in. I'll show you."

It's one of those crazy moments that happen now and then, reporting crime. Someone asks for my trust, and my gut is all I've got to go on.

I nod. "Okay, sure."

He smiles and turns. I enter, and when he shuts the door behind me, I don't feel the warning twinge of fear. Good sign.

"It's this way," he says, and he leads me past the immaculate living room and through a doorway.

The kitchen is a warm, bright yellow, and morning sun streams in through a wall of windows on the east. "This is really nice," I say, and I mean it.

A large center island is topped with a slab of butcher block, and on the wood sit huge heaps of vegetables: carrots, celery, peppers, potatoes. Several fat yellow onions sit on the side, uncut.

What strikes me is how big the piles are. Each one alone could easily fill a pot.

I pull up a stool. "What time did you get up this morning?"

He glances at me. "Let me just finish this one," he says, and his knife blurs through a stalk of celery, thunking against the board like machine-gun fire. I remember what he told me about working the cold line in a restaurant. He must have been pretty good before Jude Taffner started his makeover.

He scoops up the fine slices and adds them to the pile, then turns to the sink to wash the knife.

"I don't know," he says, his back to me. "Three o'clock?"

I look around. If the white-and-crystal living room was Judith Taffner's domain, then this kitchen is surely her husband's. The top of the white fridge is rounded, vintage, and there's a booth in the corner: yellow benches, cool metal-edged table, like in a diner. Funky. A rusted sign that says EAT HERE hangs above the table. Evidence of Chloe is everywhere. Dozens of her smiles beam from photographs stuck to the fridge. Finger paintings are taped to it.

The lower kitchen cabinets have been painted with black chalkboard paint, so Chloe can sit and draw while he cooks. Chalked rainbows and stick figures romp across the cupboard doors.

I look at Luke Jourdan's back. Broad shoulders. Muscles obvious, right through the T-shirt. His triceps ripple.

He turns to me, carefully wiping the knife with a white towel.

"Nice idea," I say, pointing down at the cupboards.

He glances. "Oh. Yeah, she likes to be in here with me. And I like her company." He places the knife in a rack. It's an expensive set of knives, the kind Uri and I would ogle in the Williams-Sonoma catalog before we'd throw it in the recycling bin. The kind Soline has on her counter. The kind of blades that slide through steak like it's warmed butter.

I wave at the mounds of veggies. "So what are you making?"

He looks down. Shrugs. "I don't know. Soup?"

"You're going to have a lot of soup on your hands."

"Yeah. Well, Chloe likes soup okay." He scoops the piles into separate plastic containers, puts them in the fridge, dries his hands, and hangs the towel on the refrigerator handle. He waves a hand toward the living room. "Let's go in there."

"Sure. Thanks," I say. We leave the warm sunshine behind and head for the white love seats. The cushions are soft. I cross my legs. "I'll be brief."

"It's okay," he says, sinking down into the love seat opposite me. "It's not like I've got a lot to do right now. The school gave me a week of leave, Chloe's sleeping again, and would you believe Jude had everything already planned with the funeral home?" He shakes his head, cracks his knuckles. "So I'm in limbo right now, waiting for the funeral home to set a date, waiting to hear from the police."

"Have they gotten the coroner's report?"

"No. But there doesn't seem to be much doubt about how it happened." He rubs his forehead.

I think back to Dr. Taffner's glazed eyes, her bruised throat, her swollen face, her brown hair snaking through water.

"Not much, I guess." I clear my throat. "And do they have any leads on the killer?"

He shakes his head and looks down at his hands in his lap. His voice is low. "I just feel so helpless. I should have been there.

I could have protected her." He looks up. "And now this guy's out there, loose, and the police tell me to just stay here, that my daughter needs me—and I know they're right—but I want to be out there, looking. I want to find the son of a bitch."

"I know."

He looks at me, skepticism plain on his face.

I lean forward. "I do know, believe me. I've been the victim of a violent crime," I say. "I know what it's like to want justice." I don't tell him that the black Beretta in my purse helped me get it.

He nods slowly. "Yeah," he says. He cracks his knuckles again. "Sitting here is driving me crazy."

No more stalling. I've built all the rapport I've got time to build.

"Mr. Jourdan, there might be a way you can help. There's some evidence that your wife knew a student whom she identified only by the initials CB. I'm wondering if you might know who that is."

He thinks, then shakes his head. "Jude had hundreds of students. Thousands, probably, over the years. I met some of them at campus events—concerts, lectures—but I didn't pay attention to their names."

"This was a student she may have spoken about recently." I choose my words. When people cheat, they like to drop the name of their lover into conversation in some innocuous way. To feel the secret closeness, the thrill. It's almost compulsive. "Someone she may have been particularly close to."

He purses his lips. "She was mentoring some interns, and she occasionally chaired an honors thesis, but she really didn't talk about individual students." He frowns. "Why? What does this have to do with her murder?"

I use my best butter-melting voice. "Probably nothing at all. I'm just tracking down a potential lead."

"But why do you care who her students were?"

"It might give us a fuller picture of your wife's activities before the murder. If I find anything out, I'll share it with the police. It might help them." I take a breath. "His first name might be Cory."

Luke Jourdan blinks three times. "His?" He blinks again, as if calculations are tumbling in his head entirely against his will. "Where'd you get those initials, anyway?"

I clear my throat again. "They were in some writing your wife had done. The name Cory was inscribed in a book that she'd apparently received as a gift."

"What are you saying to me?" He rises to his feet. His voice is deadly quiet. "What are you saying? Particularly close? What does that mean?" He steps toward me, leans down, and grabs my shoulders. "What are you not saying?"

"Mr. Jourdan, Mr. Jourdan," I say, rising to my feet as well. His hands drop away from me. They clench and unclench at his sides as I speak. "There's some suggestion that this student, this CB, knew your wife well. We'd like to question him in connection with the murder."

"Is he a suspect? Was she being stalked?"

I let the silence rest between us for a moment. "The nature of their relationship makes that a possibility. But not a likely one."

He stands there, staring at me for long moments. "The nature of their relationship," he repeats dully. Then, as though someone unplugged him, he drops to the white cushions. "Fucking Jude," he says, his voice low. "I fucking knew it."

I keep my voice quiet. "What do you mean?"

"Oh, I don't know." He rubs his hand over his eyes. "I don't know. There was something. There was always something wrong, some little thing she'd find to get upset about. And even when there wasn't, something just always felt . . . wrong." He shakes his head and looks at me, like he's waiting for me to explain it. We look at each other. I can't help him. He shakes his head again. "She didn't seem happy. Or she seemed happy, but not happy enough. Not happy like I thought she'd be." His voice catches. "Not happy like I was."

"So you had a feeling." I think of the numbers scrawled in blood on the dead woman's skin.

"I'd ask her what was wrong, and she'd brush me off. Yeah, I had a feeling. But I never thought she'd really—Jude was a good person. She worked hard. She had values. She was always talking about her standards. She wouldn't have—" His voice thickens and skids to a halt.

"Mr. Jourdan, I'm so sorry." I cross over and sit next to him, laying a hand on his broad-boned wrist, hoping it's not the wrong move. His skin is warm and smooth.

"Call me Luke." His laugh is bitter. "I think we're past mister."

"There's a chance I could be wrong about the relationship. That's why it's important to find this Cory B."

He shakes his head. "Search me. Honestly. I've got no fucking idea." His chest rises and falls inside his gray T-shirt, as if he's deliberately calming himself down. "Excuse me."

He lurches to his feet and disappears into the kitchen. I hear a cupboard door bang softly shut. When he comes back, he's holding two Old-Fashioneds, each with a finger of brown liquor. He sets one down on the table near me.

It's eight-thirty in the morning.

"No, thanks," I say, despite wanting it.

He collapses into the love seat next to me and tosses the whole thing back in two swift gulps. Then he glances over at me. "You sure?" he says.

I smile and nod politely. He reaches over, grabs my glass, and knocks that one back as well. He coughs a little. Wipes his eyes.

"Martine," he says. "You should ask Martine."

"Martine?"

"Jude's closest friend. Martine White Elk. She teaches at Tulane, too. I forget which department. Sociology? I don't remember. They went out together a lot." He laughs again, a harsh laugh. "If Jude was up to anything, and if she told anyone, Martine would be the one."

I'm nodding. "I'll see if she'll talk with me."

He snorts. "Good luck with that."

"What do you mean?"

"You'll see."

8

Twenty minutes before eleven, I arrive early to talk to Uri, who—
aside from the hotel's easy proximity to Tulane—is the reason I
chose The Columns as a rendezvous spot. He's working behind
the long mahogany bar of the Vic when I get there.

Something catches in my chest at the sight of him. I hug him
too hard and take too long to let go.

"It's different around the house with you gone," he says. Before I have the chance to feel touched, he adds, "Serene. Quiet."
He laughs. "Tidy."

"Nice." I punch his muscled arm. "So how's Brian?"

"Oh, he's great," Uri says, but his smile fades, and he doesn't
meet my eyes.

"What?" My hands settle on my hips, waiting. "What is it?
Dígame."

"He's really great. He's just . . . busy."

"Busy?"

"And tired. I mean, I knew that residency was hard. I get it.
But he's tired all the time, and a little . . ."

"A little what?"

"Oh, I don't know. Nothing. He's fine. We're fine. And you're still liking it over at your friend's place?"

I let his artless change of topics ride. "It's cool," I say, squashing whole paragraphs of my ambivalence into two words. "Look, I've got a *favorcito* to ask you."

"Name it."

"I'm working a story, and I'm going to interview someone here in a few minutes."

"In here?"

"Out on the porch, I think." This early in the day, the sunny veranda seems more appropriate than the velvety brown womb of the Vic.

"No worries. I'll wait on you myself."

"Thanks, but it's not your service I want, so much as your powers of observation. I want your sense of her."

"Oh, cool." His smile comes back. "I'm in." An aspiring novelist, Uri continually writes sketches of the bar patrons anyway— for possible future use—so he studies people. He used to come home late from his shift and entertain me with impressions. I miss that.

"Let's set you up at fourteen," he says, leading the way to a small round table laid with gleaming silverware and thick white linens. "It's the easiest one to watch."

So I'm sitting here, breathing the April air and enjoying the birdsong and the rustle of oak leaves, when up the stairs walks a woman in jeans, boots, and a white T-shirt. She's tall. Her black hair falls in a thick shining sheet to the small of her back. There's a leather bag slung diagonally across her lean frame, and when I rise to my feet, her lips curve smoothly into a hard smile.

"Martine White Elk?"

She nods. We shake hands. She's a good five inches taller than I am. All of her movements have an unusual grace and slowness, like she's moving underwater or in some other thick, fluid medium.

The source of Luke Jourdan's tension with Martine, I realize, is sex. Pure, unapologetic, amoral sex. Martine White Elk is the girl that fathers warn their sons about and envy them for. A bad influence, as they say. Not the kind of friend a man would want his wife to have. He'd want to have her himself.

Martine folds herself into the chair like an erotic act. Leans back. Crosses her legs. Gazes coolly at me from beneath lowered lids. Blinks.

"Absentee Shawnee, from Oklahoma," she says.

"Did I ask?"

"I just get it out there. Otherwise I become everyone's all-purpose third-world exotic nothing." Her eyes slide over me like a caress. "But this isn't about me." She leans across and drags her fingertips lightly across my wrist. They feel like heavy silk. "You want to talk about Jude."

"Yes." I hold out my press pass.

She briefly eyes it, then nods. "Go ahead."

"Her husband, Luke, said you might be able to help me."

"Sure," she says. Her voice is husky, like it comes from deep in her chest or deep in a dream. "Anything to catch this guy."

"Good. Then let me cut to the chase. I'm trying to learn the name of a Tulane student Jude knew. Someone she may have been particularly close to. His initials are CB, and his first name may be Cory."

She looks at me for a long moment, registering nothing. There's the faintest stiffening of the muscles around her eyes. It's almost as though I haven't spoken. Then she leans back in her chair and folds her arms.

"You must have mistaken me," she says softly, "for something other than Jude's friend."

I keep my smile gentle, nonintrusive. "I appreciate your loyalty. I do. That's how I'd want my own friends to answer." I lean toward her. "But I want justice for Jude, and I think this student, this Cory B, can help."

Other people shake their heads when they mean no. Martine White Elk merely shifts hers: a fraction to the right, a fraction to the left. It still means no.

"Jude was killed by a maniac in the park," she says. "How's some kid supposed to help you?"

"I'm trying to build a picture of her activities in the days before she was murdered. Now, it's possible that her attacker chose her randomly—that he was an opportunistic rapist and killer, and she just came along. Right place, right time."

"Wrong time," she corrects me.

"Yes. But what if he wasn't an opportunistic killer? What if he watched her, stalked her, chose her? Then figuring out where she was, where he might have seen her, could help the police locate the killer." She's watching me, weighing my words. "Because right now, the police have exactly no suspects in custody. And according to her husband, she went pretty much nowhere except the office, the park, and dropping off Chloe at daycare. But I have a hotel receipt that says she spent some part of a day and night right here at The Columns last month, and a journal entry that says she was sailing on Pontchartrain last Sunday." I sigh. "Look, I'm sorry. But if I can find this Cory B, I can find out where else she might have gone. Somewhere the killer might have spotted her."

She watches me, unmoved.

We sit there, staring at each other.

"Look," I say. "Other women go to those places. Other women are still at risk." I play my last card: guilt. "The way she died—it was bad. You don't want that happening to someone else." We sit there, our knowledge of Jude's death hanging in the air between us.

Finally Martine squints, as if deciding, and leans forward. "Luke can never know."

I nod. I don't tell her that Luke already knows plenty.

Cory Brink, as it turns out, is a fifth-year senior, living near Tulane in a sweet apartment on the corner of Jeannette and Pine. For Jude, the affair started out as a lark, a diversion, but the deeper in she got, the more it felt like more. She wanted to leave Luke, but according to Martine, Cory Brink pulled away every time she brought up living together. She was planning a divorce, but Cory, on the verge of graduation and with an abundance of family connections, had no intention of fettering himself. Jude was alternately ecstatic and distraught when the two women met for their weekly lunches.

"But she never wanted Luke to know about the affair," Martine says. Her finger taps my wrist. "You've got to believe that. She always talked about what a good man he was: a good husband, a good father to Chloe. She didn't love him anymore, but she didn't want to hurt him. She wanted a clean divorce and a fresh start."

A fresh start. I feel a pang on Luke's behalf, remembering his Whole Foods story. I imagine him taking the chard, past its prime, from her hand. He was supposed to have been the fresh start, but ended up being the stale thing she wanted to discard.

"Can I ask you a question, Martine? I mean, it might sound

strange, but it gets at her state of mind. Did Jude Taffner ever really love her husband? Really?"

She blinks slowly at me. "How well did you say you knew her?"

"She was just my professor. But I did the math. Luke came along: right place, right time." Or wrong time, for him. "She wasn't getting any younger. The opportunity was there. She took it."

"Jude was my friend. Her choices were her business." She folds her arms across her chest. "Personally, I try not to judge."

"Personally," I say, "I call it like I see it."

"That must be very fulfilling for you." She stands abruptly.

"I like it okay."

She turns and strides down the steps, her hips swinging smoothly, her shoulders thrown back.

"Wait!" I say, but she keeps walking, and I sit there, watching her turn left onto the sidewalk and disappear.

"Besides being smokin' hot?" says Uri. I'm on the phone with him as I drive to Cory Brink's apartment.

"Yeah, besides that."

He laughs. "What'd you do to piss her off? You have a knack."

"I'm lucky that way. What else?"

"Self-possessed. Smart. Self-made. Hiding something."

"Hiding what?"

"Can't say. But you could see it in her body language. Closed, careful, even while she was putting on a show."

"Yeah," I agree. "She was hiding something when she first sat down, but then she gave it up."

There's a pause on the line as he considers.

"I think so," he says. "Probably. What's this all about, anyway?" he asks. "What's the story?"

"I'm not sure yet." I turn onto Broadway, pass a fraternity house and The Boot, the college bar where I used to hang out, and make my way to the corner of Pine and Jeannette, where I scan for a parking spot.

"Nola," he says, "is anything wrong?"

"Maybe not." I whip the Pontiac around and wedge it into a spot. In the grass by the curb, a hip-high pyramid of beer cans glitters. "*Mira,* I've got to go, but thank you. *Mil gracias.* You're a jewel."

"Of the first water," he replies.

9

Like I said, there are good nights with Bento. And then there are bad ones. Like the night we had a week ago.

Bento's bed. He's lying back on the pillows, and I'm on top, the way I like it, my hips swiveling like they're on a pivot, his beautiful brown chest and belly beneath me, his hands gripping my hips. The Moorish mirrors reflect infinite Bentos and Nolas, all working it. My arms are up over my head, my hands in my hair, and all shall be hot, and all shall be hot, and all manner of thing shall be hot, and I'm Shamhat, I'm Shakira, I'm the Kama Sutra live hot girls—when all of a sudden, he fucks it up.

"*Querida*," he says, reaching up to stroke my face. "Look at me."

It's like all the music stops. Just grinds to silence. His dark eyes, I can't look into them.

"*Querida*," he says again, and other love words.

I splay my hand on his chest and focus on it, my spread fingers against his skin. The ovals of lacquered scarlet. The heat of him. Focus. Breathe from my belly. Stay in the moment.

But when I glance back at his face, I can't help it: he's changed.

A cartoon, a bloated simpering fool, murmuring his dumb en-dearments. Disgust fills me fast, like a house fills with water, and I hate him and I hate myself and I need to be gone.

My hand on his chest pushes me back and off him, and I'm up and dressing, scattering the pieces from the backgammon board he'd placed so carefully on the floor. He's sitting up, the sheet pulled around his hips.

"What is it?" he says. "What's wrong?" But I just shake my head, mute, my mouth sealed tight because, sick and furious as I am, I do not want to blow this, I don't. I can't let the bile flood out of me. I mutter some words about a sudden stomachache that we both know aren't true.

Before he can even pull on his jeans to follow, my feet are in my shoes and I'm out the door, and I'm gunning my Pontiac down dark streets, my hand fumbling in my purse for my cell, and then I'm glancing back and forth from its small bright screen to the road, thumbing to *C,* calling Shiduri Collins at one in the morning and hearing my voice husky in the dark cool capsule of the car:

"It's me. It's Nola. It happened again."

On this block, most of the houses are a bit battered. It's a college rental zone: lots of partying, lots of turnover, lots of kids for whom respect for others' property is optional.

But the address that popped up on my iPhone for Cory Brink is a well-kept two-story house with a fresh coat of quiet green paint. The lawn has been recently mown. Gardenia bushes blossom beneath neatly pruned crape myrtle trees. Jude Taffner would have been reassured by it all.

When I get to the top of the stairs, I lean on the doorbell and then wait for a full minute. I'm almost ready to give up and leave, when the door is opened by the prettiest douche bag I've ever seen.

He answers his door shirtless, his muscled torso baked tan, his hair bleached nearly white by real salt and real sun.

"Cory Brink?"

He smiles lazily and looks me up and down. Nods. Like moving his lips would be too much trouble. He's wearing two-hundred-dollar board shorts, canvas deck shoes, and one of those bead-and-twine necklaces that suburban boys affect. He's an undergraduate who owns a sailboat big enough to have sex on.

Nothing about him seems marked by the recent and violent death of his lover. His bright blue eyes have only the casual, self-absorbed social fearlessness that comes with a lifetime of un-touchability and being catered to. It's a feeling I don't know from personal experience, but I've seen it often enough. I've thought about what it leads to.

I introduce myself, show him my press pass, and invite myself in to ask a few questions.

Cory Brink waves me inside toward a white leather sofa. I make myself comfortable, my skirt sliding a little. On the granite-topped coffee table sit *The Thing About Life Is That One Day You'll Be Dead* by David Shields, a couple of well-thumbed *Esquire*s, and a purple glass bong as tall as a toddler.

"You want a beer?" says Cory Brink.

I realize I'm thirsty. "Some water would be great." While he's gone, I inventory the room: ESPN blaring from a flat-screen the size of my Pontiac, soccer cleats kicked off by the door, white leather recliners, a deflated backpack, posters of Jimi Hendrix and Green Day, a framed photo of a beautiful young blond woman on the deck of a yacht. I lean forward to study her. She's half Jude Taffner's age.

The white carpet is striped by recent vacuum-tracks. Someone cleans regularly, and I doubt it's Cory Brink.

There's money here, but everything seems typical, even banal. This is the guy Jude Taffner wanted to talk books and music with?

He returns with a plastic convenience-store cup, sets my icewater down on the granite, and settles himself into a recliner across from me, his browned pecs and abs on generous display as he leans back and jerks the footrest horizontal. He lifts the remote to mute ESPN, like a young king lifting a scepter, and looks me full in the face.

The head of Cory Brink tilts, and he stares at me in the silence for a long moment. He squints. "Do people tell you that you look like J.Lo?"

I nod. "Yeah, that's fine," I say. I take a long swallow of the water. It's cold and good. "Nice place."

"Yeah." He nods. A cool, lazy motion.

"Do you rent?"

"Nah. My parents bought it." He shrugs. "Investment property. You know."

I nod like I do. "And they pay someone to come in and clean up after you? Someone to do the yard?"

A ripple of mild surprise passes over his face, shifts to irritation, and then disappears. "Yeah. You doing a story on student housing or what?"

"I wish I were, Cory. I really wish I were. But unfortunately, I'm here to ask you about Dr. Taffner."

His eyelids drop just a millimeter. "What about her?"

"Can you talk to me a little about your relationship?"

The blue eyes narrow further. "She was my professor, junior year. Some journalism class."

"Ah." I nod earnestly and write in my notebook. *Douche bag*, it says. "And are you a journalism major?"

He laughs. "As if. No way. Business."

Of course you are. "Yet Dr. Taffner's notes indicate that she recently took you along on an interview. You weren't interning?"

"Naw. Just along for the ride."

"Indeed. And whom were you interviewing?"

"Just some politician guy. We went out to his house and Dr. T did the talking. I just hung out." He rubs his hand through his hair in a way that college girls no doubt find endearing. "His place was sweet."

"Senator Claiborne?"

"Yeah, I think so. He had this house right on the lake. North shore. Awesome dockage."

"Did you play any active role in the interview at all?"

He glances up at the ceiling as if scanning his memory. "I asked some questions, I guess. They had cool horses. Racehorses. I asked the guide-girl and the stable guy some questions about them."

"What kinds of questions?"

"Like, where they're bred, how much they cost, that kind of stuff. And then when we met the senator guy, I asked him about his campaign. I'm pre-law. Got accepted into LSU law. My dad wants me to go into politics someday. I don't know, though."

"And did your relationship with Dr. Taffner extend beyond the academic?"

He sits there, smiling lazily, saying nothing.

"Would you like to comment?"

"Not really."

"I'm sorry, Cory. This must be a very difficult time for you."

Again a mild ripple shifts the flesh of his face. There's a pause. "Why difficult?"

"I'm so sorry for your loss."

He pushes the footrest down and sits up. "What loss?"

"I'm sure you've heard. Dr. Taffner was killed yesterday morning. Murdered."

He squints. "You're fucking with me."

"I'm afraid not. It was in today's paper."

"Who reads the paper?"

"I'm serious, Cory. She really did die. She was attacked not far from here, in Audubon Park, during her morning run. The killer strangled her."

I watch him carefully. His surprise seems genuine. But that's all it is. Surprise. Not guilt. Not grief. Not anguish.

"Shit," he says slowly. He pulls his fingers through his pretty mane again. "Does her husband know?"

"Yes, he's been informed."

"And her little girl?"

"Did you know Chloe?"

"No. But I knew about her. Jude talked about her sometimes." Mere seconds have passed since he learned of her death, but he's already speaking of her in the past tense. No denial here.

"Chloe knows. But she's quite young. She doesn't really understand yet."

"Aw, man. This really sucks for them."

"Yes. Yes, it does. And Cory, the police are currently trying to find her killer, so—"

"It wasn't me, man." A hint of anxiety darkens his eyes.

"No one thinks it is. But we're hoping you can help us with our inquiries. If you could provide an alibi . . ."

"Yeah, sure. Definitely. When did you say it happened?"

"Monday morning, between five and six A.M."

"Oh, dude," he says, "I am *never* up that early."

"Hmm. Yes. But is there anyone who can corroborate that?"

"Yeah. Vanessa, my girlfriend." He gestures toward the framed photo of the blonde, and I feel a pang of pity for Jude Taffner. This boy is what she wanted to ruin her marriage and leave her daughter for.

"If you could give me her contact information—"

He does, and I write it down.

"Cory, we're interviewing Dr. Taffner's known associates in order to identify the locales where she usually went. Places where her attacker might have first seen her and become interested. The police aren't sure, but it could have been a stalker. So anywhere you might have gone together, restaurants, clubs . . ."

He's nodding slowly. "I can't get in trouble for this, right? I mean, they can't keep me from graduating, can they?"

"Yes. That's correct." I feel another pang of pity for Dr. Taffner. She's in the morgue being autopsied, and he's worried about commencement.

He nods. "Then yeah, we had a thing. But we didn't go out. She mostly came over here. She'd park over on another street, walk up the alley, come in the back way, after dark. Just for a couple of hours, usually."

"Did she know about Vanessa?"

"What, do I look like an idiot? No. And Vanessa sure as hell didn't know about her."

"Dr. Taffner's notes suggest that you took her sailing."

"A couple of times. She was game. She liked it out there." He grins. "Once we got far enough from shore, she was pretty . . . uninhibited. She didn't care if people saw us going at it. From a distance, I mean." I remember the lines from Jude Taffner's journal, the open secret on her desktop: *Three times on the deck we made love, in front of God & everyone. I felt 21 again.* Cory Brink shakes his head. "It's unreal about her dying. She was a fun lady."

Stirring epitaph.

"Cory, I also have in my possession a receipt from The Columns, the hotel on St. Charles. Did you and Dr. Taffner ever spend the night there?"

"We went there, yeah. But we didn't spend the whole night. She checked in, then I came later, and then we left around midnight or one. Separately." He nods and taps the side of his nose like we're in a movie. "Very hush-hush."

"Why would she have risked going to a hotel so close to the university with you?"

"Yeah, I didn't get it, either. She kept talking about how it was our anniversary and stuff. She had champagne sent up, flowers, all that."

"Anniversary?" I'm surprised. "How long were you together?"

"Three months. I don't know why she made a big deal about it." He stares at the picture of Vanessa. "It was kind of embarrassing, tell you the truth."

"Did you ever go running with her in the mornings?"

His gaze swings back to me, startled. "Fuck, no. She would never have gone for that. Besides, like I said, the Brinkster's not up that early."

I sigh. Of course he refers to himself with an annoying nickname in the third person. "Okay. But do you know where she usually ran? Her typical route?"

"No. Look, I don't even know where she lived, okay?" His hands move impatiently through the air. "She was hot, I flirted, she went for it. That's it."

"There was a book in her desk, signed by you. A gift."

"Oh, yeah. That." He sighs. "Early days, that was. I saw this Johnny Depp movie about Hunter Thompson in Las Vegas. He was, like, this crazy journalist. So I ordered the guy's book online. First edition. Set me back beaucoup bucks. Worked, though. She was all turned on."

An entire love affair, one-sided and fueled by illusion. I sigh again.

"Thank you, Cory. I think you've told me all I need to know."

"Cool." He nods with self-approval. I wait for him to rise to his feet and usher me to the door, the way people usually do when an interview ends, but he sits in his recliner, watching me, nodding and smiling like any congenial stoner.

I gather my things and let myself out.

When I get back to the Pontiac, which has been quietly baking in the sun, it's noon. I get in and check my phone. A text from Calinda says, "Call me." I roll down the windows, start the motor, and dial her number.

She doesn't even pause to greet me. "You're not going to believe this," she says. "Forensics just came in on your vic."

"And?"

"Nola," she says. "Get this. There's no evidence of rape."

I pause, remembering the scene. Definitely the scene of a sex crime. "No semen? No damage to the soft tissues?"

"Nothing."

I stare out at the line of parked cars in front of me. "What about the blood?"

"Porcine. Available at any butcher."

"People buy blood?"

"My poor dear innocent. Yes, people buy blood. Some recipes call for it. And this is New Orleans, remember. People do weird shit here."

I rub my temples. "So it was all staged?" The ripped clothes, the pulling down of her underwear, the blood, the feathers . . . "The real point was to kill her. The rest of it was window dressing."

"Looks that way, yeah."

"A diversion," I say, my mind flicking through options. "A delay tactic."

"But anyone with half a brain would know the delay could only be temporary."

"Which argues against the obvious prime suspect—"

"The husband," says Calinda.

"Yeah." Luke Jourdan had more than half a brain. "If he was the doer, there'd be no point in throwing the cops off the scent for a day or two, unless he was going to run. Which he hasn't. He's sitting right there on Nashville Avenue. I saw him this morning." I close my eyes and pinch the bridge of my nose. "On the other hand—"

"Yeah?"

The words come out reluctantly, because I feel sorry for Luke Jourdan. Handsome Luke Jourdan who's kind to his daughter and who cooks. I might even like him a little bit. "He did have motive. The vic was screwing a Tulane student."

"Ooh. Bad professor."

"Quite bad, apparently. And she was planning to file for

divorce." I watch as a young woman comes out of one of the apartment houses, a small bundle of clothes hugged to her chest, and weaves her way down the sidewalk.

"So if the husband found out—"

"And if he were the angry type—"

"But would a husband leave his wife all stripped like that?" I can hear Calinda's consternation through the phone. "And sexualized? For public consumption?"

"If he was mad enough about the affair, he might want to expose her. Humiliate her."

She clucks. "That would be cold. Does he seem that cold?"

"He seems—" I think for a moment. "He seems calm. Controlled. If he's a killer—and I don't think he is, Calinda, I really don't—he'd be an organized one, capable of planning ahead. And he's easily strong enough to do it." Those muscles. "He knows her routine." A chill runs through me as I realize how much opportunity he'd really had. But I remember sitting next to him on the love seat, his warmth with Chloe, his skin smooth under my palm. Was Luke Jourdan a consummate actor?

"What about the Catholic props?" asks Calinda. "The whole Satanic thing."

"Not sure. Could be pure red herring."

"Is he Catholic? Or was she?"

"I don't know. I'll ask."

"Ask?" Her tone is horrified. "Nola Céspedes, you stay away from that guy. Hear?"

"Did my lawyer friend just tell me how to do my job? Because—"

She laughs. "Yeah, all right. Backing off. Just be careful, okay? I'm just saying. Because your judgment isn't always—"

"Excuse me? This is how you back off?"

She laughs again. "Okay, okay."

But I trace the long white scar that circles my arm. She's got a point.

"Hey." I try to change the subject. "How's it going with the sperm-bank fellas?"

"Nola." Her voice lowers conspiratorially, and I can hear her smile. "I think I might've found one. You got time to meet up later this week? I'll show you his profile."

"Sounds good. Find a time and text me."

"Will do. Listen, you take care now. I mean it."

We say the usual affectionate things and sign off. The air blowing from the Pontiac's vents is finally cool, so I roll up my windows and pull into traffic.

10

When I step onto the front porch of Mahonia Applewhite's dilapidated shotgun cottage in the Upper Ninth Ward and knock on her door, it's two o'clock in the afternoon. The sun presses down hot and strong, and I'm glad of the shade. Taut green Astroturf covers the floor of her porch. The yellow cushions on her metal glider are faded but clean, and a sweet, spiced scent comes from the purple petunias that flourish in coffee cans on the porch rails.

A small, bent woman materializes on the other side of the screen to peer at me. She's wearing a yellow dress and house-shoes, and her crinkly white hair is drawn back from her brown face in a bun. I introduce myself and show my press pass.

She looks me up and down, then jerks her chin.

"I thought from the phone you was white," she says. She unlatches the door and pushes it open for me. "Come on in. You want some tea?"

Mahonia Applewhite ushers me inside. There's no air conditioner running, but the jalousie shades have kept the room cool and dark, and it has that gentle, peaceful, much-washed smell of old houses.

"Go on and set yourself down," she says, and I take a seat on a mustardy tweed sofa, its sharp angles edged with piping, authentically 1960s, not some recent *Mad Men* facsimile from CB2. Faded family photos cluster together on top of a bookcase: a long-ago wedding, children's school portraits. Two diplomas from Xavier University hang framed on the wall. Mahonia Applewhite disappears into the kitchen, her house-shoes rasping softly on the linoleum, and returns with two glasses of iced tea.

"So, I suppose you want to know about my husband," she says, leaning to place both glasses down on coasters on the coffee table. Her fingers are permanently bent with age, curling in toward her palms. She sinks with a little sigh into a blue vinyl armchair.

"Yes, ma'am, if you don't mind." I pull out my silver Olympus. "Would it be all right if I record our conversation?"

She looks at me askance, hesitates, then nods. "You go on ahead. I don't care who hears what I got to say. The Lord knows the truth, and the truth will out."

"Yes, ma'am." I press the small Record button, and the red light starts to blink. "Ms. Applewhite—"

"Missus," she says. "I'm not one of these newfangled women. I was his wife."

I nod. "Yes, ma'am. Mrs. Applewhite, I believe Dr. Judith Taffner has been here to speak with you. A journalist from Tulane."

"Yes, she came over here just like you did. Asked me all about Jonas and guns and the day he died. Sat right where you sitting, matter of fact."

"I've read the story she wrote about your husband, and I'd like to help get it into print. Bring attention to your case."

"Then you better watch yourself, young miss. Look where it got that lady."

Her face is settled, calm, her hands folded in her lap.

"You've heard about her death, then."

She nods. "I read the papers. I watch the news. I'm old, honey. I'm not dead."

"And you don't believe Dr. Taffner's death was a random murder?"

Her smile is wan. "I been in this city my whole life, dear, fearing God and doing His work, and there ain't one thing I'd put past the NOPD. If they can lie and cover up one killing, they can lie and cover up another."

I consider for a moment. "You might be interested to know," I say slowly, "that the coroner found no evidence of sexual assault, though the crime was staged to look like a rape-and-murder."

"Mm-hmm." She folds her arms across her thin frame, rocks slightly to and fro. "That right there's just exactly what I'm telling you."

"Do you know anything about the two patrol officers who were in the car when your husband was shot?"

"Never seen them. Not then, not ever. Never want to."

"There wasn't much coverage of the story in the newspaper at the time of your husband's death."

"Barely an inch." She nods and keeps rocking. "A man's whole life, barely an inch. And since then, nothing. I called the police department a dozen times or more, but I guess a little old lady is easy to forget about."

"I'd like to make sure your husband's case gets the investigation it deserves."

She nods again. "That's what you said on the phone, dear. That's why you sitting here." She takes a long cool sip of her tea and swallows, her eyes never leaving me. "That'd be real nice. But like I say, you best watch yourself."

I ask about the details of the day, and what Mahonia Applewhite tells me tallies with Dr. Taffner's write-up. Two officers, a hot day, no witnesses, her seventy-one-year-old husband with a shotgun blast in his chest, and a gun found by the body—a gun of which Mahonia Applewhite had never seen hide nor hair in her fifty-two years of married life.

"Why do you think there were no witnesses?" Her street had been busy and bustling when I'd pulled up, crowded with cars and people passing.

She nods. "Most houses was still empty on account of Katrina, folks scattered to kingdom come and hadn't come back home yet. Getting evacuated to Utah and all that mess. Some of them folks never did come back." She stares off. "If there was witnesses, they was too scared to step up."

"Why haven't you sought legal counsel?"

She waves a hand at the room. "Do I look like I got that kind of money? My daughter says leave it alone, trust on the Lord. And I'm trying. Jesus knows I am trying. But my trust is running low, I have to tell you. My Jonas trusted in the Lord his whole life. Clean living, no violence, good neighbor. Put our kids through school, every last one. Didn't get him no farther than an early grave."

"There are groups that might help. The ACLU, the NAACP—"

She laughs softly. "Child, keep your alphabets. I don't barely go off the block except for groceries and church. This my best dress right here." She smooths a deprecating hand down its plain yellow cotton. "How'm I supposed to get them big downtown people to notice me?"

I nod. I know what she means. After coming up in the Ninth myself, I felt unsure in downtown situations for years.

But fear can be a kind of fuel.

"Mrs. Applewhite, when this story breaks, those downtown people will be coming to you. You'll have lawyers lined up around the block."

Her eyes are distant, disbelieving, her tone flat. "Now, wouldn't that be something," she says.

Before heading back to the *Times-Picayune* office, I drive southeast on Florida Avenue and cross the bright blue bridge over the Industrial Canal, curious to see how things are going in the city's hardest hit neighborhood. Until Katrina, the Lower Ninth Ward, which is bounded on three sides by water—the canal, the Mississippi, and Bayou Bienvenue—had one of the highest percentages of African American home ownership in the country. Generations of family and friends lived within shouting distance. Now, almost four years after the hurricane, most blocks have only one or two occupied houses still standing.

I cruise slowly on broken asphalt through the new-growth forest, vines twining over everything, rich and green. In the vacant yards, weeds grow as high as your neck. Oleander and lantana blossom and sprawl. New Orleans soil is unusually fecund, thick with thousands of years of alluvial silt from the Mississippi. In the wake of Katrina, with the houses demolished and the people gone, nature took back the land. Crape myrtles, golden rain trees, and Chinese tallow trees, which grow six feet a year, thicket the empty lots. Reports abound of wildlife, pushed inland from the levee by the risen river: raccoons, opossums, armadillos, king snakes and garter snakes, even coyotes. Hawks and falcons circle overhead. Ospreys fish in the bayou. A white egret takes slow, majestic steps across the street in front of me, unfazed by my car.

I pass the raised beds of an organic garden and the simple, old-school homes that one organization has rebuilt with volunteer labor. Driving down Tennessee and then up Deslonde, I check out the strange, futuristic boxes of the Make It Right houses, certified LEED Platinum and topped with solar panels.

But beyond those few brave blocks, the forest is claiming the land. There are no amenities. There's nothing—except a sense of home—to come back for. There's no fire station, no supermarket, no hospital. Lots still lie filled with rusting, jagged debris, and worse. Dead bodies get dumped in these woods.

Only the most tenacious and courageous former Lower Ninth residents have returned. They come back with their savings, their children, their hope. They stare out from their new porches across a wasteland.

A wasteland for humans, that is. For nature, it's a bonanza.

Like it is for the tour companies that bus rich tourists through.

I hang a right on Claiborne and head back upriver.

I drive through hot streets to the *Times-Picayune* building, drafting the Mahonia Applewhite interview in my head. It's not like I think I'm the great Latina savior of the Ninth Ward, that by telling people's stories I can bring them justice, like white folks doing sloppy good in Africa but changing nothing, or some sci-fi fantasy version of the 1960s South, where white people just told the story of their black maids and made it all better.

It's not that I think I'm a savior. It's just that telling people's stories is my compulsion.

We didn't see a lot of Latina journalists at Tulane when I was there getting educated, but one did stop by as a distinguished visiting lecturer. I was so excited that I cut classes to attend every event: every panel, every talk, every lunch with students. She was tall and slim and long-boned, pretty, a New Mexican of the kind that called themselves Hispanic, and she'd gone to Harvard on a full scholarship before heading down to Central America during the 1980s to cover the civil wars. Her dark eyes had that bleak, tough look of having seen everything. And still getting up in the morning. No time to indulge depression. You get up and you write it.

"It's one of life's most profound privileges," she had said from the podium, "one of the most intimate gifts, to be able to tell the stories of others."

Some smarmy guy from the audience stood up during Q&A and accused her of silencing the subalterns she wrote about. What gave her, with her Ivy League education, the right to speak for anyone else?

"Privilege exists," she said quietly into the mic. "The power of voice is not distributed equally. We know that. The only thing you can do with privilege is to grip it like a baseball bat." The whole room paused, silent, waiting, barely breathing. "And swing it with all your might at injustice."

I loved that. At twenty-one, I loved that image. Grip. Swing. I love it still.

In the blessed gray cool of the newsroom, I'm at my desk, typing and shaping the Mahonia Applewhite interview, when a call comes in on my cell. It's Luke Jourdan.

I answer right away. "Nola Céspedes. What can I do for you?"

"Was it you?" His voice is loud and angry.

"Sorry?"

"Did you break into my goddamn house? Jesus. Fucking media. I always heard it was like this, but—"

"Wait. Mr. Jourdan, wait! I have no idea what you're talking about. I've been interviewing subjects all day, and I've been in my office for the last hour."

There's a pause. When he speaks, his voice is dubious. But quieter.

"How am I supposed to believe that? You could be telling me anything. How would I know?"

Ah. Trust isn't his strong suit right now. He's paranoid, muddled by grief.

I soften my voice. "Mr. Jourdan, a break-in can be very disturbing. I know. I've been ripped off twice." It shocks you, disorients you, leaves you feeling vulnerable and raw in a way you can't shake. "I understand why you're upset. But I promise you, I've been busy with interview subjects all day, and I can prove it."

He's silent.

"I think the most important thing you can do right now is to contact the police, and then figure out what's been stolen." Not that the NOPD will do much. Personal-property thefts aren't high priority in New Orleans, as I know from personal experience. Oh, the cops'll come take your statement, sure, and smirk while they're doing it. Your stuff's long gone, and they know it. They just go through the ritual Noh drama of filing the report.

"Nothing's missing," says Luke. "Things are just—moved. Out of place. Drawers open. Jude's office is a mess."

"It's been searched?"

"That's why I thought it was you. I thought you wanted more information for your story."

"My story's over." And that's not how I play. Generally. "Was any kind of threat left behind? Any message?"

"No."

"So it wasn't a warning." I tap my pen on the desk. "Which means they were looking for something. Something specific."

"But what?" he says. "What could anyone be looking for?"

More important, who?

"You need to call the police," I say. "Tell the detective what happened."

There's a long pause. Then he clears his throat. "Listen. I'm sorry for getting on your case. This has been such a mess. These last couple of days—I feel like I'm not even in my life anymore."

"You're not," I say. "Everything's different now."

"Yeah. Well, anyway."

"Don't worry about it. But trust me: if I need information, I'll knock on your door and ask you."

A tired smile warms his voice. "Yeah, okay. Thanks."

"Speaking of which," I say, "are you Catholic, or was your wife?"

"What? No. Episcopalian. But we don't go to church much. Why?"

"Just an angle the DA's office is looking into. The murderer used rosaries and Satanic symbols."

"Oh," he says quietly. "Yeah."

Seconds tick by. I see Jude's body again, its macabre decorations. I imagine Luke imagining it.

Finally, he clears his throat. "Hey, I'm going to take your advice, by the way. I'm taking Chloe to Jazz Fest tomorrow. It will do us both good. Get out of the house, get our minds off things."

"That's great. That's a good idea. It's okay to take breaks." I don't know who died and made me a therapist, but it feels true enough. The sorrow will be ready and waiting when they get home.

"Yeah," he says. There's another long pause, and I think he's going to say something else, but he doesn't.

"Well," I say, "take care—"

"That Cory B," he blurts. "Did you find anything out?"

I inhale slowly. I've been hoping he wouldn't ask. "I did. And I'm sorry. He confirmed that your wife was having an affair."

There's a long silence on the line.

"Okay," he says finally, his voice tight with tension again. Loud. Stiff. "I guess it's better to know. Thanks. I guess."

"I'm really sorry."

"Yeah," he says. "Me, too." He hangs up without another word.

I breathe in relief. Better that his anger grab him than that he ask me for Cory B's last name. I already know how easy Cory is to track down, how close by—how he would open the door with no shirt on, stoned and mellow and smiling, not expecting the wrath of a cuckolded man.

I finish my write-up of the Mahonia Applewhite interview and spend the rest of the afternoon blending my own impressions with the draft that Jude Taffner wrote.

When I shut my computer down for the evening, twelve reporters are still working in the newsroom, and the heavy gray blanket of night is lowering over the city as they sit, hunched at their desks, eyes locked on their screens. When I call good night, they barely grunt.

In my growling car, I head for Fabi's apartment in the Quarter. The dusky air is still flooded with heat. It's Girls' Night. Lights twinkle and neon signs glow on the old French and Spanish buildings, and the streets are crowded. With Jazz Fest, the city is crawling with tourists, and parking's hard to find. The streets are full of revelers, college-aged and trying to act all badass. I find two of them propped against Fabi's brick building, already weak with drink.

"Hey, baby," one says, and I brush past them and let myself inside. I punch the number of Fabi's apartment onto the little silver squares. When the inner door buzzes, I take the stairs to the third floor and knock.

"Nola, hey!" Fabi pulls me inside and hugs me hello, her body fragile in my arms.

I love Fabi's apartment the way I love pictures of Disneyland. With white walls, floors of glossy golden pine, and pink velvet sofas and drapes, it's a girly dream boudoir. Chandeliers tremble in every room, and large mirrors hang in wide, antiqued-gold gilt frames, doubling and tripling us back to ourselves.

Fabi gives us salad, curried tofu, and pineapple sorbet, together with her TED Talks on the virtues of veganism and the evils of agribusiness.

When she pauses for breath, we manage to catch up on work and men. Calinda shows us on her iPhone the photograph of the donor she chose. "My new baby daddy," she says, "if that turkey baster thing worked." He's cute, smart, and young—a med student—and he has a little reddish undertone to his skin. "And tall," Calinda says. "Look." She scrolls down the description and taps the screen with a gold fingernail. He's six one, two hundred pounds. "No short fat babies."

Calinda, best described as plush, refuses to apologize for her perfectly average weight. But she sees how things go for thinner women. We all do. Soline and Fabi try not to rub it in.

We talk about Carlo, who still frustrates Fabi with his frank materialism and devotion to her. He gives her necklaces from Tiffany & Co., when she wants him to be out building houses for the poor.

"Hmm." Soline presses her lips together. "Stockbroker. Restaurateur. Maybe not the odds-on choice for altruism?"

"Oh, I know. I know. Leave me alone." Fabi's hardly one to talk, anyway, here in Little Versailles. She tours us around her newly redecorated guest room under the eaves, with its single bed and its dormer windows overlooking the street, sweet as a schoolgirl's attic, and we all ooh and aah at the pretty changes she's made.

We take our cappuccinos—made with fair-trade coffee beans, of course, and organic coconut creamer—out to her balcony, which overlooks art galleries, bars, and throngs of tourists, and settle into her white wicker chairs. On a schoolteacher's salary, she could never afford to live here, but her parents were so appalled at her first postcollege apartment—a monkish, shabby place in Mid-City, not so different from the one I'd shared with Uri—that they'd immediately kicked in a thousand a month if she'd just live somewhere respectable, like the *gente decente* that they are. So we get to sip cappuccino on one of the prettiest little wrought-iron balconies in the Vieux Carré.

Talk turns to Soline, whose first wedding anniversary has just passed. We peer through a new scrim of distance at our friend now; she's on the other side of something. We all want to know how married life is.

"Well, honestly, it's kind of hard," she says softly, tilting her head to one side, running a finger along the rim of her porcelain cup. A silence falls over us. Soline, who glides through life on a breezy smile, is complaining.

"What do you mean, hard?" My curiosity shivers to life, fueled by something more personal than mere compassion. Given my own struggles with Bento, I need to hear this.

Soline's voice stays soft. "The club's doing good. Real good. And you know I'm happy for him. It's his dream. His baby." All the tourist guidebooks now list Code Noir as a must-see nightclub. The hottest bands vie to play there. People come in droves, and money, presumably, is pouring in. "But it means he's gone a lot." Her tone turns wry. "And running a club's not a nine-to-five job. He's out until two, three every morning. Five or six nights a week. And he's tired a lot." Her laugh is tender. "At least I get it. I know how it is. I know what it takes. When I was getting Sinegal off the ground— Well, y'all remember."

We did. For months, we'd barely seen her. She'd worked all hours to get her shop into the headlines and into the black. Now it ranks among the best boutiques on Magazine Street.

"Can't he hire a manager?" Fabi asks. Her boyfriend Carlo has two, and they run his upscale Italian seafood restaurant in the Quarter. But that's different. He's a stockbroker. His restaurant is only his hobby. Code Noir is Rob's dream.

"He's got a manager," says Soline. "He's got an accountant. He's got four bartenders and two DJs. But he still feels like he needs to be there on the floor every night, a presence. He's got to put his stamp on it. Everything's got to be perfect." She shakes her head. "Not that I blame him. No. I admire him. I'm the same way. He's got a vision, and he's seeing it through." She sighs. "It just doesn't leave us a whole lot of time together." She looks hesitantly at Calinda. "And not that we're thinking about it right now," she says, "not in any serious way, but it doesn't seem like the best kind of situation for starting a family." She watches Calinda's face. She's aware of the baby fever. She's being delicate.

"Hmm." Calinda's lips are pressed together. I can feel her change the subject before she does it. "Family aside, what kind of impact is all this having on the old uh-huh?"

Soline laughs. "We've still got it. When we get it."

"It's the *when* I'm talking about."

"Okay." Soline's smile is shy. "So maybe not as often as I'd like."

"Hoo, girl," says Calinda. "If that goes, it all goes." She turns to Fabi and me. "Not that I know. I'm getting this from magazines."

"Me and Rob are all right," says Soline, looking down, her long lashes grazing her cheeks. "We're still good. It's just—hard, is all I'm saying. He's very . . . focused."

"There's something else," I say suddenly, and her eyes flash up at me. There's a long moment of silence. "There is, isn't there?" I say. "There is. Come on. What is it?"

Her white teeth sink into her lip. "It's nothing," she says. "People wear perfume to clubs. It's nothing new. He always came home smelling like liquor and sweat and perfume. It's no big deal. It just goes with the territory."

"But?"

Her eyes flash at me again. "Yes, all right. Lately he's been coming home smelling of the same particular perfume."

"Which perfume?" Fabi asks. Oh, Lord. Drugstore or designer? Trust Fabi to care. She wants to classify the girl.

A little line appears between Soline's waxed brows. "Dior, maybe. Miss Cherie or something like that. I don't know."

"Oh, Soline." Fabi's eyes are dark with concern. Presumably

if it had been some cheap perfume, the other woman—if there is one—could have been dismissed. Fabi and her class issues.

"Hey," Soline says, her tone sharp. "It's not time to commiserate. It could be nothing."

"Have you asked him about it?" I say.

She takes a deep breath, lets it out. "I promised myself I was not going to be that kind of wife. If me and Rob are going to be together for the long haul, and Code Noir stays strong, there's always going to be a fresh crop of twenty-one-year-olds there, wearing their little nothings and working their mojo like they invented hips."

"Ain't that the truth," says Calinda. "That was us, not so long ago."

"Exactly," says Soline. "And I promised myself I would not lose sleep." She closes her eyes, breathes. Opens them again. "He chose me," she says.

"Yes, he did," says Calinda. "'Cause the man's got brains."

"I tell myself: I'm a good-looking woman. I'm well educated, I'm financially independent, and I'm emotionally stable. I am, in other words, a catch."

"That's all true," says Calinda, "but—not to go lawyer on you—there are plenty of catches in divorce court right now because their husbands cheated."

Soline nods. "Rob knows where he'll be if he ever cheats. Out. Over. Done." She shakes her head as if shaking off the topic. "So I am not going to let myself worry. I'm not going to get all paranoid. I'm going to trust him. Unless and until I have a reason not to." She shakes her finger at us. "A reason, mind you. Not a suspicion."

"But you've got a pre-nup, right?"

Soline nods again. "We do. But that's not the issue here. The issue is how I want to live my life. What kind of marriage I want to live in. Do I want to be checking his collar for lipstick and his pockets for phone numbers? Or am I going to love him and trust him?"

"There's love and trust," I say, "and then there's ignoring the evidence."

She just laughs. "This is exactly what I get," she says, "for having a lawyer and a reporter for friends. Look, I'm just going through the first-year jitters. That's all. I'm sure everything's okay."

We all nod, and smile, and encourage her, but when she leans to spoon some more sugar into her cappuccino, we glance at one another.

Quizzed about Bento, I hustle through the abbreviated version—we're doing great, lovely, fine. I don't mention my troubles in bed: how I flash back to the rape and have to stop, or get so tense that it hurts to do it, or burst out crying afterward. How I'm embarrassed. Or just irrationally hate him. How it's not the way I want him to see me—messed up, broken, vulnerable—so I withdraw. How it was all a lot easier when he was just a hot stranger.

Instead, I tell my friends about Jude Taffner, Cory Brink, and Mahonia Applewhite. And there's still Senator Claiborne, whom I'm planning to interview myself, and his wife's mysterious horse sales.

Calinda and Soline are all over the Applewhite story.

"Send it to me," says Calinda. "I'll take it to the DA *tomorrow*."

I protest that I haven't yet interviewed Cinelli and Doucet, or their superiors. That it's all just a mess of notes so far.

"Doesn't matter. Send me what you've got. Let's get this ball rolling."

"And I can give Mrs. Applewhite's number to my mama," says Soline. Her mother, a circuit court judge, is retiring next year. "She's got NAACP connections who'd love to hear about this." She slips inside to Fabi's living room for a second and returns with her white Birkin bag. "Here," she says, pulling out a little notebook and a silver fountain pen. "Write it down." I find the number on my cell phone and scrawl it, unaccustomed to the weight of a metal pen in my hand, the pleasurable smoothness of the nib's slide. "And what you said about her dress," she says. "What would you say her size is?"

I squint to picture her in my mind. "She's tiny, but she's got a little old-lady belly. Maybe a four?"

"The issue," says Soline, "can be addressed." We all grin. It's plain that she's mentally scanning the inventory of Sinegal. "Every lady needs a good dress or two," Soline says sternly. She nods at me and lifts an eyebrow. "Something you could stand to contemplate."

11

It's only ten o'clock by the time my friends and I have suffi-
ciently solved, in theory at least, the problems of the world, but
I'm tired when I head home in the Pontiac. It's been a long day.

It's finally cool out, and I leave the windows down as I drive
home to St. Charles. The night breeze rushes in, and I play
WWOZ's R&B show loud on the radio. When I get to Soline's
building, the security gate opens electronically with my keycard, and I pull into the lot, where I park between a Volvo and a
Saab.

Crossing the pavestones on foot, I hear a voice yell, "Hey!"

A figure stands outside the steel fence. The voice is high and
sweet, familiar. A female voice. Unthreatening. I move closer.

Loosed from context, the figure is unrecognizable. She's my
height, with a mass of dark curls.

"Who is it?" I say.

An exasperated sigh. "Who do you think?" Her hands are
curled around the bars, and I draw closer. She shifts, and a band
of light gleams across her face.

Marisol. She's only thirteen, but someone could take us for

twins. In the dark, at least. Seeing her week by week, I hadn't realized how much she's gradually grown over the past year.

"You're as tall as I am," I say, still registering.

"Duh," she says. "So are you letting me in, or what?"

"Sure. Sorry. Of course." I key the gate open. When I hug her, she smells like plums—incandescent juicy plums, sweet like the cheap drugstore perfumes teenagers wear. "What's going on, mi'ja? Do your parents know you're here?"

"Rosie dropped me off." Her nineteen-year-old friend from the apartment complex in Metairie. Not the best influence, in my view. Marisol shrugs. "If you want to talk, can we go inside?"

"*If*? You show up on my doorstep in the middle of the night, and you say *if* I want to talk? Of course we're talking."

She sighs.

"It's just that my dad's being so crazy," she says.

My senses stay on alert as we enter the building and climb the stairs. Crazy how? Inside Soline's apartment, I flip on the lights and we settle into soft white sofas while Marisol complains about her father's increasingly strict rules and how he wants her to go only to church and to school, and otherwise stay home to help her mother with the five younger children. How he grounds her every time she's five minutes late getting home.

I've always liked Señor Cruz, but this level of control is new. Is he just afraid for his daughter, who looks increasingly mature and lovely? In the sketchy area off Veterans where they live, full of self-storage units and cheap apartment complexes, careful monitoring of her whereabouts makes sense.

Marisol shows no signs of damage. Just ordinary teenage frustration. "I love my dad," she says. "I do." She rummages through the little purple backpack and pulls out a phone. "He got me this, even though he says kids don't need cell phones, blah blah. And you know. He's my dad. I love him. But then he never lets me talk to anybody. Cook and clean, cook and clean. And take care of the babies. It's like he thinks I'm the maid." She tosses her shoulders. "*Hello.* I have a life. It's like he thinks we're in Mexico or something." She checks her texts, then puts the phone back in her backpack. "And who has an eight o'clock curfew—on the *weekend*?"

"And your mom? What does she say?"

"Pshht. She's so tired she doesn't care. She wants the help, you know? And she basically agrees with him about girls and stuff. She grew up in a *village*."

I'm nodding and listening, balancing Marisol's need to be heard with the fact that a few miles away, her parents have got to be freaking out. I let her talk for a few more minutes before digging my own phone from my handbag. "Let's just let them know you're all right."

Her eyes widen. "God, no." Her voice rises to the edge of panic. "Haven't you been listening? They'll come down here and take me back." She crosses her arms, shakes her head. "I am not going back to that—that *Angola*."

Ah, teenagers. That magical land where an eight o'clock curfew equates with state prison.

"Technically, sweetie," I say, remembering the guidelines of Big Brothers Big Sisters, "you're not allowed to stay overnight with me. It's in the rules."

"Oh, my God," she says, jumping up and pacing the room in a flurry of frustration. "I am not going back there. I won't."

"Okay, okay. *Cálmate.* Just let me talk to them and see what I can do."

"They'll send the police."

"Don't worry." I tap the number. "The police don't have time to deal with runaway girls," I mutter, listening to the phone ring. An unfortunate truth. I've seen the fallout on too many late-night calls. Rapes, stabbings, beatings. Girls as young as Marisol.

Her mother picks up, and we have a quick conversation in Spanish: hers initially panicked, mine rudimentary. The upshot is relief.

Señora Cruz tells me Marisol's bedtime, and when school starts and ends, and a dozen other anxiety-fueled details. With each instruction, the fear eases out of her voice, but she can't seem to stop talking. She finally ends with how Marisol needs to drink more milk.

Then there's a sudden silence on the line, and then I hear her husband's voice. I can hear the layers in it: anger, fear, concern.

Still struggling with my Spanish, I explain to him that Marisol's upset and wants to spend the night—Marisol holds up three fingers and pushes them at me—okay, maybe a few nights here with me until she feels better.

I promise to take care of her, imagining the lawsuit Big Brothers Big Sisters could bring.

But I don't have any language to tell a father why his daughter doesn't want to talk to him. She stands across the room, shaking her head.

After we hang up, I help Marisol settle into Soline's guest room.

"Oh, yeah," she says, dropping her backpack on the white matelassé bedspread and looking around with satisfaction at the plush furnishings. "This is way more like it." I wonder uneasily if Soline's well-appointed guest room, which Marisol has seen on Saturday visits, is simply more desirable than the cramped brown bedroom she shares with her three younger sisters. While

I understand, right down to my marrow, what it is to want better—and while I don't mind sharing Soline's apartment—I don't want to be lied to, either. Or used.

"Do you need some pajamas?"

"No. I got some." She digs through her backpack and pulls out a tight soft log of pink nylon. Gravity unrolls it in a swift swirl. It looks like a gown a grandma would wear, like something from Kmart for $8.99.

"Looks like you're good, then."

"Yeah."

"You hungry?"

She shakes her head. "I ate."

"Do you need any toiletries?"

She shakes her head again, pulling out a toothbrush and a hair pick.

"You know where the bathroom is."

She nods again.

"Well, okay, then." I stand there awkwardly. "So, good night."

"Buenas noches," she says, stepping forward to slip her arms around me for a quick embrace, light as a moth. *"Gracias,"* she whispers into my shoulder.

It takes Marisol a good hour to get settled, by which time I've showered, drunk a cup of hot chamomile tea, and written in the journal Shiduri Collins makes me keep now. I log my feelings awkwardly, practically in code, hoping to God no one ever finds the little red notebook I keep stuffed between the mattress and box spring.

Finally, Marisol's door closes, and everything is quiet in the apartment.

Down the hall from her room, I lie awake in the dark, thinking through the facts of the Taffner case. A woman dead, the apparent victim of a ritualistic sex crime—but no sex crime. So we could have an impotent ritual sex killer, for whom all the rosary and feather bullshit is sincere, or a killer of random women who has no particular sex compulsion but just wants to take the police for a ride.

But the victim was cheating on her husband, who's automatically the prime suspect anyway and now has even more motive. Punishment. Revenge. But Luke Jourdan hadn't seemed to know about the affair—though he could just be a great actor—and the murder method was fairly elaborate and misleading for a crime of passion.

Cory Brink, though he wanted to extract himself from Dr. Taffner's increasingly serious notions of romance, didn't seem like a viable suspect, either. Self-interest seems to be his North Star, and in a strict cost-benefit analysis, the trouble he could get into for murder far outweighed the nuisance of dumping a woman.

Dumping a woman. I see Jude Taffner's dead body in the dark air in front of me and have to blink it away.

Cory Brink's not likely. This murder had required more effort and planning than Cory Brink, with his good looks, money, women, and sailboats, had ever had to muster.

Which left the entire rest of the world.

Unless Mahonia Applewhite's suspicions were correct, in which case the New Orleans police force had reason to shut Dr. Taffner up. Since the crime investigation was in their hands, it would be easy enough to obscure evidence, delay the process, pin it on some random serial killer who must have skipped town. Too bad. File it and let it grow cold.

It's weird to contemplate killers while a thirteen-year-old girl sleeps just down the hall. I listen for her breathing and hear nothing. Soline's condo is large. It's not really a place for a kid. Not here, not with me. In that high school class where you carry a boiled egg around for a week to learn how hard it is to parent, I went through three eggs, secretly boiling them up at home. The one I finally turned in on Friday, which I'd made fresh that morning, was still a crushed gray mass of egg-pulp, smashed in my backpack by books.

And what will I do with Marisol tomorrow? We usually visit for four hours, max, and I'm always worn out when I drop her off. What will I do with a kid all day when I've got a murder to investigate?

Saturday

12

On Saturday morning, Marisol and I are sitting on Soline's re-production French provincial sofa, eating cornflakes and drinking cappuccinos, and I'm wondering what I'm going to do with a teenager for the next fourteen hours, when my cell phone rings.

Luke Jourdan, reads the screen. Great. What will he accuse me of this time? I pick it up.

"Nola, hey."

"Hey."

"Listen, I'm taking Chloe to Jazz Fest, like you said, and I was just— I'm just wondering— She likes you." There's a long pause full of unspoken apology. "You're good with her." His voice is tentative. "We've got an extra ticket—"

I look over at Marisol, munching away, watching me curiously. The answer to my problem might be right in the palm of my hand. Jazz Fest could be a great place to kill two birds with one stone: keep Marisol occupied, and keep pursuing the story. Luke Jourdan may be innocent of his wife's death, but if he's not, this could be a great chance to observe him, to learn more about Jude. And in a public place, he'd be no threat to me or anyone else.

"Hang on a sec." I mute the phone. "Mari, how'd you like to go to Jazz Fest?"

Her eyes light up. With her mouth full of cereal, she nods like a maniac. I smile and unmute the phone.

"All right, then, but I need to bring my Little Sister. She's thirteen." A thought strikes me. "She's good with little kids."

"Sure. Great. Listen, though, I only have the one extra ticket." His voice falls. "Jude's."

"*No problema*. We can buy one for Marisol at the gate."

"Do you want to meet there? At about ten?" Jazz Fest runs all day and is a mad scene. With kids, we'd be wise to go that early.

"Parking's crazy. Why don't I come to your place, and we can ride over together? Then we only have to find one space."

"Sure." He sounds pleased, like my overture means I've forgiven him for yesterday. "Sure," he says again. "Come over when you're ready."

I glance at Soline's beautiful wooden clock on the mantel. It's just after nine o'clock.

"We'll be there by quarter till. Ten at the latest."

We hang up, and Marisol claps her hands. "It's like a big music party, right?"

"Yep."

It's also like a huge bacchanal, with thousands of fucked-up, sweaty adults mashed together and dozens of bands playing at top volume. But I don't say that. I've always had a good time at Jazz Fest. There's a children's tent. It'll be okay.

Marisol is nodding happily. "Yeah, that's what kids at school say. I never thought I'd get to go."

"You're in for an adventure." The other thing about Jazz Fest is that it's a small, small world. You never know who you'll run into. At any given moment, half of New Orleans is there, carousing. You could run into your doctor, your lawyer, your sixth-grade teacher, your boss, your ex.

Marisol looks at the clock. "But you said quarter till." She jumps to her feet, cereal bowl in hand, and bestows upon me a look of horror and shock. Her voice is panicky. "How'm I supposed to get ready?"

I guess I've forgotten what it's like to be thirteen. I hear the clatter of the bowl in the sink and then her footsteps skittering down the hall. I flip on the local weather. Sunny, humid, high of eighty-seven. Sighing, I haul myself off the couch.

When my Pontiac pulls up in front of the Taffner house, Chloe is waiting on the porch, excited to see us, eager to meet Marisol. Even Luke's weak smile looks genuine enough. His eyes are tired, but the crinkles at their corners are real. It strikes me again that he's a good-looking man.

After we've all introduced ourselves and gone inside, the girls run off to Chloe's room.

I keep my voice quiet as we sink to the love seat. His knees are close to mine, and he smells like limes. "How's she doing?"

"She's okay. It comes and goes." He shrugs. "She's clingier than usual, and she cries more easily at little things. She asks about Jude, and I explain, and then an hour later she asks again."

"That's pretty typical." I've worked the crime beat long enough to know.

He nods. "Yeah, I think she's doing all right."

"And you? How are you doing?"

His laugh is low and baffled, his brown eyes hurt. "I'm a mess," he says. "I'm pissed, which makes me feel guilty as hell, since how can you be angry at someone who died in such—" He breaks off, takes a breath. "And I'm crushed, like I can't breathe. I loved her. I still love her. And I'm still kind of in shock." He spreads his empty hands between us and gazes down at them, as if he's trying to read his own palms. A tremor runs through his strong fingers. "I don't know who I am now, what I'm supposed to be without her. Worse, I don't know who Jude was. Not really. Not anymore."

I take his hands in mine and grip them firmly. "You're Chloe's father," I say. "That hasn't changed."

Just then, the girls burst into the living room. Marisol's eyebrows shoot up when she sees us touching, and I drop his hands abruptly. She likes Bento. I'll have some explaining to do.

"¡Ándale!" I say, clapping my hands and rising. "Let's go hear some music." I dust my hands on my hips.

"Yeah!" yells Chloe. Luke checks her little fuzzy-puppy backpack. Juice boxes? Handi Wipes? Sunscreen? Hat? Bug spray? Check, check, check.

"It's just Jazz Fest." I laugh. "Not the Amazon."

"You wait," he says. "You have a kid, you'll see."

We finally make it out the door and down to the curb. "I can drive," I say.

"Sure. No, wait. Chloe's car seat. Let's take my Jeep." It's a nice one, olive green, built for off-road antics but so far unscratched. An expensive toy for city people who want to look like they're not.

We climb in, and I can tell Marisol likes getting to ride in the open air. She's asking Chloe her colors. "But do you know them," she asks as I'm buckling in, "in Spanish?" At home, she's pressed into childcare service by her tired mother—and resents it. Here, she's reveling in the easy rapport she's able to build with a stranger.

Luke's a smooth, deft driver, which always makes me like a man more: nothing showy, no gunning it when the light turns green. We glide through heavy tourist traffic like it's butter, chatting lightly about the weather and the bands we hope to see. It's the second and final weekend of Jazz Fest, and people come from all over the country—all over the world—to see it. As we approach the Fairgrounds, the streets are jammed.

Luke slows, and we all watch for a parking space as we crawl down the narrow neighborhood streets of Mid-City, but the only spots left are the ones for fifteen dollars in someone's private driveway. New Orleanians are nothing if not entrepreneurial. Luke chooses one at the edge of the Fairgrounds and pulls out two crisp bills, waving my crumpled dollars away.

When we enter, it's still early, so there are stretches of grass where the girls can play freely and we can walk behind them, talking. It's not the crush of drunken bodies it will be later on. We let them run ahead for a while as Luke talks quietly about the business of death: the certificates to be obtained, the insurance companies to be called, the obituary to be written, the funeral services to be arranged—all of it troubled, in his case, by the ugly new knowledge that his wife was cheating.

"How can I write an obituary that honors Jude the way it should?" he says. "When what I really want to write is a headline like, 'MURDERED WIFE BETRAYS LOVING HUSBAND'?"

I consider. "It would get tweeted a lot."

"Great." A wry smile flashes and then disappears. He shakes his head. "She was the journalist. Not me."

A few seconds tick by. I realize what he's asking. Hinting at. It takes a few more seconds to overcome my reluctance. "Do you want some help?"

His eyes swing over to me. "Really?"

I try not to sigh audibly. "Sure." Once people know you can write, they're always asking you to write for them. In the Desire Projects, lots of folks weren't that literate. I've written love letters for people, letters to landlords, letters of complaint. It feels weird. Now I'm supposed to write an obit for a professor I couldn't stand?

Ahead of us, the girls gallop, and we trek behind them down the long stretch of lawn. Blades of grass, battered by last weekend's revelries, are just beginning to straighten up. By nightfall, they'll be flattened.

Luke has brought a large blue blanket, and by the time we find a show we like, the girls are panting and ready to sit for a while.

"We're hummingbirds!" Chloe declares. "*¡Chuparosas!*" She glances at Marisol, who nods in approval. Chloe drops down cross-legged beside me and roots in her little backpack for a juice box. She holds it up and breaks the straw from its side. "And this is my flower!" With her rosebud mouth sipping and the bright brown hair falling into her shining eyes, she's an adorable child. A child whose mother had wanted to leave her behind. And now had, permanently.

Marisol looks around. She glances at Luke and Chloe, then eases closer to me. Her voice is quiet. "Can we go in the shade?"

We look around. No tent or shelter is nearby. The audience area for this soundstage, like most, is uncovered, open to the sun.

"How come?"

She lowers her tone further. "My mom doesn't want me getting dark."

The words snap out before I think. "Are you with your mom right now?"

It's not that I want to undermine her parents. I just hate that internalized-racism bullshit.

A grin seeps slowly onto her lips. "No."

"And do you have sunscreen on?"

"Yes." I'd watched her smear it on at Soline's apartment, and I'd done her shoulders, which the little pink tank top left bare.

"All right, then. So chill."

She keeps grinning and starts teasing Chloe about her juice box. Chloe loves it, delighted to be the center of an older girl's attention.

I glance over at Luke, whose eyes are soft, watching them, and when he looks suddenly at me, I feel shy. His eyes fill with something dark and serious, and his glance drops, just for a moment, to my lips.

Sweating slightly, grateful for the breeze, I turn to watch the band.

The day passes easily like that. Whenever the girls get restless, we fold up our things and wander for a while, and then find a new place to set up camp. At noon, we eat lunch on the grass. As the hours drift by, the fairgrounds fill up with more bodies, and the crowds grow more raucous, more inebriated. The air is dustier, the grass mashed to a pale mat. Now when we walk somewhere, Luke hoists Chloe onto his shoulders, and I keep Marisol, who says she's too old for holding hands, right in front of me.

At about three in the afternoon, the girls are hungry again. We choose one of the many booths that spill delicious smells into the air, and I get in line to order for all of us. Marisol comes along to help me carry everything, and Luke and Chloe wait a safe distance away from the crush of people. The line creeps forward slowly, the heat of the day blaring down. When we finally push our way to the counter, I place our order with a big bearded Cajun guy who wipes his hands on his white apron: jambalaya for Luke, gumbo for me and Marisol, alligator sausage for Chloe, and cornbread muffins and cold drinks all around. Fabi's voice in my head chastises me for our planet-destroying choices, and waves of oven heat ripple out from the booth as we wait for our order, which is finally plunked down on the counter with a "Y'all enjoy now, *cher.*"

Our hands full of food and drink, our pockets stuffed with paper napkins, Marisol and I weave our way carefully to where Chloe's head sprouts above the crowd.

When we get close, I jerk to a halt. A couple of yards away stands Cory Brink, his arm draped casually around the neck of a blonde who might be Vanessa the girlfriend. They're surrounded by six or seven similarly lithe, sleepy-eyed, hopelessly cool college-age kids.

Body language says it's a complete coincidence. Luke doesn't know them; they don't know him.

Cory Brink's lids lift fractionally when he sees me. His way of expressing shock, I guess.

"Hey," he says, with a lift of his chin.

"Hey," I reply.

Vanessa's eyes flick up and down me. "Who's this?"

Luke has turned to watch us with equal interest.

"No one," I say loudly to Cory, ignoring the girlfriend, ignoring Luke. "You must've thought I was someone else." I step away from Cory Brink and his tribe of pretty people and turn toward Luke and Chloe. "How about let's go to the children's tent?" I say brightly, like it's the best place on earth.

"Yeah!" Chloe says.

Out of the corner of my eye, I see Cory Brink take the hint and slouch off with his friends. They melt into the sea of moving bodies.

But Luke is adding it up. He swings Chloe down from his shoulders. "Who was that?"

"No one," I say. "Just a mistake." I glance over my shoulder. Cory Brink is nowhere. "He's nobody, Luke. Some guy who thought he knew me."

He glances down. Chloe's imploring little face looks up at him, her eyes wide. He glances toward where Cory Brink disappeared, and the struggle is plain on his face.

"Come on," I say, lifting the food and nodding at the girls. "Let's go eat. It'll be cooler in the tent."

"Christ," Luke mutters, staring into the crowd. But he bends and lifts Chloe onto his shoulders again. We set off, passing small white tents marked with red crosses for people who drink too much, or become dehydrated in the heat, or suffer a real emergency, the kind that brings ambulances shrieking from their quiet dormancy on the perimeter of the fairgrounds. We wend our way slowly through the sweaty crowds. The heat is building. When I'm jostled and cold soda splashes on my arm and shoulder, it feels good. The sun dries it to a sticky sheen.

When we finally duck inside the big white children's tent, some mandolin band is singing about sunshine and the number five. We find space at a long plastic table and spread out our lunch. Luke's jaw is rock tight, but everyone starts to cool off. While our food may be terrible for the planet, it's delicious, and the Cokes are cold and full of fake energy. Chloe cheers up, watching all the children dance around in front of the stage. She takes only two bites of her alligator sausage before declaring it officially "yucky" and sliding down from the bench. "Can I, Daddy?" she says, jumping up and down.

"Sure," Luke says, and she dashes off. The three of us sit there in silence, eating, drinking, and watching Chloe twirl like an ecstatic pint-sized Sufi. Marisol's eyes dart back and forth between Luke and me.

"They're not bad," I say, gesturing toward the stage, although songs about bunnies and harmony aren't my thing.

But Luke's too distracted. "Yeah," he says blankly, his mind obviously on the tremendous pleasure it would have been to fill Cory Brink's lazy, entitled smile with a fist. Not that I'm projecting.

The cool shade of the tent is a pleasant relief, and it's cute to watch Chloe as she spins and hops near the stage, but once the food's gone, Marisol's restless, checking the schedule. A steel drum band starts in ten minutes.

"Can I go?"

I look at the map. It's across the fairgrounds. "Not by yourself."

Luke rouses himself from his fog of bloodlust or grief or whatever it is. "You two go," he says. "Chloe's good here, and if she gets tired"—he pats the folded blue blanket—"I can put her down for a nap." Plenty of little kids are crashed on the grass nearby, despite the general hullabaloo. Their parents sit with their eyes closed, wearing that look of stunned, grateful exhaustion parents have when their kids stop moving for ten minutes.

"Are you sure?"

"Of course. Go enjoy the band, and just come back here when you're done."

"You have my cell number, right?" Losing each other in the crowds of thousands would be easy to do.

He nods. "So, no worries. See you when we see you."

"All *right*," says Marisol, like the cool part is finally going to start.

It takes more than ten minutes, and when we finally make it to the Fais Do-Do Stage, the throng is thick and already writhing to the soft pongs of steel drums. Marisol and I slip in among the dancing crowds. She flashes me a quick grin and then turns to watch the band. Slowly her arms lift over her head, her wrists graceful in the air as she sways. She turns again and briefly smiles at me, her face lit with pleasure, then turns back toward the stage. When a couple of guys my age check her out, I shoot them the *mal de ojo*.

The band is good, and for a few welcome moments, clouds block the sun, and a breeze freshens the air. The soft metallic chime of the drums feels light and happy, ebullient, and I let everything drift from my mind the way the singer says I should. Marisol is here and safe and happy. I'm here and safe and— A whiff of the dreadlocked white hippie chick dancing nearby catches me right in the throat. *Put your arms down, darlin'. I don't need to know that much about you.*

What I'd love to have in my hand right now is a beer or something stronger to spill me into full-blown mellow, but the Big Sister policies are strict on that score, so I just hum along and let the drums move me. When a hot guy checks me out, I smile back. One song lilts into the next, and the next, and it's a beautiful April day in New Orleans. All may not be right with the world, but it never is. Right now, right here, the music and the sun feel damn good. The singer croons to us to just let go, let go, and I do.

When sirens blare, chopping through the music, I startle as if I've been asleep. Lights flash blue and red. From different directions, an ambulance and a cop car are plowing slowly through the crowd.

Instantly, I'm a reporter again. Crudely triangulating, I pinpoint the spot where the two vehicles' trajectories will converge, and that's the place I race toward, sprinting and weaving toward where the action is, pushing and sliding between sweaty shoulders, drunken curses flung in my wake.

On foot, I'm faster than the cops and the EMTs, and when I arrive, people are backing away in a growing oval of space, beer cups in hands, staring down shocked.

On the trampled grass lies Cory Brink, a red flood pouring from his side, his eyes fluttering slowly and more slowly and then rolling quietly back, their blind whites turned up to the sky.

Sunday

13

The light in the Church of the Holy Rosary is clear and soft. On Sunday morning, I'm wedged at the end of the pew beside Marisol, who wanted to sit by *mi mamá*, who adores her. My mother's girlfriend, Ledia, a devout atheist, is at home cooking Sunday dinner for us. Tamales, I believe. Which is good, because I could eat six of them right now. My stomach rumbles stubbornly, its voice more compelling than the priest's. He's yammering on about peace and forgiveness.

I'd gotten to the scene of Cory Brink's murder just before the police and EMTs did, so I was able to snap three quick photos with my cell phone of his dead body on the ground before they arrived, yelling, "Back up! Back up!" and pushing the horrified crowds away. Once the news and manner of the death began to ripple outward, some people swarmed for the exit gates—whether in fear of a random killer, or because they had their own reasons for not wanting to be questioned by the NOPD. Others converged upon the crime scene, curious, holding their video cameras up above the heads of people blocking their view. It was easy to see how it could have happened: the crush of people, a quick knife thrust under the ribs, his body staggering and falling like just another drunken reveler.

The paramedics removed Cory Brink's body quickly, and once I'd seen everything I needed to see, I let myself melt back into the wall of bodies. Marisol, to my surprise, was right behind me. She had followed my squirming dash through the crowds to get there, and something in me felt pleased and proud that she'd kept up. But her lips were slightly open, her eyes wide with shock. I took her hands and squeezed them. "It's okay," I said. "You're okay." She nodded. She sometimes talks pretty tough, but she's still a kid, after all. A dead body's a dead body. "Come on," I said. "Let's go find Luke and Chloe."

As we headed for the children's tent, I thought with unease of Luke. He'd been out of our sight for over an hour. I'd unwittingly ID'd Cory Brink for him.

But that would mean that he'd located a weapon—and I hadn't seen any usable blades in Chloe's puppy backpack or folded into the blue blanket. Luke could hardly have stabbed Cory Brink to death with a juice box. He'd need to have swiped a knife from one of the food booths. Moreover, it would have meant either taking Chloe with him, which would surely have slowed him down—not to mention traumatized Chloe—or leaving her among strangers until he got back. He seemed like too good a father for either choice.

But who else wanted to kill Cory Brink? Even if his girlfriend Vanessa had somehow found out about his affair with Dr. Taffner, girls like that don't kill when men cheat; they move on—or acquire jewelry. Besides, she'd been the one screaming, her hands to her throat, her hands in her hair. When they'd lifted his body, she collapsed like her legs just stopped working. If she'd killed him, she deserved an Oscar.

When Marisol and I got back to the children's tent, Chloe was groggy, just waking up from a nap on the blue blanket, and Luke lounged on the grass at her side, propped on an elbow. He lifted his chin in the direction of the sirens. "What's going on?"

"That guy got killed," Marisol said rapidly. "That guy we saw when we got food."

I nodded. Why fool around? There was no point in concealment now.

"Cory Brink," I said, watching Luke's face.

He sat up in a hurry then. "What?"

"Stab wound to the side." I keep my voice low. "Killer knew what he was doing. He bled out before the ambulance got there."

"Oh, Jesus." Seconds ticked by as he stared in the direction of the crime scene. "But why?"

"Good question. Is there some connection?"

"Connection?"

I glanced at Chloe, then back at Luke. I didn't want to say *Some connection to Jude's death* aloud.

"Oh," he said. "Wow." His voice was low and troubled. Which didn't stop me from covertly inspecting him for blood spatter. There was none.

We began to pack up Chloe's detritus, our cheerful façade of normalcy shattered.

That was okay. I had things to do.

Luke drove us in the Jeep back to his house, where we said our quick good-byes. I stroked Chloe's hair as I climbed out. "Good-bye, baby," I said. I didn't expect to be seeing her again.

Marisol and I climbed into the Pontiac's hot oven and took off. I wanted to get back to Soline's apartment.

In the car, I pulled out my phone. "Never do this," I told

Marisol, steering with one hand and dialing Calinda with the other. "Do not talk on your cell phone when you drive."

"I'm *thirteen*," she said.

Calinda picked up. "What's going on, babycakes?" she said.

"You're not going to believe this." I told her about the Brink killing and Luke's proximity. About the fact that he had motive, opportunity, and a way with a kitchen knife.

Marisol stared at me while I spoke.

"Do you think he did them both?" asked Calinda.

"If he did, he's got the smoothest act I've ever seen. He's a good dad. Total Boy Scout."

"BTK was a Scout leader."

I glanced over at Marisol, who was listening like there'd be an exam later. I gave Calinda all the details I knew and hung up.

"You suspect *Chloe's dad*?" Marisol said.

"Like I said, I don't personally think he's the one. But he could be. He had every reason to be mad at that guy, and he was out of our sight when it happened."

"He's *nice*," she said. "He's sweet, and Chloe's so cute." She crossed her arms and turned her face to the passenger window. "I don't know how you can even think that."

"It's my job to think," I said.

She snorted. "It's your job to *write* stuff," she said. Her tone turned mournful. "Anyone would be lucky to have a dad like that."

I drove for a while. Dusk was falling when we pulled up to the steel security gates of Soline's parking lot and slid inside.

Marisol clomped up the stairs next to me and gave me the silent treatment for the rest of the evening.

It was fine with me. The silence gave me time to phone Bailey and call dibs on the story, to sit at Soline's desk, writing it up and filing it with the *Times-Picayune*.

It gave me time to call Detective Winterson with my new information.

I told him everything I'd learned about Cory Brink in the past three days. He responded with an occasional grunt, and when I finished, he was silent.

So I spelled it out. "The two murder cases could be linked," I said.

"Thanks," he drawled, making it into a three-syllable word. "I'm always so grateful when reporters tell me how to do my job."

"Look, I'm just saying that Luke Jourdan had motive and opportunity in both cases."

"You know," said Detective Winterson slowly, his words grinding and rumbling like trucks on gravel, "what strikes me as *unusual* is that *you* happened to show up when the Brink boy died. Just like when the Taffner body was found."

A long pause grew on the line.

"What are you saying?"

"Murders are down. What's a poor journalist to do?"

"Oh, you've got to be—"

"Seems to me you've had a run of good luck lately. Awful good luck."

"Give me a break. Like I'm going to—"

"You covered the Taffner story, didn't you?"

"You know I did."

"You writing this one?"

I paused. I'd just filed it. A rush of illogical guilt flooded me. "Well, but that doesn't mean—"

His chuckle was a grim sound. "Folks ought to watch out around you. That's all I'm saying."

"Fine. Remind me to share information."

"Aw, poor me. How'm I ever going to solve the big, bad crimes?"

It wasn't the first time I'd hung up on a cop.

Hunger and the dinner hour softened Marisol's heart, and she deigned to come out and see what her soulless Big Sister might be cooking.

"I'm wiped," I said. "How about pizza?"

This was apparently acceptable.

Reginelli's is on my phone's list of favorite contacts, and I let Marisol make the call. "No Coke!" I hissed, the extent of my pseudo-parental nutritional guidance. After ordering a shrimp pesto pizza with Calamata olives and feta, she rattled off my address by heart. I was startled for a moment, but of course she knew it. She found her way here alone. It sort of touched me, that my home address was something she'd committed to memory.

Half an hour later when the buzzer rang, I jumped up, slid on my flip-flops, and grabbed my keys.

"Can't you just buzz them in? Like on TV?"

"Could do," I said. "Call me paranoid, but I'm going down." And I did. I handed the guy the cash through the bars, and he lifted the pizza over the fence. Nighttime in New Orleans, a single woman living alone. Not paranoid. Realistic.

We sat on Soline's white upholstery, paper towels handy, eating our pizza and staring at an episode of *George Lopez*, its volume low.

Marisol pointed up at the map of Cuba, which hangs on Soline's wall now. "So are you going to go there or what?"

I looked at it.

"I don't know," I said. "Sometime, I guess."

"Why don't you just go already?"

I'd talked before to Marisol about my mother, about my grandparents, who died working the cane fields in southern Cuba. They raised my mother on what was once, long ago, a plantation, and which continued after the revolution to be agricultural land. As a young woman, freshly orphaned, she'd taken her chances with the Mariel boatlift and never gone back.

"I don't know," I said. "It's no big deal. My life is here. I don't need some fancy roots trip to find out who I am."

"Hmph." She nodded, chewing, and then took a big swig of her cold drink. "So why do you have it hanging up there?"

I picked up one of Soline's silk pillows and threw it at her, laughing. "*¡Basta!* I don't need this grief from some little teenager."

She laughed and grabbed the pillow, waving it in the air, threatening.

"Hey," I yelled. "Don't you be touching that with your greasy pizza fingers!"

She jumped up and ran toward me, giggling, the pillow raised over her head. It all kind of went downhill from there.

Two hours later, Marisol was tucked in for the night, and I was cross-legged on Soline's king-sized French provincial bed, eating the last cold slice of shrimp pesto pizza, when my cell phone rang.

Luke Jourdan's voice was harsh and urgent. "Come over," he says. "I found something. I did something. I have something to show you."

"What?" I said. "What did you find?" There was a pause, and fear trickled through me. I thought of Cory Brink's upturned eyes, the bright red blood spilling out of his side. I thought of little Chloe, asleep in her bed. I thought of crime scenes where betrayed ex-husbands gunned down their own children in revenge. "What did you *do*?"

"Just come," he said thickly. "You need to see this."

Before I left, I checked on Marisol, who was breathing steadily in her sleep. I wrote a note and left it on the floor of the hallway, where she'd be sure to see it if she woke up.

Leaving the condo, I locked the door carefully. Was it okay to leave a thirteen-year-old alone in the middle of the night to go investigate a story? What kind of mother—if the day ever came—could I possibly manage to be?

I hurried down the marble steps, keys in my hand, worrying about whether Marisol would be frightened if she woke up. Was this the mommy guilt that women's magazines always anguished about? This heavy, anxious sense of responsibility—was this what Jude Taffner tried to escape?

I got in the car and drove to the dead woman's house.

The door opened before I'd knocked twice. When I stepped into the dark living room, Luke Jourdan's bloodshot eyes locked on mine. The air felt hot and electric and black.

Then the smell hit me. Something was burning.

He turned, and I followed him into the kitchen.

In the sink, papers smoldered.

Thank God.

"What are they?"

"Letters," he said. "Jude's letters to me. When we were dating. She used to write me, send them through the mail." He laughs, choking. "I thought it was romantic."

"It *was* romantic," I said. It was her best hopes written down on paper. Too bad they hadn't worked out.

He could have saved the letters for Chloe. One day, she could know that her parents—once, for a little while—had loved each other. That she came from love and hope.

But Luke wasn't thinking of the future. He was thinking of the past, the false version of it he'd believed, the lie it had turned out to be. And like anyone betrayed, he wanted to destroy it, destroy the evidence of the fool he'd been. Pain with a lighter.

But surely this didn't count as news. Why call a reporter late at night?

"What did you want to show me?"

In the darkness, he turned from the sink and looked at me, the glow of orange embers flecking his eyes. He stood there, silent, clenching and opening his fists. His need spun and crackled around him like hunger, like anger, like desire.

Suddenly, I knew what was coming. He'd found nothing. There was nothing he wanted to show me.

He caught my wrist and crushed me to the kitchen counter, pinning me with his hips.

I closed my eyes. When his mouth lowered to hover above mine, whiskey fumes swimming like a fog around us, I hung in the moment, suspended, letting him, heating up with the contact thrill of being ravenously, illicitly wanted.

But it was Jude he wanted, not me. Jude he wanted to fuck, and Jude he wanted to punish.

I pushed him away, twisting free.

He grabbed me and shoved me up against a wall, his whole muscled body firm against mine. My knees went liquid.

I have a weakness for violence.

A weakness I have to fight, Shiduri Collins tells me, if I ever want to be well. If I ever want to be healthy, happy, normal. I have to fight it like addiction.

My will stirred sluggishly within me. I heard the sound of Shiduri's voice in my head. All I wanted was to grab his hips and kiss him back and let it happen, hard and now. The violence of stranger sex, a violence and urgency that good, safe, interesting, respectful Bento can't provide.

My forearm drove up against Luke Jourdan's throat, and he gasped. His dark eyes narrowed. He pushed my arm away, gripped my shoulders. Shook me hard. Slammed me against the wall. My shoulder blades and head knocked against the plaster.

Suddenly I saw: it wasn't dirty hate sex for fun. It wasn't getting back at Jude with a hot young stranger. It was the pent-up rage of the good man betrayed—the bottled, well-muscled fury of years of shopping and cooking and keeping the kid, only to learn that his wife had been out fucking a pretty boy in her spare time. A rage that was turned on me now. I was the one who told him. I was the one who ruined the peaceful illusion that all was well.

His dark eyes clouded. The danger was real. If I could have struck a match near his mouth, it would have sparked the fumes.

"Luke," I said. "Luke."

His grip on my shoulders tightened and burned, and he looked at me with hatred. I'd covered enough domestic calls to know how badly this could end.

"Chloe," I said. "Is Chloe okay?"

He froze. And somehow that question shifted him, flipped

him to another gear, the habitual gear of caring for his daughter. His hands loosened, and his eyes changed.

"You can't do this," I whispered. "Not with Chloe here." His hands dropped away from my shoulders, and he stepped backward. He stood there, swaying a little.

The front door was still open. I ran.

This morning when I woke, there were three messages from him on my cell phone, slurring his drunk apologies. When good guys go bad, they can't cope. They don't know what hit them. They don't know what's always inside us.

The third message asked, "So, would you still be willing to write Jude's obituary?" I deleted his voice. After my shower, I stood in front of Soline's steamed mirror. Gray fingerprints marked my shoulders.

Church feels like a safe place to be.

Marisol is scrubbed and sweet, as if pizza and a bath and a good night's sleep have transformed her into a different kid. She knows from long experience how to sit still through Mass, and my mother looks beatifically happy to have a temporary, pretend grandchild sitting next to her.

Me, I'm thinking of Ledia's tamales. I can't wait to drop Marisol off at school tomorrow morning and get back to my life.

Monday

14

The explosions always start in the south, where the refineries are. From the window, I watch the hot toxic clouds billow upward, dark gray. Orange flames flicker down low.

One fire touches off another, and the dark clouds swell and surge toward the city. I gather my gun, the jugs of water, damp cloths for my own face and the face of my mother, who is somehow always staying with me when the explosions begin.

We tie the wet rags over our mouths and head down to the car, knowing the smoke will sink as it moves over us, that we'll be like children in grade-school safety films about house fires, needing to crawl down low where air is still breathable—and we will be low, hunched in my Pontiac, heading north on I-10 with thousands of other little metal boxes of desperation. But not low enough, and the smoke will drop lower and lower until there is nowhere for us to go.

I wake up gasping, sick with a thick fear I can't shake.

New Orleans hums on oil. The industry lies under everything else: the law offices in the CBD, City Hall, historic preservation, tourism, and the mansions on St. Charles. Oil is the big-bellied sugar daddy who writes checks for it all, and the wise do well not to forget it.

But me and my apocalyptic nightmares, we can't seem to get wise.

Marisol's a freshman at Grace King High School in Metairie, so I swing through and drop her off on my way north. It's Monday morning, and I'm in a foul mood. Kids. Why do people have them? I'm heading to Mandeville, where I'll interview Senator Claiborne, whose secretary has given me the hour between nine and ten o'clock.

The morning air is thick and cool, so I leave my windows down as the Pontiac glides up onto the Causeway Bridge. Twenty-four miles of four-lane highway raised on pilings above Lake Pontchartrain, it used to be the longest bridge in the world. My tires find an easy rhythm—*ka-chunk ka-chunk*—over the sectioned road, and the vast waters of the estuary stretch out, shimmering and silver, on both sides. With the breeze in my face and the easy drive, the hangover of my bad dream fades away. I feel my shoulders drop, the tensions of the last few days falling behind me as the city shrinks in my rearview mirror.

When my cell phone rings, it's Calinda, and there are no preliminaries.

"Listen," she says. "The police got to your boy Cory Brink's apartment Saturday night after the murder. Someone had already been there. As in, searching the place. As in, drawers open, couch cut up, the works."

"Thanks," I say, taking it in. When Luke had accused me of searching his house, I'd half-thought he was just grief-addled, paranoid. I tell Calinda what he'd said. "Two people dead who knew each other. Two domiciles searched by person or persons unknown. What did the vics have?"

"Or what did someone *think* they had?"

"Or . . ." I break off, not willing to say it aloud.

"Or what?"

"Nothing. Listen, I've got to go."

I don't, but I need to think.

"Later," she said, and clicked off.

Luke had told me his house had been searched, but I had only his word for it, and though I'd told him to call the police, I'd never checked to see if he'd filed a report. What's more, he'd told me it had been searched only after I'd explained the likelihood of his wife's affair.

Half an hour later, the Causeway sets me down in Mandeville, a town of about twelve thousand on the north shore of the lake. In the 1800s, it was agricultural land, and then a town. Steamboats carried vacationers across from the city. The bridge was built in the 1950s, and in the 1960s and '70s, Mandeville was a sleepy little bedroom community. Pine trees shaded the old neighborhoods. Kids played ball, camped in the swamps, and swam in the lake on hot days. Now, swollen by white flight, Mandeville's an upscale suburb with malls and coffee shops, po'boy shacks and La Madeleine cafés.

If I turn right, I'll end up at the lakefront, a three-mile swathe of lawn and oaks where the locals jog and roller-blade, and where Fabi's parents' white plantation-style mansion sits across the street, its French doors opening onto a wide veranda that faces the lake.

Instead, I turn left. West. Toward new money and the senator's home. Slowing to twenty-five miles an hour, then fifteen, I pass mansions that get bigger and grander as I drive. On the left, a colossal Italianate manor of peach stucco stands. It's new, hideous, and completely out of place—one of the structures thrown up after Lake Pontchartrain washed the original houses away during Katrina. It looks like the house of a Colombian drug lord, plopped down among the wooden Creole cottages and shotguns and plantation-style houses, blind to the vernacular. Its peach paint is almost fluorescent in the morning sun. I keep driving west.

The senator's place is hard to miss, since it's the only horse farm around. You need a lot of land to pasture horses, and lakefront property costs top dollar, so the north shore of Lake Pontchartrain is a pricey place to raise Thoroughbreds—which isn't, if I understand correctly, a cheap pursuit to begin with. With the risk of tropical storms and the difficulty of transporting a lot of horses in a weather emergency, the location seems like a strange choice.

I give my name at the gate. The guy in the booth checks it against his computer, checks my ID and press pass. Wide white panels slide open, and I pull through.

The paved driveway cuts between white-fenced fields, barns, and paddocks on the right. When I arrive at the senator's mansion, it reminds me of any number of old Louisiana plantations, of Moss Manors, of Tara in old movie stills. Fat columns stretch to the roof. A broad veranda stretches in front.

I pull up to the house and get out. The front door opens. A young woman, perhaps twenty-five, comes swiftly down the stone steps. Her golden hair falls smooth and shining to her shoulders, her gray pantsuit looks like it's been cut to her slim body, and her black shoes have a low, discreet heel. She's about the prettiest little shill for the capitalist petro-state you ever saw.

"Good," she says, holding out her hand. "You're on time. I'm Mindi Manning, personal assistant to Senator Claiborne."

Her clasp is cool and firm, an efficient, capable handshake. I catch a whiff of expensive musky rose and jasmine. Chanel No. 5. If she hadn't announced herself as a PA, I'd have guessed daughter. Maybe even young trophy wife.

"Nola Céspedes," I say.

"Yes. May I see your credentials?"

I pull out my press pass.

While she inspects it, I look at her. Up close, her facial features are sharp and bony. Her wrists are freckled. Mindi is not a rich girl's name.

She nods at the press pass and hands it back. "Welcome," she says.

"Where you from, Mindi?"

She looks startled. "Slidell," she says, dropping her eyes. She glances back up at me, a quiet pride blooming on her face. "But I live here now."

"Really? Right here in the senator's mansion?"

"In the staff quarters. It's convenient." She flashes a professional smile. "Shall we tour the stables?" She turns me neatly away from the manor house and begins to walk, and I realize three things.

First, everything about Mindi Manning, including the perfume, is aspirational.

Second, she's a smooth operator—she knows how to fit in, to move up—but being asked about her origins rattles her. There's a subsonic frequency I catch sometimes from people who used to be poor—something about the way their pronunciation slips on particular words, for example, or the rough ease in a gesture—that stirs an echo in me from the Desire Projects of my childhood. Often, when I get to know them better, I learn I'm right. Over one too many drinks, perhaps, I'll suddenly hear about food stamps and government cheese, or seven kids in a two-room apartment, or dirt floors in a shack so far out in rural Mississippi the roads don't have numbers or names. But those aren't things people tell you up front. I can relate. I'd kept my background a secret from everyone for a long time. Even now, only Bento, Marisol, and my closest friends know. With this girl, it's something different, something even stronger, something that thumps through me like the hard, sure throb of a single pulse beat. She's like me; I know she is. Layers and masks. *Ma soeur, mon double.* Mindi Manning comes from poor.

Third, I'm not getting my full hour with the senator.

"Excuse me," I call at Mindi Manning's gray flannel back, and she halts in midstride. "I was supposed to interview the senator from nine to ten."

"And you will interview him," she says, "but the senator is occupied at the moment, and he would very much like to have you see the horses." Without waiting, she takes off again. I follow.

We enter the barn. It's cool and clean, the floor thickly blanketed with fresh sawdust. At our end, there's a tack room on one side and an office on the other. Six spacious stalls line each side of the broad aisle.

"I've never been inside a barn before," I say. To my surprise, I like it: the thick leather scent, the smell of hay, the jostle and whickerings of the horses in their stalls. A hoof rings against wood. Long brown muzzles and gentle eyes turn to see who we are.

"Stable," Mindi says, correcting me. She reaches up and

scratches the white blotch on one horse's forehead. Its large dark eyes close, and air blows softly from its nostrils. "Pretty, aren't they?"

I nod. I stroke its cheek. First time I've ever touched a horse. I reach into the stall and slide my hand along its satiny shoulder. "How many does the senator own?"

"They're really Mrs. Claiborne's," she says. "Usually between twenty and twenty-five. She sells off some of the younger ones, especially this time of year. There's another stable just like this one."

The horse's shoulder is smooth under my hand. "They're nice," I say. It's true. The warmth, the muscle, the bone. It's an honest feeling.

"Yes," she says, and her smile, for the first time, looks genuine. Our eyes meet, and there's a flicker of something—something soft, some shyness, some kind of wordless appeal. It's as light and fleeting as the brush of a moth wing. A sudden connection. And then it's gone.

"Come on. I'll show you." She leads the way back outside, and after the cool shade of the barn, the sunlight makes me squint. Mindi walks to the white fence, and we put our hands on the rail and look out over the senator's pastures. Now I see the other barn, along with a track.

"Is that where they practice?"

"Yes, that's where the trainers work them."

I pull out my pen and notebook. Might as well make the most of it. "And they're all Thoroughbreds?"

"Yes, bred to race. Shadowfax Farms has had significant success at bringing home cups at the regional and national levels." Her speech sounds rehearsed. "Moreover, we're proud to say that the farm's record is spotless regarding illegal drug use, jockey injuries, and track breakdowns. Mrs. Claiborne has very high standards."

A young brown horse canters slowly across a pasture, and I watch. A horse running is a beautiful thing and well outside my purview.

But money, I know about. "These cups. Do they come with cash?"

She pauses, drawing in a delicate, patient breath as if I've said something rude. "Many of the purses are substantial, yes."

I'm about to ask how substantial when a small man bursts out of the stable and storms toward us, fists clenched. As he gets close, I can see that he has green eyes, a sharp chin, and at least three days' worth of stubble. He's Latino, maybe Mayan. And he's short. Probably the shortest man I've ever seen in real life. Petite.

"Where the fuck is Joe?" he yells up into Mindi's face. He has no accent, sounds like he's lived in Louisiana all his life.

It's interesting. She doesn't even flinch, like being yelled at by angry men is routine for her.

"That's right." Her voice is calm. "You haven't worked with us for a while."

"Bingo, genius." His brown hands are small, the size of a child's, but they're calloused and lean like a man's. "So where the fuck is Joe?"

"I'm sorry to be the one to tell you"—and she does seem sorry—"that Joe passed away last week." She turns to me. "Our stable manager," she explains. "A wonderful man, and excellent at his job. Much missed." She turns back to the jockey. "It was sudden. Unexpected. Terry's over at the other building if you have questions."

"Damn right I have fucking questions. What's my schedule?

Which horses am I working? And where the fuck is my bonus for Saratoga?"

Her smile is smooth as Teflon. "Terry can help you with all of that. Please be sure not to disturb Mrs. Claiborne with your concerns."

He turns away muttering. "Oh, I'm going to disturb someone, all right, if I don't see that bonus . . ." His jerky footsteps carry him quickly away.

"The talent," says Mindi. "So high-strung." She flips a strand of blond hair out of her face.

"What else can you tell me about the horses?"

"Well, all of Mrs. Claiborne's animals are pedigreed, purebred. They come from some of the finest stock in North America. Her family has been in horses for generations, so it's a real passion and legacy for her." Again, her words sound canned, like she's mouthed this tour script many times before.

"This manager, Joe. The one who died. What happened?"

Her blue eyes look calmly into mine, and her tone doesn't waver. She puts on a face of professional condolence. "Very fine employee. A great loss to Shadowfax Farms. There was an accident," she says. "I don't know much about it."

"And his last name was?" My pen hovers over my notebook.

She stares at me for a moment. "Shorter," she says. "Joe Shorter."

JS. The initials in Judith Taffner's list of notes. A dead man.

Mindi Manning brightens and gestures toward the house. "Shall we?"

Apparently, we shall. But if we think we're going to see the senator now, we're very much mistaken.

15

Mindi Manning escorts me up the stone steps and through the tall double doors. In the foyer, I stop, shocked.

The inside of the Claibornes' house has been gutted. The outside may look like history, like tradition, like every Louisiana coffee-table book filled with glossy photos of magnolia trees and plantation manors. But it's just a shell. Inside, everything is new, modern. The rooms are larger than they should be, as if walls have been torn out, and the ceilings are at least twenty feet high. The old-style furniture is new and seems built for some race of Scandinavian superhumans. Everything's grandiose with fresh possibility and promise. Beyond a wall of glass, the lake stretches from side to side like a gray steel stripe.

"Intimate, isn't it?" I murmur.

She glances at me. "After this lovely 1840s lake home suffered severe damage during Hurricane Katrina, it was renovated expressly for the Claibornes in 2007. They're completely committed to rebuilding and investing in the community."

In other words, they got the house for a song after the storm, when a lot of buildings on the shore were destroyed. Some owners called it quits and moved north. The Claibornes moved in with their money and snapped up the acreage. Suddenly their impractical choice for siting a horse farm makes sense. You can't put a price tag on the positive PR that comes from post-Katrina rebuilding.

Mindi Manning waves at the shiny tan stuff under our feet and smiles with pride. "The floors are terrazzo."

I pull out my camera. "Do you mind?"

"Of course not."

Of course not. This whole place is a stage. It's designed to be photographed, to hold catered parties for two hundred and fifty donors at once. I snap a few shots. Chandeliers the size of oil barrels dangle from the high ceilings. It's a perfect setting for the Claibornes themselves, who come from old-money Louisiana— old land, old antebellum wealth—but whose ambitions are larger than life.

"Is Senator Claiborne available now, do you think?"

Mindi Manning checks her white Chanel wristwatch, its large face rimmed in diamonds. Or her very good white knock-off wristwatch, its face rimmed in rhinestones. Whichever. "Not just yet," she says. "But come join me on the veranda."

I sigh—more HGTV bullshit—and follow her out through glass doors as tall as a tree. Why would a PA in her twenties be wearing a watch worth more than my car?

Outside, the wind off the lake feels like a caress, and some invisible servant has thoughtfully placed a tray with two tall glasses of iced lemonade on the curved stone railing. Mindi lifts one and sips it. "Mind the pulp," she says, smiling. "It's fresh squeezed." I wonder how many times she's done this routine.

I lift my glass. "Nice," I say. Meaning the lake, the view, the lemonade, the nifty way our elected officials manage to live like royalty while whining in Washington about the need to cut so-cial services to the poor and middle class.

While I wonder if I'm ever going to see the senator, Mindi delivers a mini-lecture on the ecology of Lake Pontchartrain and the great strides that have been made to restore it to its origi-nal state. She reels off statistics about rebounding populations of brown pelicans, bald eagles, and various species of fish. The senator, she assures me, has contributed so much to the cause.

Right. The same senator who voted time and again to gut the EPA. The senator who's known for the catchphrase, *We all want clean air, but*. . . .

Finally, at exactly 9:47, she leads me back inside, up a wide staircase, and into the senator's office. At last.

Lined with shelves of books, his office is a larger, redder fac-simile of the presidential Oval Office, photogenic as a stage set. I flash to *The Great Gatsby* and wonder how many of these leather-spined volumes have been read, by anyone, ever.

From the leather chair behind his desk rises Senator Caleb Claiborne, lean, fit, and classically handsome, with silvering hair and a deep tan, the sleek achievement of expensive groom-ing, tooth whitening, and focus groups.

"Hello," he says warmly, "and welcome." I know from Jude Taffner's profile that he's sixty-three, but if I saw him on the street, I'd guess early fifties.

He exudes the warm, assured ease of a lifelong golden boy, and his shirt is the kind that made Daisy Buchanan cry, a cot-ton so thick and fine it has a sheen. The cuffs are turned back, and his wrists are broad and browned and strong. He looks like a man who knows his way around a tennis court, a boardroom, Geneva.

Yet the lines in his face are earnest, open, and the light in his blue eyes looks real. He's wearing a red tie, but it's loosened, the way I like ties, and his suit jacket is tossed over the back of a chair. He looks like a man who's here to work.

He puts out his hand, and I move forward to shake it. His grasp is dry and firm, and he gives me a little extra squeeze and smiles into my eyes like he's sincerely glad, like we've known each other for years and he's delighted to see me again.

I introduce myself.

"Lovely," he says. "Wonderful to have you here." He turns and places a fatherly hand on Mindi Manning's shoulder. "Thank you, Mindi, for bringing Ms. Céspedes to see me," he says, pronouncing my name correctly, and then waves her toward a little desk at the side of the room. She smiles coolly, steps across the thick, silencing rug, and folds into her seat.

The senator settles back into his chair. To his right, an American flag hangs from a brass pole. Next to the flag stands a tall, broad-shouldered Latino in a navy pinstriped suit. Dark eyes, dark curls, skin the color of mine, and a wide-legged stance that makes me guess he's more muscle than aide. He probably comes in handy at photo ops, too: visual proof that the senator doesn't suffer from Hispanophobia.

As I settle into the proffered chair, I smile invitingly at the Latino guy, but he doesn't smile back.

A lot of men don't. It's this rule or agreement they have: *Leave the smiling to the ladies. Leave the nods, the encouragement, the little affirming noises of agreement and appreciation to the girls.* The Latino guy stares through me, his face a handsome, empty mask.

But I trust his bland unwelcome more than the unsettling charm of Senator Claiborne.

I pull out my Olympus and press it on. "Thank you for making time to see me." All ten minutes of it. I open my little notebook and click my pen.

"Yes, my pleasure," the senator says warmly. "I'm glad you wanted to talk." When his eyes lock on mine, there's a strange, electric focus in his gaze. It's unnerving and pleasurable all at once, being the recipient of his high-wattage attention. He doesn't look merely at my face, as people generally do, or at my eyes, but into my very pupils, as though he's slipping through their thin black tunnels and straight into my brain. With his broad shoulders and strong jaw, Senator Claiborne radiates a palpable aura of old-school masculinity, the kind that promises to take care of me forever—if I'll just give him my trust, my vote, my wallet.

"Senator, I know you plan to run for reelection again next November. Is that correct?"

"Yes, that's right. Claiborne 2010," he says, nodding, his blue eyes sincere. "Best thing for Louisiana. Best thing for America."

As banal as his words are, there's an undeniable glow about him. This is the thing people mean when they say *charisma*: that ineffable magic, the thing you can't fake. It's heady stuff.

I expected slick. I didn't expect this. His charm throws me off balance.

I check my notes. "Senator, can you tell me if your donor base has shifted over the past couple of years?" I'm thinking of the cryptic note Jude Taffner wrote: "Dem donors."

"No, not at all. We've got a great set of American values and a good strategy to win. Nothing's broken. No need to fix it."

"But sir, I mean in terms of the current economic crisis." Anything to break through the façade of his planned, canned rhetoric. "Will you propose any shifts in policy as part of your campaign, to attract a broader set of donors?"

"Ah. Ah." He taps his index fingers together. "Well, of course

I'll support strategies that respond flexibly to current realities." He stops like that was an answer, like he's done.

I wait. He *is* done. His charm begins to fade. Same old song-and-dance.

He squints suddenly. "You know," he says, "you look just like someone on television." He glances at the Latino guy. "That girl on *30 Rock*—the one Alec Baldwin dates?"

The other man clears his throat. "Salma Hayek, sir." Nice voice. Deep, with a bit of a rasp. A whiskey voice.

"*That's* the one." The senator turns back to me and beams congenially, as though he's just paid me the highest possible compliment. "Salma Hayek."

Yeah, okay. Moving on. "Senator, Ms. Manning was telling me about your support, here on the local level, for clean water. And Lake Pontchartrain is certainly doing better." In the corner, Mindi Manning straightens, smiling to herself. I've reported something good back to her boss. Maybe he'll give her a pony.

He nods. "Yes, yes. We've stopped the dredging, stopped the dumping. The numbers are looking good."

"I think my readers at the *Times-Picayune* will be very pleased to hear about your role in that."

"Good, good." He smiles expansively, nods again.

"So, can you tell me if your environmental support extends to the national level? If, for example, you might be prepared to push to reinstate the ban on offshore drilling in the Gulf? Or take other steps that might appeal to progressive voters?" I'm shooting blind.

The head keeps nodding, but the smile fades away. The steepled index fingers tap, tap, tap. Behind him, the handsome guy tightens subtly all over. If he's muscle, he's not dumb muscle.

"My position on America's energy needs," says the senator,

"will remain the same. We need to tap and maximize our own energy resources, including our unused oil beds, to reduce our dependence on foreign oil and our reliance on unstable nations in the Middle East."

"But you've always voted to support U.S. invasions of oil-rich countries, up to and including Iraq."

His jaw pulses like a little mouse, and his blue eyes go flat. The temperature in the room plummets. "Those wars, young lady, were initiated to defend America's freedom and the freedom of our allies. They are political wars for political reasons, not economic ones." He glances at the clock on the wall. "Ah," he says, "look at the time." A pale semblance of his former smile returns, and he rises. "This has been most pleasant. You can assure your readers that my positions and policies will remain unchanged. Best thing for Louisiana, best—"

"Thing for America. You said." I rise, too, but my Olympus stays on. "Just one last question, Senator. Are you familiar with a Dr. Judith Taffner, a Tulane professor who was writing a story about you?"

The silence that falls on the room is long and strange. The senator's glance flicks to Mindi Manning. If nods are exchanged, I can't see them.

"Yes," he says slowly. "I believe she came out here to interview me."

Mindi Manning nods. "That's correct," she tells me. "Just like you."

"Dandy," I say, turning to her. "Did she get the same royal treatment? The stable tour, the lemonade on the terrace, the whole nine yards?"

Her chin lowers half an inch.

"And in the stable, did she happen to meet Joe Shorter?"

Her cool eyes appraise me. Her lids slide down over them and rise slowly back up. "I really don't recall."

"Were you aware," I ask the senator, "that both Dr. Taffner and the student who accompanied her here to the interview have been murdered within the last week?"

The senator's eyes widen, and he looks genuinely surprised and pained. But it's hard to know what's genuine when someone's been acting for the public for forty years.

"No, of course not," he says. "That's terrible. Tragic." He takes a breath, pauses. Silence reigns in the room. When he begins to speak again, it's as if he's located the correct script for the occasion. "The violent crime rate in New Orleans remains one of our great challenges, but it's one that our fine officers in the police force are working on, and that we will continue to pursue with all the resources at our disposal." Sound bite.

"Dr. Taffner was unable to finish her article about you before she was killed. However, her notes suggest that you may be receiving donations from Democrats, and I'm just wondering why that would be. Would you care to comment?"

His jaw pulses for a moment, as if he's considering saying no. Finally he speaks. "That is a complete and utter fiction," he says. "I can assure you, my base has not changed. My positions have not changed." Gone are the senator's charm, the magnetism, the marvelous semblance of love. His hand waves dismissively, and the Latino muscle guy steps forward. "I don't know where you've gotten your information, young lady, but you're sadly mistaken."

The muscle takes me gently by the elbow, steering me out of the room. I'm ushered downstairs by the handsomest Latino I've ever seen in a suit.

"Why do you work for that guy?" I say.

He's silent. Our feet tap across the wide terrazzo floor together.

He smells good, like woods and musk, and he's not wearing a ring.

"What's your name, anyway?"

He opens the front door, and I step out onto the wide stone steps in the sunlight.

"You want to get coffee sometime? Talk about it?" I fish out a business card with my number. "Figure out where you went wrong?"

The door closes. I put the card back in my bag and head down the steps to my car.

16

Back in my black Pontiac, I blow past the buildings of Mandeville and onto the Causeway, mashing the gas in frustration. By
the time I get back downtown, two hours of my life will have
been spent learning nothing, except that Joe Shorter was the
senator's stable manager, that now he's dead, and that all Lati-
nos don't support their own political interests any more than
Kansans do.

By eleven A.M., I'm at the *Times-Picayune* office, digging online for dirt. I'm thinking that if Mindi Manning comes from a
tough financial background—as my gut tells me she does—
then her backstory could be great material to fold into the profile of Senator Claiborne. Human interest. Including her story
could humanize the portrait of the senator and complicate his
patrician narrative. What's Mindi Manning's background? What
drove her to work for him: a paycheck? Proximity to power? Or is
she a true believer?

But Mindi Manning keeps a pretty low Internet profile.
There's no bio of her on the senator's Web site and nothing on
Facebook. But she's on LinkedIn, bless her striving heart, and I

learn that after graduating from Slidell High she went directly into the Marines. LinkedIn doesn't say where she was stationed. After that, she got a BA in political science, magna cum laude, from LSU, where she was a member of Chi Omega sorority.

So when the Mannings couldn't send her to college, the military could. Okay. But why'd she choose the toughest branch, the one whose brochures read, "There are no female Marines. Only Marines"? Why would someone choose to purge away gender, and then come back and pledge a sorority? Upwardly mobile ambition? The desire to blend extreme toughness with extreme femininity? It's the mandatory recipe for contemporary female success.

I search the white pages for every *Manning* in Slidell. There are only three households, and Mindi Manning is still listed as a resident at one, though she's been long gone from there. I jot the address down.

I'd like to investigate the handsome bodyguard, too, if that's what he is, though I confess my motives are a little more polluted in his case. But without his name, it's hard to do much.

Then I look for Joe Shorter. The obituary pulls up quickly, and there's a photo: a kind-looking face, warm brown. Forty-seven, married, with no children, the victim of a hit-and-run. His widow, Irene, lives in Madisonville. Back across the damn lake. Another fifty-mile round-trip. I look up her street address.

Shifting gears, I submit a request to NOPD for the Jonas Applewhite case file. I write and file a couple of routine stories from police reports, fact-checking on the phone. A fourteen-year-old boy who shot up a convenience store in Tremé. A rape-murder down in Algiers. A hit-and-run by a silver Saturn on North Broad. "New Orleans police are investigating. . . . There is no other information at this time." The usual.

The newsroom isn't like it used to be. It was always frenetic, but now there's a jittery energy, a nervousness, that wasn't here before the recession hit. Not that we're supposed to call it a recession in print. But everyone's got at least one friend who's been pink-slipped. Here at the *Picayune,* where circulation's down, we're all watching the editor Bailey's door. One of these days, he'll come out. He'll walk to one of our desks. He'll say, "Come talk with me for a minute." And that'll be the end of our career, because it's not like other papers are hiring. They're closing their bureaus, closing their doors.

Calinda says I should think about law school, since I like facts and research and arguing. Since I don't back down or scare easily. Maybe. Soline says I should get licensed as a private investigator. It's just a forty-hour course, and I'm good at digging dirt. But the only people who'd read my reports would be my clients. Not sure I relish writing for an audience of one, reporting on stolen jewelry and cheating wives.

Jude Taffner's career choice—the haven of academia—might have left her insecure in the classroom, like Professor Guillory said, but it's one I've been considering. "Go to grad school," people say. And I've already done the hands-on part, so I wouldn't have to feel nervous and half-baked like Dr. Taffner. I could get a masters, a PhD, and find a job within the shelter of some big university, like she did. Long hours, but summers off.

But that ease shows in her work, in the texture of her prose. Both of the features I pulled from her desktop are full of long, compound-complex sentences. Leisurely, written for readers with time on their hands. They're elegant and correct, but it's the elegance of the drawing room, of teacups carefully raised, not of a horse race: fast, muscular, hurtling toward the finish line, where fractions of a second count. Her leads—did she even have leads?—were buried deep in her stories, subtle and oblique. Not like real news, where you break the story in the first paragraph, and each succeeding paragraph becomes more and more disposable, so that readers get the core information first, in case they have to quit reading.

Leisure sounds good sometimes. To have a comfortable, quiet office with leather chairs and a door you can close, instead of a metal desk among fifty other metal desks in a vast gray newsroom, with reporters barking back and forth at one another or into their cell phones. Adrenaline and caffeine and deadlines. Cynicism. Exhaustion. A fast and permanent burn.

Maybe a certain smugness in one's prose is a reasonable price to pay. A certain complacency.

I don't know. Leisure and shelter and tenure didn't save Jude Taffner. Not in the long run.

That afternoon, despite the mad swarm of kids and cars outside Grace King High School, Marisol finds me with some weird teen echolocation system and slips into the Pontiac beside me.

"Hey," she says, then leans back and closes her eyes as I pull into traffic.

I drive, asking the questions I've seen moms ask on TV. "How was school?" "What did you learn today?" Marisol's replies are just as obligatory. Only when she launches into a blow-by-blow account—apparently in real time—of the latest spat that's split her circle of friends does her voice light up. Rises in outrage. Drops to a hushed shock. "And then you know what she said?"

I don't. Dear God help me, I do not. And I don't know what

I'm supposed to do with a teenager for the two or three hours before we can reasonably begin eating dinner in front of the TV.

"Hey," I break in. "I have an idea."

She gasps and glares at me, appalled that I've interrupted, insulted by my clear lack of interest in her saga. She folds her arms and stares through the windshield.

"Come on. Do you want to go to the shooting range?" It's a bad idea. I haven't cleared it with her parents. And the national Big Brothers Big Sisters organization might not be too crazy about the notion.

But it changes everything. Marisol turns to me, her eyes shining.

"Oh, my God," she says. "Totally."

The Shooters' Club in Metairie is only six miles away, so the drive takes no time. The shy teenager at the counter with the big, clumsy hands and a puppy-tumble of blond hair is happy to get us both rigged up with earmuffs and targets. I can't tell if his sweet eagerness to demonstrate everything is for me or Marisol.

In our aisle in the gallery, I show her how to hold the Beretta, how to load it, how to work the safety, how to grip and aim. My hands are nervous on the gun, as they have been ever since I killed Blake Lanusse.

But Marisol doesn't notice. She's rapt, nodding, glued to every word. When I demonstrate a shooting stance, legs apart, arm braced, she mimics me perfectly. If her high school offered ballistics, she'd be an honor student.

We send the clipped target gliding away down the aisle, and I fire off a few rounds to demonstrate. My wrists quake, as they always do now, and I struggle to hold steady. Shiduri Collins says that killing can traumatize, that I need to process the trauma I inflicted on myself.

I just want my mojo back.

Then it's Marisol's turn. Her wide-legged stance is *que* cute, like Angie Dickinson, and she empties the clip fast like she's in a B movie. In her mind, she's probably Angelina Jolie.

"Hey, now," I say when she's done and we slip off our muffs. "*Cálmate.*"

I flip the switch that brings the paper target swooping toward us. She's destroyed his hips and the air around his head. Her hand covers her mouth as she laughs.

"Take your time," I say. "Aim." I tell her to focus on the torso. It's your best chance for a kill shot. "If someone's coming at you, that's how you'll stop him. Don't mess around aiming for legs. Leave that to professionals. Legs move too fast. I hope to God you never need to pull a gun, but if you ever have to, you shoot to stop him."

She nods. I send Mr. Target fluttering back again and watch her reload.

This time, she's slower, more careful. An intent gleam grows in her eyes, and a kind of quietness falls over her. When we retrieve the target, all her new shots have speckled his upper torso.

"Good. Much better."

Her grin is proud.

We stay for an hour, taking turns, and Marisol gets better with each clip she drains.

"Okay," I say finally. "Got to wrap it up."

Reluctant, Marisol unwinds her fingers from the black metal and moans like we're leaving Disneyland.

Unique kid. We may not be the most typical Big Sister–Little

Sister pairing in the history of the organization, but they sure matched us well.

We drive out into the warm evening with the Pontiac's windows down, and the wind whips our dark hair around our heads like we're twin Medusas. I veto Marisol's dinner request—McDonald's—and drive us home to Soline's apartment, where I make wild rice, sauté tofu in olive oil and tapenade, and steam up some broccoli and cauliflower. Fabi would approve. But that's as far as my parenting efforts go, though Soline's dining table beckons. We eat in the living room, watching *Friends* reruns.

During a commercial, I mute the TV. "So how'd you like that today, shooting?"

She chews, thinking. Swallows. Nods.

"Yeah," she says. "Not bad."

After dinner, she unpacks her backpack across the table like Rommel driving deep into Egypt. Protractor, calculator, schoolbooks, notebooks, phone. Once her territory's marked, she sits quietly, doing her homework, with which I do not offer to help, since I need to shower and dress for my date with Bento. Makeup, perfume, hair. A pretty scarlet dress and peep-toe heels. Marisol whistles when I come out to say good-bye.

"Yeah. Listen, there's flan in the fridge, but save me some. TV off by nine, lights off by ten."

"You said all that already," she tells the ceiling.

"And when can you answer the landline?"

She sighs. "Never, unless it's you and you tell me to pick up."

"And under what circumstances can you leave the apartment?"

"If there's a fire."

"Right."

"I'll be *fine*," she says. "My mom leaves me by myself with the babies all the time."

Yeah. No comment. "Look, if anything comes up, call me, okay? If you need anything."

"Would you just go already?"

I lean and kiss her forehead. "Be good."

She snorts. "You be good." There's a teasing glint in her eye. "Don't stay out all night."

"Yes, all right. I'm going." I grab my keys, my little lamé clutch, a cream-colored cashmere wrap that Soline left behind.

Can a thirteen-year-old leer? "Tell Bento hi," she says, grinning.

Fifteen minutes later, I'm sitting in the lovely walled garden of Martinique, a bistro on Magazine Street. The thick walls are red brick, and green vines tumble over them, lit with tiny twinkling lights. Inside the walls, the sounds of street traffic are muffled. All you hear are the murmur and laughter of diners, the clink of silver and china, and the scrape of metal chair legs against the patio's cement. Waiters glide to and fro, carrying duck breasts cured in sugarcane, Gulf shrimp, sea scallops, and pork brined in Creole mustard.

I'm here with a snowy white napkin in my lap and a man in my face.

"Why haven't you returned my calls?" he says.

Nice, Bento. Great romantic opening. His handsome face is half anxious, half suspicious. He's ordered a bottle of Cabernet, which sits open on the table, breathing—more calmly, I hope, than I am. I am not into being told what to do. But is this control or concern? I wish, as I often do now, that I had Shiduri Collins on speakerphone.

"Where have you been all week?" he asks.

I pour myself a glass, take a slow breath, and explain about the two murders. About how Jude Taffner had been my teacher long ago. I tell him how Marisol showed up at my gate like a lost puppy. How Jazz Fest turned into a blood fest.

His face softens into concern, and I make myself reach across the table to put my hand on his. "But I'm sorry," I say. "I should have called."

The truth is, I'm glad of the excuses. Things have gotten thick and sweet and heavy with Bento. It's too much, and too soon. It's enough to indict me that my account of the last few days omits the Latino muscle's nicely filled pinstriped suit and the way my knees went weak in Luke Jourdan's kitchen.

I'm attracted to other people. To Bento, not so much anymore.

Which is perverse, given our chemistry. It's not like the man's not attractive. It's not like he doesn't have skills.

The waiter comes, and Bento orders. I'm still full from dinner with Marisol, so I ask for just a salad.

I want to tell Bento that none of it's his fault. It's not even my fault, according to Shiduri Collins, who keeps assuring me that my reaction is completely normal. What feels like loss of interest, she says—or even disgust, like the other night—is a defense mechanism. For survivors of rape and sexual abuse, the more emotionally intimate a relationship gets, the harder it becomes to sustain an erotic connection. Warm, open-hearted, intimate sex leaves us too raw, too vulnerable—making us prey to flashbacks and nightmares. Instinctively, we avoid it.

It's the unconscious reason, Shiduri Collins says, that for years I restricted my sexual experience to one-offs with strangers. If I can objectify the guy, I can objectify myself, which is much emotionally safer than bringing my whole self to the bed. I just can't. Too risky. So distance or sudden disgust kicks in to save me from all that. Or so the theory goes.

Or maybe I'm just bored.

Our food comes. I fork up my arugula, and Bento eats with an exuberance I used to find sensual. I used to find it fascinating when he exclaimed over each flavor like an aspiring food critic.

Now I wish he'd just shut up and chew.

Instead, we chat politely about his work, my work, his friends, my friends. He has a colleague who's completely over his divorce now. Would Calinda be interested?

I think of Handsome Sperm Donor and her plans. "I'm not sure," I say. "I don't think so."

It's the slowest dinner in the history of civilization. Since I've already mentioned the fact that I need to get home to Marisol, he politely doesn't invite me back to his place. When the check comes, I put down a twenty for my share.

He sighs. "When will you let me take you out properly?"

I rise and bend to kiss his mouth. "Good night," I say. "I'll call you."

"*Querida,*" he says. His hand grabs mine, and he looks up into my eyes as though he's about to speak.

Guilt floods through me, or irritation, or both, and I smile brightly and pull away. With a little wave, I head across the patio, not looking back, pulling the cashmere tight around me even though the night's still warm.

When I pull the Pontiac into traffic, I don't head for home.

Shiduri Collins always says that I should call her when I get in a mood like this. That I shouldn't resort to old coping strategies.

But seriously, who calls their therapist at nine o'clock on a Monday night?

The band Papa Grows Funk plays a weekly gig at the Maple Leaf Bar, so I drive in that direction. It's hard to find a parking space in the cramped, crowded streets, but I finally nab a spot a few blocks away and make my way to the bar.

Inside its red walls, it's easy to get lost in the crowd of shifting, rhythmic bodies, the loud, thrumming funk, the multiple shots of vodka, the cloud of marijuana smoke that hovers like a ghost above us. I dance and drink and flirt like I'm single and there's no kid waiting at home, like this damn city isn't rife with murderers and freaks, like I've got nothing to do and nothing to fear.

The memory of Bento fades under the influence of the thumping bass, the brass, the vodka, the bodies of strangers pressed against mine. I face a man whose dark eyes pull me in, and our bodies square off. My hip follows his hip, my shoulder his shoulder. A slight smile curves his lips. He lifts one hand, an invitation, and I place mine in it, lightly, a still point of connection. I like it, the elegance of that contact, no grinding, no ass-grabbing, just the breath-light touch of palm riding palm as our bodies twist and rock to the throbbing funk.

The song ends. We smile at each other, and I sidle off into the crowd. That's all I want, and I find it, again and again—though some partners have significantly less subtlety, their hands urging against my ribs, clamping the small of my back and dragging me toward them—but I find it, the release of movement, for two full sets, between which I stand at the bar, winded, drinking iced vodka and acting very interested in my cell phone.

By the end of the evening, Bento and the threat of domestication seem far away, like distant pinpricks of light on a muddy horizon. The pleasantly worn, sore, fleshy pads of my heels distract me from abstract concerns like love.

There's a way in which dancing can bring one very close to ecstasy. That immersion, when one's muscles merge with the bass line, the drum line, and thought sails away: the abandon, the relief of the emptied mind. The moment when all the monkeys finally quit their chatter and you can hear the tree itself. When just to breathe is bliss.

To stay there, to dwell, to lodge in that deep silence instead of returning to the world of conflicts, of stories, of competing political agendas and murders at dawn—that's the privilege of monks, high in their ancient mountain temples or their little desert caves or walking in unison, heads bowed, down the cloister arcades of old stone abbeys.

The rest of us have only these little respites, whether we find them in church or at the end of a needle or very close to the body of a handsome stranger who smells of the ocean in a hot, close club on a Monday night.

And then we return to the world.

At one A.M., right on the brink of another icy shot of Ketel One, it suddenly hits me: I have to drive Marisol to school in Metairie in a few ungodly short hours. Which is just wrong, in every way. Don't school administrators read those studies about the biorhythms of teenagers?

Clutching my tiny lamé bag, I slip through the bodies of strangers and into the cool night air, completely one hundred percent fine to drive, not weaving, not stumbling even in heels. A few tired-looking women are gathered around the door, smoking their cigarettes hungrily, and their men's heads turn when I pass.

I strike off in the darkness in the general direction of my car, wondering if a shower tonight is really a necessity. Can one drive a child to school when one's hair reeks of pot smoke? The lights and noise of the club recede behind me as I navigate the narrow streets, my heels clicking on the asphalt and cement. It's a black, quiet night, and my Pontiac has apparently melted into the ether. I keep walking.

At last, after several wrong turns up tiny lanes, I spot the baked finish of my car down the block. All the tiny shotgun houses that line the road are dark now, and only a few tired streetlamps cast a pale glow down onto the silent street. I step out to walk across.

Suddenly, an engine guns loud and close on my left. Headlights flash on—high up, a truck or an SUV, a big one—and there's a roar of motor, and six thousand pounds of metal veer into the lane and bear down.

Adrenaline rocks through me, pushing my legs fast across the street, and then I'm crouched down between two parked cars, twisting to watch as the SUV speeds past, a dark vehicle, black or navy or dark green, with its rear plate blacked out. No license number. I stay crouched, my heart pounding.

Just crouch. Just breathe. Wait.

Will it come back to try again? Will it stop and cut its motor? Will someone get out? Someone armed?

But the engine fades as the SUV roars into the night. The red pinpricks of its taillights swerve around a distant corner and disappear in the dark.

I'm here in the night, crouched between bumpers, my hand on the warm metal of a stranger's car. The SUV's exhaust fumes hang in the air, thick and stinking.

No one from the nearby shotgun houses comes out to see if

I'm okay. Apparently, no one saw or heard what happened. Whoever the driver was, he picked his moment well. A dark night, a deserted street. A woman alone, leaving a club, tipsy, unsuspecting.

But was it random, or was I a chosen target? And had he really missed, or was it meant to be only a warning?

When I'm sure the SUV's not coming back, I stand up.

I've always heard that fear will shake you stone-cold sober. It's true. No more giddy dance steps juke my feet as I move slowly to the middle of the empty street and stand there, breathing heavily, my hands shaking.

I walk to my car. Sober now for sure. The drive home is furious and quick.

Who? And why?

Tuesday

17

At six A.M. on Tuesday morning, I startle awake and sit up in bed, staring out Soline's window at a dawn full of fog. I'm exhausted, confused, yet on full alert. I dreamed of being chased.

Even after showering and dressing, I'm uneasy. When Marisol and I pull out through the steel security gate, I count four black SUVs parked on the side street. None of them moves into traffic after us, but I watch the rearview mirror all the way to Metairie. If someone's tailing us, he's really good.

Which is worse.

My random comments to Marisol are distracted, but she's too absorbed in her cell phone to notice. I'm glad when she gets out of the car and heads toward the school with a swarm of other kids. Away from me, away from danger.

My brain's still hazy when I pull out of the school's drop-off zone, so I head for the shooting range. Practicing with Marisol left me itchy for more. I park, open the trunk, and grab a few cartridges from the arsenal of ammunition I keep there.

I've only had the Beretta for four years, since the Wild-West lawlessness after Katrina convinced me—along with half of

New Orleans—that it was time to carry a gun. Some of the places I've gone on the crime beat, I've been glad to have it.

A different guy checks me in, a heavyset, middle-aged guy who's reading a guns and ammo magazine and barely looks up. Standing in the aisle at the shooting gallery, firing off round after round into the face of my target, I find a little peace. Thought stops. My wrists tremble, but I ignore that. My head clears. There's just the squeeze, the release, the loud crack, the connect: all one. All smooth. My Beretta swallows clip after clip after clip, and my brain shuts up. Load. Brace. Fire.

This is the mental space that awaits me, Shiduri Collins promises, if I can just learn to meditate properly. She's outlined all the health benefits, the improved mood, et cetera. But sitting cross-legged staring at a rug just makes me squirm.

For Zen tranquility, I'll take a loaded semi-automatic.

When I've spent all the ammo I have, I'm clear, calm, focused. And I have a plan.

Driving fast to the Upper Ninth Ward, where I grew up, I call Evie Wilson. We say hello, and I hustle through some quick catching up. I ask if she's busy right now.

"Nuh-uh. Just washing dishes. What you thinking to do?"

I describe my plan and the role in it for her that I'm proposing.

She whistles. "Sure, I'm in. Sounds like a good day's work if there ever was one."

"Thanks, Evie. Is it okay to pick you up in"—I glance at the clock on my dashboard—"twenty minutes?"

She laughs into the phone. "Girl, you're not fooling around!"

I'm not. "Does that work?"

"Sure, sure," she says. "I'll be ready."

Evie Wilson—Evie Downes as was—grew up near me in the Desire Projects and remembers us as friends. But when I got out of the neighborhood, I stuffed all that to the back of a mental drawer so hard that when I turned up on her porch in 2008, investigating a story, I didn't recognize her face. When she told me her name, I couldn't place it.

Evie had the grace to forgive me, and we've been getting together every week or two since then—usually for lunch, since her kids are in school and that's easiest for her. We get burgers and fries and reminisce about old times, half of which I can't recall, but scraps come back as she talks. We talk about my job at the newspaper, her work at home raising three children with no man. Her husband—she was married by senior year—got killed by an IED in Iraq, and she makes his army pension and her own small convenience-store paycheck cover the bills. She talks about the crime, the drugs, and the worries that are part and parcel of living in the Upper Ninth. Sometimes she asks me what college was like.

The fog has burned off and the day is bright and clear, with easy clouds chugging slowly across a blue sky, when I pull up to Evie's battered white shotgun shack on its narrow street full of nearly identical houses. She's waiting on the porch in a flowered dress, a little blazer the color of apricots, and apricot pumps. I jump out as she crosses the yard.

"You look a picture of pretty," I say, and we hug. She smells like buttercream icing, and a small gold cross lies nestled, as always, in the hollow of her throat. "Thank you so much for doing this."

"You kidding me? I never played reporter before." We get in the car, and as I drive over to the block where Mahonia Applewhite lives, I coach Evie about what to say. Folks in the Ninth are notoriously and understandably loath to talk to outsiders, especially official outsiders. I'm Latina and grew up here, and my Pontiac is nothing impressive, but with my press pass, professional clothes, and light skin, I read as white. Part of the system. Not to be trusted. If I were to barge in by myself asking questions, the neighbors would surely clam up. My hope is that Evie at my side will soften my strangeness as I go door to door, asking if anyone witnessed the shooting of Jonas Applewhite. That we'll look like neighbors, community organizers.

It seems like a good plan. When we park, get out, and head for our first house, the two of us look about as threatening as a couple of Jehovah's Witnesses.

When we mount the rickety wood steps of the first little white shotgun house and knock, it's a comfort to have Evie by my side. But no one's home. At the second and third, people answer the doors, and Evie and I do our spiel, but they weren't back in town right after Katrina. No one saw the Applewhite shooting.

The little houses are packed close together, all painted with cheap white paint that blisters and peels. The yards are little scraps of tired grass already browning this early in the year. At the fourth house, we don't make it up the steps before a man yells, "Get the fuck off my porch!" and a pit bull hurls itself against the screen door.

"Whew," says Evie when we get back to the street. "This ain't going so well."

I laugh. "Welcome to journalism."

She smiles at me uncertainly.

We move to the opposite side of the block, across the street from the Applewhite house. At the corner house, a man with a Schlitz can in his hand opens the door and peers at us. "I done voted," he says. "Get along out of here."

"Sir, I'm Nola Céspedes from the *Times-Picayune*. Grew up a few blocks away."

"And I'm Evie Wilson, your neighbor from over on Pauline Street."

"And I done voted, like I told you."

"Please," I say. "We're here about the police shooting of Jonas Applewhite. We want to help Mrs. Applewhite get justice."

His eyes narrow. "Don't know what you're talking about. I ain't seen nothing."

The door slams.

"Some folks," Evie murmurs as we walk back to the street.

We have no joy at the sixth and seventh houses, either. At the eighth house, no one's home.

At the ninth, a young woman opens the door in short-shorts and a top that looks like a handkerchief strung on a ribbon. It barely covers her breasts. Her collarbones jut, and the tops of her hipbones are visible above the waistband of her shorts. She stares dully at us as we introduce ourselves and say our little piece about getting justice for the Applewhites.

She stares for a moment. "Huh?" she finally says.

I repeat our question. "We just want to know if you saw anything."

She sways a little and puts a hand against the doorframe. "Did Brickie send y'all? 'Cause I ain't got nothing."

I'm about to state the question another way when Evie lays a hand on my arm.

"You take care now," she says to the girl. "Take real good care." To me, she says, "Come on." She takes my arm, and we head back down to the street. "No blood out of that turnip." She shakes her head. "These young sisters. They just break your heart."

The next house looks no different, but there's a new Toyota parked out front, and when we knock, the door is opened by a broad-shouldered, good-looking man, early thirties, in gray work-pants. His Lube King shirt has a patch on the chest that says DEREK.

We introduce ourselves, and Derek sizes us up. "You got ID?" he says. "From the paper?"

"Sure," I say, digging in my handbag. No one else has asked. He takes it and reads, then nods.

"Yeah," he says, looking more at Evie than at me, "I saw the shooting." He gestures toward Mahonia Applewhite's house, across the street and three houses down. "I could see pretty good from my living room." He pushes the screen door open wide. "I'll show you."

Evie and I glance at each other, then follow him in. The house smells clean and cool, like cedar.

"What's your last name?" I ask, and he tells us it's Johnson.

"I was sitting right here," he says, indicating a cracked green armchair that faces the window. He stands behind it and taps its back as he talks, gazing out at the Applewhite house as if watching the scene replay. "The cop car was driving real slow down the road. Jonas out on his front porch, working on something. They stop, yell something, and get out the car. He come down his steps, holding a wrench in his hand." He shakes his head and turns to us. "And they just opened fire on the man. Six, seven shots maybe. Freak my shit right out, let me tell you. I jumped up. Stood here watching."

"Then what happened?" I say.

"Two cops. White. One tall and built, one just regular height but wiry. They looked at Jonas, looked around, but no one was out on the streets. Not that I could see, anyhow. They looked kind of worried, talking for a minute. Then the tall one opened the trunk, got out a gun, dropped it on the ground next to Jonas. Used a rag, I think, to hold it. Picked up Jonas's wrench and threw it in the trunk. The skinny one went back to the car and called it in. Ambulance came after a while."

"What did they do while they waited?"

"Just stood there, talking. Looking around. Nervous like. Took a few pictures."

"What did you do?" asks Evie, her voice soft with sympathy.

He looks at the two of us, his brown eyes sad and distracted. "Y'all want to sit down? I got some Dr. Pepper in the fridge."

"Sure," says Evie. "That'd be real nice."

He disappears, and we sit on an old brown plaid sofa. "What do you think?" she whispers.

He walks in before I can speak.

"Thank you," Evie says as he puts a can in her hand. "This is real nice and cold." He hands me one. The cold rush of sugar and caffeine is good after the heat of door-to-door canvassing. He drops into the green chair.

"So have you told your story to anyone?" I ask.

"Look, I'll be real with you," he says. "Number one, that shit scared me. Number two, I make a terrible witness. Credibility issues," he explains. "I been in twice on possession, once on unarmed robbery." I feel Evie sit up a little straighter, alert. "Kid stuff," he says. "Nothing serious. I was fifteen, sixteen. Just being a fool. I cleaned up a long time ago. But who's going to put me on the stand against a cop? I'm just a working man with a record."

"I'd believe you," Evie says. I glance at her.

"So would most folks up here," he says. "But you know how that's gonna play down at the courthouse."

"And you don't know anyone else who was back home at the time?" I ask. "No one else who might have seen the shooting?"

"Oh, I know for sure old Chester was home." He nods and points out the window. "Chester McNair. See Miz Mahonia's house? Two houses to the left. That's him. And I'd lay money he saw every damn thing. Nobody sneeze on this block without he sees it." Derek laughs. "Always been that way. Nosy old fucker." He glances at Evie. "'Scuse me."

"That's all right." Evie laughs. "There's one on every block, seem like." She turns to me. "Remember old Miz Jackson in Desire?"

I smile like I do.

"So you think this Chester McNair saw the shooting," I say.

"I'd put my paycheck on it. He was home. He's retired. It was the middle of the afternoon. But when I asked him about it after, he just looked at me like I was smoking something. Didn't say nothing, one way or the other."

I nod to Evie and set down my half-full Dr. Pepper can. "Sounds like we need to pay Chester McNair a visit." I rise, and Evie follows, smoothing her flowered dress. Derek rises to see us out. At the door, I pull out a business card and hand it to him. "You think of anything else, call me. I'm going to talk to the DA's and see if you'd work as a witness. That okay with you?"

He pulls in a deep lungful of breath and nods. "Yeah," he says. "I can do that." Then he turns to Evie. "How about you? You got a card?"

Her eyes go shy. "No."

"Here," I say, pulling out a pen. "Write your name and number on the back of mine."

He holds the card out to her, smiling, and she quickly scribbles her name and number. I thank him again, but Evie says nothing until we're down in the street and Derek Johnson's door is safely closed. Then her fingers wrap around my arm. "Girl," she breathes, her voice on the edge of giddy, "you're going to get me in trouble with the Lord."

I smile. "He seemed to like you all right."

"That is one beautiful man. And employed, too."

"He is the Lube King, after all."

She slaps my arm. "Behave." We laugh our way across the street like we're in eighth grade, like we're not in one of the poorest, most murderous neighborhoods in a struggling city. Like we're not on the trail of a story that could explode like a hot mess on my head. Like we're just friends out having fun, and suddenly I get a flash—whether it's a memory or déjà vu or just my imagination—of what it must have been like when I was friends with Evie Downes back in the day.

"Come on," I say. "Let's talk to Chester McNair."

Chester McNair is seventy if he's a day, a stern little man with glasses and a faded grandpa cardigan the color of wine. His voice sounds like it's coming through rust. When we introduce ourselves and explain the purpose of our visit, his eyes grow sly.

On the day of the shooting, no, he wasn't home. He wasn't clipping his hedges, tidying up the yard after the mess Katrina had left behind. He wasn't kneeling, cleaning up the scrubby growth around the base of his gardenia bushes, when he heard the single whoop of a police car's siren and looked up. The officers did not get out of their car and yell to Jonas Applewhite, who came down off his porch with a wrench. Chester McNair stayed on his knees, not watching through a gap in the hedge "big as my hand" as Jonas Applewhite jerked and fell, as the officers prodded his lifeless body, as one went to the trunk and got the pistol that they let fall next to Jonas Applewhite's dead hand, as they picked up the wrench. Chester McNair didn't hear them radio it in. He didn't see the EMTs pull up in their ambulance and lift away the body of the man who'd been his neighbor for three decades.

Evie and I stand on his porch as he tells us everything that didn't happen. A clean porch, freshly painted. He doesn't invite us inside.

"Why didn't you tell anyone?" I finally say.

"Nobody asked," he snaps. "Forty-two years now I've been living on this street. I've seen plenty of things I never told no-body. This here's just one more. Keep yourself to yourself, stay out of folks' business, you be all right. Sixty years ago my mama told me that, and be damned if she ain't right." He glares at us.

I nod. "But if a case went to trial against those officers, would you be willing to testify?"

"Huh. I ain't no fool." He snorts and crosses his thin arms across his chest. "I read the paper." He nods at me. "*Your* paper. I know how this here city works."

"We're just trying to get some justice for Mrs. Applewhite," says Evie.

"I respect Miz Mahonia," he says. "I do. I'm sorry she lost her man. But testify?" He shakes his head, and his chuckle rasps across the air. I catch the smells of stale, sour coffee and old age. "You gonna get me witness protection? Who's gonna protect me? The same cops I'd be ratting out? Their buddies?" He shakes his head again. "No, thank you. I ain't got much in this life, but I'm glad to say I got the sense God gave me."

Learned helplessness, they call it in kidnapping and domestic abuse cases: the willingness to stay silent and obey when the victim has been made too painfully aware that the captor has all the power. What's lost is the sense that there's a world out-side—a world where fairness, justice, and decency are possible.

I'm not sure what it says about his decades in the Ninth and his perusal of the news, but Chester McNair has a bad case of learned helplessness, and a lot of people in these blocks share it. Powerlessness, hopelessness, the sure sense that the system is rigged to work against them. It's the current that flowed through my whole childhood in the Ninth. Despair.

And for good reason. Marred by racism, violence, scandal, and corruption, the history of the New Orleans police force is a bleak one. The force first formed in 1805, just two years after the Louisiana Purchase, primarily in response to white fear of black slaves. Back then, the police styled themselves as a military unit. They slept in barracks, marched in formation, and carried muskets, sabers, and flintlock pistols. At night they swept the streets for unruly slaves. Fast-forward a hundred years, and the police were in bed with racists and organized crime, enforcing segregation, keeping folks in their place. The twentieth century wasn't much better. Sometimes the Danziger Bridge shootings—and now this one—seem like merely the latest eruption of the fear and hatred that have always snaked under this city.

We push Chester McNair little harder, but his thin jaw sets, a right angle of stubbornness, and he finally tells us we need to be moving along.

We walk down his steps and out toward the street again.

"Well, if that ain't frustrating." Evie sighs. "What are you go-ing to do?"

"I'm not sure," I say, turning it over in my mind. "Talk to

Calinda, I guess—my friend at the DA's. After that, I don't know. He could be subpoenaed." I smile at her. "You've been great, Evie. A huge help."

She smiles her sweet smile back. "It's kind of fun, what you do."

I nod. "It is."

"You get to be nosy. Get all up in people's business."

" 'Poking and prying with a purpose,' " I quote. "Zora Neale Hurston."

"Ooh, I love her. You ever read *Tell My Horse*?"

And we chat about books as we walk back to my car in the heat and I drive Evie back to her little white shotgun.

18

When I pull my car into the lot at the *Times-Picayune* office and get out, it's almost noon. The air has grown hot and sluggish, with low dark thunderclouds off to the west.

I'm thinking about Jonas Applewhite and his wrench, about Cinelli and Doucet cruising the Ninth on a hot, bright afternoon when the city had been destroyed. More than a hundred and eighty-two thousand houses, ruined. Maybe theirs.

I'm thinking about good shoots: the necessary ones, the ones you have to make to save yourself or someone else.

Sometimes you're lucky. You know for sure which kind of shoot it is before you pull the trigger.

But sometimes you can't know. You're thrown in the hot thick of it, and the stakes are high, and there's no time to think. You move on instinct, hoping for the best, hoping your instincts are pure.

And sometimes they're not.

It's true for all of us. We're always in a context that's bigger than we are and moving fast. We can never see all the pieces. We've all got our lurking pockets of prejudice and fear. And the

Ninth is a scary place. Cops get killed there. Show me someone whose vision's not tainted by the past, and I'll show you a saint.

Which is not to say I'm letting these bastards off the hook. As I ride the escalators up to the third floor, I call information and get first Tony Cinelli's number and then Darryl Doucet's. I call and leave messages for each of them. Just the basics. "Hi, this is Nola Céspedes from the *Times-Picayune*, and I'd like to speak with you about the shooting death of Jonas Applewhite in the Ninth Ward."

I remember the way Doucet sat parked in a squad car in front of Luke Jourdan's house, having just broken the news of his wife's death. I imagine a cop car pulling up in front of my mom's place if I'm right about all this.

Inside on my desk, the fax of the police report for the Jonas Applewhite shooting has come in.

I read it and learn pretty much the same details that Jude Taffner's draft sketched out: the shooting, the time of death, and the names of the two patrol officers, the ones I've just called.

What's new is the name of the commanding officer on the case: Tom Winterson. Who's now Detective Winterson. Who just happened to be the first to arrive at the scene of Jude Taffner's murder. Who took my statement. I remember his hard, lined face, his professional solicitude. His card, still in my wallet.

I pull it out and dial his number.

Then I hang up.

Had Jude Taffner done the same thing? Had she called Tom Winterson and asked for an interview, only to end up with her hair in a lake?

I take a breath. Think it through. Dial again. I'm routed straight to voice mail. "Detective Winterson," I say. Keep it vague.

"This is Nola Céspedes from the *Times-Picayune*. We met after the recent murder of Judith Taffner in Audubon Park. I'd like to ask you a few questions about a related case." I leave my number and put the phone down. I stare out across the sea of metal desks, the gray computer monitors.

What if Tom Winterson himself had acted as the cleaner? I picture his hands on Jude Taffner's slim throat.

My phone rings, and I grab it, looking at the screen. But it's Evie Wilson.

"Hey, girl," she says, her tone electric. "You are not going to believe who called me."

I laugh. "He didn't waste any time, did he?"

"Derek Johnson!" She gives a muffled little shriek, like her hand's over her mouth. "Can you believe that? He called me up."

"Don't even tell me you're surprised."

"Are you kidding me? I'm a mother. I'm middle-aged."

"You're *thirty*."

"Well, with three kids in the house, I feel middle-aged, let me tell you."

"Well, apparently you don't look middle-aged to Derek Johnson."

"Nola, he wants me to go *out*."

I laugh again. "Of course he does. Where's he going to take you?"

"Hold on a minute." She clears her throat. "I said he wants me to. I didn't say I was going."

"Are you kidding? Of course you should go."

"Nola, you don't understand. I've got responsibilities."

"He asked you to go out, not move to France with him."

"Still. You know what I mean."

"No, I don't know what you mean. Raymond's been gone how long now?" Her husband went to Iraq right out of trade school. Blew up. Left her with three kids and loneliness.

"That's not the point."

"You're allowed to have a little fun. Your kids won't perish if you go out for an evening." I pause, thinking back to his warm smile, his broad shoulders. "And he's pretty cute, you've got to admit."

She stifles something that sounds like a giggle. "He *is,* isn't he? And he was such a gentleman on the phone. 'Would you like to join me?' and all that."

"So where's he want to take you?"

"Out to dinner. Some place called Ignatius, down on Magazine Street."

"Ignatius? Evie, that's a really great place. Your man's got taste."

"He's not my man, Nola."

"He could be."

She laughs. "Girl, you're going to get me in so much trouble."

"Evie, it's just a date."

"I know, I know." She pauses, and her voice gets serious. "But it's been such a long time. And you know I never did date much to start with. Met Raymond in school, fell in love, and that was that. Here I am, three babies later. Been a mama as long as I wasn't, just about. I don't know how to go out on no real date to a restaurant and all. And he's so fine-looking. What am I going to talk about?"

"It's not rocket science. You ask him questions about what he likes to do, and if he's a nice guy, he'll ask you questions, too. You eat some food, drink some wine, and one thing leads to another." I think of Bento. "If you're lucky."

"I don't know."

"What have you got to lose? He's young, he's cute, he's gainfully employed. . . ."

"Yeah, I know all that. Believe you me, I know it. Or I wouldn't have even been thinking about it. It's not like I ain't been asked, you know, all these years. The old fools they got up in here. Just never been anyone worth saying yes to."

"And now maybe there is."

"Yeah."

"And you're scared."

Her voice gets small. "Yeah." There's a long pause on the line. "I feel all . . . all fluttery inside, Nola. Ain't felt this way since high school."

"And?"

"And he could be wrong."

"Wrong?"

"You know. Not what he seems like. Or just wrong for me. How you supposed to tell? There's some crazy people up around in here. He could be fronting. No telling what he's really into."

"You want me to do a little checking for you?"

"What do you mean?"

"I could dig around online, see if anything comes up. I could ask my friend at the DA's to run a background."

"Huh." The line's quiet so long I think it's gone dead. "I never thought of that. That's kind of cold. Does that seem right?"

"Right? Half the women I know do it."

"Before they go on a date?"

"Before they so much as have coffee with a guy. You want me to check him out for you? I'd be happy to."

"Are you allowed to do that on your computer there at work?"

"Sure. Really, I ought to check him out anyway. Derek's

involved in the Jonas Applewhite case, as a witness, and if he's going to be credible, then he's got to be pretty clean."

"And you'd tell me what you find?"

"No problem."

"I told him I needed to check my schedule and call him back. So I could just tell him I need a couple of days to think about it—"

"A day. Tell him a day. It won't take me that long."

"A day." I hear her thinking it over. "And then I'll tell him if I can go or not."

"Yeah." I smile into the phone. "But, Evie, I think it's going to be fine. I think he's a really nice guy. And Ignatius is a really nice place. Good food. Quiet atmosphere. He's taking you out somewhere good—not to show off, but to show you a good time."

"What if he's no good with kids?"

"Evie."

"Well, what if?"

"He seems nice. And that's a bridge you can cross when you come to it. *If* you come to it. Y'all might not hit it off, and then it's not an issue."

"What if he's good with kids, but then my kids don't like him?"

"Whoa, there. He's asking you on a *date,* and you're already calling family therapists."

"All right, all right." Her chuckle is warm on the phone. "So maybe I'm tripping a little."

"Just a little."

"I'm sorry. It's just been a long time."

"That's okay. You called me, didn't you? You didn't freak out on him."

"No, I did not."

"So you're good. That's what friends are for."

"True that." I hear the warmth in her tone. "Well, I tell you what. I never did think, when we went knocking door to door for a dead man, that I'd end up finding me a live one." She bursts into laughter, and we chat a bit more. When we hang up, I turn to my computer. I open a basic background-check program. *Johnson, Derek,* I type in, and his address.

He comes up clean, aside from the juvenile record, and I'm not surprised. I send Calinda an e-mail with his name and stats, asking her to get back to me when she can.

I yawn and stretch, feeling the fatigue from last night. Online, I'm checking the directions to Joe Shorter's house in Madisonville, where I'm scheduled to interview his widow this afternoon, when something strikes me. Madisonville isn't far from Slidell, where Mindi Manning's family lives. Maybe half an hour. I could go check out her old home. I'll be nearby anyway. Two birds, one stone.

I shut everything down, unlock my filing cabinet, and pull out the bills of sale for the Thoroughbreds. I put them in my purse and head for my car.

Grabbing I-10 northeast out of the city, I speed all the way to the Twin Spans, the bridge that carries me across the narrow eastern end of Lake Pontchartrain, hovering above the silver water for four and a half quick miles. Down on dry land again, I catch the Old Spanish Trail into Slidell and beat my way through back streets to the edge of town.

Why I'm so curious about Mindi Manning and her background, I can't precisely say. Maybe because, for a reporter, any whiff of a secret provokes curiosity. Maybe because, like me, she works to hide her past. Maybe because of that soft moment of connection in the stable, when something real seemed to flicker in her eyes.

I reach her street and slow down, cruising slowly until I find the house number painted on the curb. I cut the Pontiac's motor and get out in the heavy heat.

It's not always good to be right.

The little blue mobile home is set far back on a lot that's as much bare dirt as grass. Weeds have overgrown the sidewalk's edges, and a tricycle lies upturned in the dirt, one wheel missing. I walk the length of the cement path, climb rickety steps to the porch, and knock. A homemade sign reads, THE MANNING'S, its letters and mistake burned into a strip of wood. Another wooden sign says, JOHN 3:16. In the yard, a torn trampoline sags slowly toward the soil beneath. I knock again and wait, counting the Black Label cans piled in a corner of the porch. No one answers.

I peer through a smudged window. There's a bare table, surrounded by six chairs. More scriptures hang on the wall. A sagging plaid sofa, a flatscreen TV, fake flowers in a plastic basket.

What was it like behind this closed door when Mindi Manning was growing up? Peaceful and cheerful, the genteel poverty of Victorian novels? But that's why they call it fiction. In the real world, domestic violence increases by a factor of five when a family slips below the poverty line. Parents talk to their children less and hit them more. When Mindi Manning joined the Marines straight out of high school, I wonder what demons she was working off. I wonder if she misses anything about this battered blue trailer. If she lies in bed at night riddled by survivor's guilt. If she forgot, as I did, the faces of friends.

Suddenly I hear the thump of footsteps inside. I pull away from the window, feeling caught in the act. The metal wall shakes a little as the footsteps draw near. There's a long pause. Silence. Someone's inspecting me through the tiny view-hole.

Then the door opens.

A man stands there. Tall, beefy, old, with reddened wattles hanging from the sides of his face. A clean white T-shirt clings a little too tightly to the softening flesh of his chest. Loose khaki pants rise too high above his bare ankles. His feet are clad in tired white gym socks. There's stubble on his face.

He squints, looks me up and down. "What do you want?"

I smile my most disarming smile. "Hello, sir," I begin. "I'm looking for the home of Mindi Manning."

His brow tightens. "What's that fool girl gone and done now?"

"She hasn't done anything, sir."

"Then what're you here for? You some kind of social worker?"

"No, sir. I'm from the *Times-Picayune*. We're doing a feature story on your daughter." I don't know where the lie comes from. It's automatic.

The laughter from his throat sounds throttled. "What in the Sam Hill for?"

"About her success. Her work with Senator Claiborne."

"Success." He says it like it's spittle. "She left her only real chance of success behind her years ago."

"Sir?"

"She left the Lord. Turned her back on the path." He sighs— not a sad sigh, but a bitter, contemptuous one. A sigh of judgment. "Shame, too. Always thought she'd do something special, that girl. She was tough. Smart. Could have done mission work. Married a preacher." He shakes his head. "You can lead 'em to the truth, but you can't make 'em drink. Better to let her go her own way than stay around here and infect the young ones."

"You have other children?"

"Seven," he says proudly, hitching up his loose khaki slacks a little, as if to honor what's inside. I feel a pang of pity for his wife. "But they can't see Mindi no more."

"Sorry?"

"She can't come back here no more. No, sir. She wants to give up on Jesus, she can give up her family, too."

"You're saying you don't allow her to come back?"

"And poison the well? No, ma'am. That ain't how we work. Them that love the Lord have got to keep our hearts pure. Or He will spit us out of His mouth."

Seriously. Like something out of Faulkner.

"What about Mindi's military service? Isn't that something you're proud of?"

"I don't know nothing about that. She just up and took off one day. Right after her high school graduation, it was. Skipped church that Sunday, gone on Monday. Never did hear from her until she was over there. Sent her momma a letter, said she's over there fighting the A-rabs."

"She got a college degree from LSU," I say quietly. "I'm guessing she put herself through."

"College." He grimaces. "Did the Redeemer go to college? Did the Redeemer have some big-time job in politics? No, he didn't. Render Caesar's things unto Caesar, and the Lord's things unto the Lord. If she wants to go off serving the things of this world, let her, I say."

"Mr. Manning, is your wife here?"

"Nora? She's here. But she don't need to be talking to no reporters."

"I'd just like to get her perspective. For the story."

"She don't have no perspective. Her perspective's my perspective. She ain't going to say no different."

"Yes, sir. But would it be possible to meet her? Just talk to her for a minute?"

He stares at me. A truck rolls slowly down the street, its loud engine unmuffled.

"Yeah. Well, all right. Can't be much harm." He backs into the living room. The floor is carpeted with a battered mauve rug, sculptured, stretching wall to wall. "Come on inside."

I step after him. The house smells of ground meat and tomato sauce and bleach.

"Have yourself a seat," he says, gesturing at the Formica table. I drag out a stiff metal chair. Its seat and back are yellow vinyl with stars on it. In a diner or a hip apartment, it would be cool.

His footsteps thump down a hallway. Now I can read the scriptures that hang on the walls. Each one has been hand-lettered with a thick black marker onto white paper, then framed in a dime-store frame:

Do not be deceived: "Bad company ruins good morals." –1 Corinthians 15:33

I have no greater joy than this, to hear that my children are walking in the truth. –3 John 4.

Children, obey your parents in the Lord, for this is right. –Ephesians 6:1

Wives, be subject to your husbands as you are to the Lord. For the husband is the head of the wife just as Christ is the head of the church. Just as the church is subject to Christ, so also wives ought to be, in everything, to their husbands. –Ephesians 5:22-24

When Mr. Manning appears in the mouth of the hallway again, he's so large that at first I can't see the woman behind him. Then they both emerge from the shadows.

Before me is the image of Mindi Manning, thirty years and a lot of heartbreak from now. Her mother's face is lined and worn, the mouth tight and unpainted, with grim grooves carved upward from her lip. Her faded dress is flowered with pink blooms. It zips up the front. Her feet wear old pink house-shoes.

Her voice is a scratchy whisper. "Carl said you wanted to see me?"

"Yes, ma'am. I just wanted to ask a few questions about your daughter Mindi."

She pulls out a chair and sits down next to me, her face turned away from her husband. A small light kindles in her eyes. "You know Mindi?" she says.

"I've met her."

"How is she?"

"Just answer the girl's questions, Mother," the man says, still standing, looming beside us, his voice loud.

She nods. "I'm sorry," she says to him. To me: "What do you need to know?"

"Well, I'm doing a story for the *Times-Picayune*. A profile about your daughter's successful career as a personal assistant to Senator Claiborne."

Beside us, Mr. Manning snorts. "Personal assistant," he says. "I think we all know what that means."

"Mindi was always a smart girl," says Mrs. Manning. "Good in school."

"Oh, yes?"

"Good grades, good in sports." Her smile is shy. A glimmer of pride shines in her eyes. "She was good with children, too. Helped with the little ones."

"Was a political career always in her plans?"

Her tired face wrinkles, puzzled. "Excuse me?"

"Did she talk about what she wanted to do when she grew up?"

Mrs. Manning's eyes dart from side to side, as if she's searching through her memories for an answer. "No," she says. "Can't say as she did. Mindi was a quiet girl. She mostly kept herself to herself."

"Did Mindi ever show any interest in horses?" I ask, thinking of the bills of sale and her ease around the senator's stable. "Anything about them?"

Again her eyes scan from side to side. She looks up. "Carl, did she?"

"Horses?" He snorts again. "How in the Sam Hill would I know what she was interested in?"

"Well," she says softly, "she did have a summer job once. Remember that, Carl? She worked for a farm one summer. They had horses. She cleaned the stalls and brushed the horses."

Carl makes a noise that's impossible to decipher.

"She liked that, didn't she?" Mrs. Manning's smile is faint and faraway. "Yes, she liked that. I know she did. She came home dirty and tired, but she always seemed happy that summer."

Maybe the Shadowfax stables were one of the job's key perks for her.

"Honor thy father and thy mother," says Mr. Manning. "That's what would have made her happy."

Mrs. Manning nods, her hands in her lap and her eyes on her hands, her smile fading.

"Is there anything else you'd like to tell me about your daughter?"

She shakes her head. "No," she says. "But if you see her—"

"If you see her," says Mr. Manning, "you can tell her the Lord sees all, and the Lord shall make a reckoning."

I rise to my feet. I want to reach out and touch the woman's flowered shoulder, but somehow it feels wrong. Like I'd start something softening and tumbling that would never be put right again, like a landslide, a hill collapsing in on itself and all the houses swallowed up in the mud. I don't dare touch her. In her thinness and housedress and straw-colored hair, she looks like a husk, like a light wind could blow her away.

"Thank you, sir," I say. He doesn't extend his hand, and I don't offer mine. He pulls the door open, and I step out into the warm spring air. The porch creaks under my feet and the door shuts hard behind me. I make my way down the steps and across the patchy yard.

19

Back in the car, I catch I-12 and head the thirty miles northwest toward Madisonville, driving through tame green pasturelands, steamy and fertile, past strip malls and bald new housing developments until I hang a left on 21 and head south under towering pines.

Madisonville is a small town, old and quaint. A library, antique shops, seafood restaurants. A river runs through it and feeds into Lake Pontchartrain. In the marina, pleasure yachts and old battered fishing boats dock side-by-side.

I find Irene Shorter's house on Bordeaux Street, cut the ignition, and sit for a moment, gathering my thoughts. The Pontiac's engine ticks and groans as it cools. Talking to the newly bereaved is never easy, never welcomed. And suggesting that a death may not have been a random accident . . .

I get out and press my car door closed and move through the little white gate of the picket fence. The Shorter home is a yellow Creole cottage with intricate gingerbread trim, freshly painted white. Yellow roses and white gardenias flower in the small front yard. A mockingbird chastises me from the branch of a young crape myrtle as I climb the steps. On the porch, two white wooden rockers sit side by side in terrible stillness.

When Irene Shorter answers the door, her dark eyes hold nothing. Early forties. Smooth khaki pants, blue blouse, neat white cardigan. Her hair is a straightened bob. I show her my press pass and give her my name.

She nods. Without a word, she holds open the door.

A tiny sitting room. Wood floors, flowered sofas, clean white rugs. She lowers herself slowly onto a sofa, like something might break, and waves vaguely at the other, so I sit down.

"Mrs. Shorter," I begin quietly, "I'm so very sorry for your loss."

Her hands fold in her lap. Her feet cross at the ankle. Her eyes look steadily at me. She's very still.

"I'm here to ask you about some documents your husband may have shown you. A problem he may have discussed with you." I'm fishing blind here, but I pull the bills of sale from my handbag and lay them on the little wicker coffee table between us.

Her eyes don't drop to the papers.

I keep talking. "These are bills of sale for Thoroughbred horses, sold by your husband's employer, Elaine Claiborne, to buyers here in Louisiana."

She stares impassively at me.

"Mrs. Shorter, please," I say gently. "Have you seen these papers before?"

Her eyes finally fall to the bills. Leaning forward, she lifts and looks carefully at each one. I watch her eyes move. She's a quick reader. I bet she doesn't miss much. She lays them all back on the table, then looks up at me and shakes her head no.

"Do you notice anything unusual about any of them?"

Her head shakes no again.

"Okay. Do you know of any reason your husband might have had these in his possession just prior to his death?"

Another quick headshake.

"He apparently gave them to a Tulane professor of journalism. He knew her because she'd been to the Claibornes' investigating a story about the senator."

A tiny line furrows the smooth skin between her eyebrows.

"Did you ever hear your husband mention a Dr. Judith Taffner?"

Her eyes quicken, but she shakes her head no again. "Wait," she says. Her gaze swings upward and off to the side. She nods slowly. "Joe went across the lake not long before—" Her voice breaks off, and she presses her hands together. "He said he was taking some papers to a white lady over there. I asked him what it was about, but he wouldn't tell me. Said it wasn't important for me to know."

My breath had quickened. "How long ago was this?"

Her eyes cloud. "Let me see. It would have to be the Sunday before—before Joe got hit. I remember telling him he should have been spending his Sunday evening here at home with me." She breathes in deeply and lets the air out in a long, silent sigh.

"Jude Taffner believed that the senator may have been accepting bribes from political donors. Somehow, these bills of sale that your husband had are connected with that. I'm trying to figure out how."

Her voice is barely audible. "Why don't you just ask her?"

"I would. But she was murdered last week."

Her eyes close briefly. A long pause grows in the room. "Then maybe you should be careful yourself," she says. She takes a deep breath, as if deciding something. Then she begins to speak. Her tone is normal enough, but calm, remote. "Joe wasn't interested in politics," she says softly. "He just loved horses. Always did, since we were kids together."

"Yes, ma'am. I understand he was very good at his job."

She nods. "Since he was a boy. Always hanging around one stable or another. I knew him since he was thirteen. He loved those horses over at Mrs. Claiborne's, and she always treated him real good."

"Do you have any idea, any idea at all, why he might have shown these receipts to a journalist?"

She thinks for a moment. "No. No, truth to tell, I surely don't. But there's someone who could tell you. Joe's friend, Bake. Monroe Baker. He's a trainer lives over in Mandeville. Knows horses like the back of his hand, and knows all the stable gossip around these parts, too. Him and Joe always used to get together and talk." She chokes a little and falls silent.

I ask for Monroe Baker's address. When she tells me, I write it down. "Mrs. Shorter, what is it that you do?"

"Teach third grade over at Madisonville Elementary. They gave me a two-week leave." Her laugh is silent, mirthless. "It's ironic, isn't it? I love kids. Joe loved horses. We never had any of our own, either one. Now we never will." She looks at her still hands in her lap.

"I'm so sorry," I say again, helpless.

"I know," she says. "Everybody's sorry." She lifts her eyes to mine and waits.

"Can you tell me about the accident?"

Her shrug is slight. "I told it all. We drove over to Coffee's Boilin' Pot to get some po'boys for supper. It was just starting to get dark. I stayed in the car, and Joe went in to get the food. He came out with the bag. He was crossing the road back to our car when he got hit. Black SUV kept right on going. Tinted windows, no plates. I couldn't see the make or model. It all happened too fast. I ran over to Joe, called nine-one-one. By the time the ambulance got there, he was gone." She closes her eyes. "Sweet Lord Jesus. Just like that." A little tremor runs through her hands.

"A black SUV? You're sure?" The vehicle wasn't described in the piece I'd found online.

Her eyes open slowly. She nods. "I saw it all."

On the drive over to Monroe Baker's house in Mandeville, I call Calinda. I tell her about Tom Winterson and his possible links to the Jonas Applewhite shooting and Dr. Taffner's murder. I tell her about the black SUV that ran down Joe Shorter. Then I tell her about the one that tried to run me down last night.

She sucks in her breath. "Nola, do you know what you're saying?"

"Afraid I do. The senator is involved. Or the NOPD. Or both. And there's a whole lot of killing going on. Joe Shorter, Judith Taffner, Cory Brink."

"And now you, potentially."

"Now me. But it's not all clear yet."

"Nola, that is not a list you want to be on. This is huge. Bad huge. You need to be careful."

"What I need is proof."

I find the address for Monroe Baker at the corner of a shady side street in Mandeville. Oak Street, it's called, but the only trees I see are tall, thin pines and fat magnolias glossy with dark leaves. Morton Baker's house is a one-story redbrick ranch with a tidy lawn and a little white carport. The bed of a blue Ford pickup juts out of it like a horse too big for its stall. MY OTHER RIDE IS A THOROUGHBRED, reads the bumper sticker. I ring the bell and wait.

A man in his fifties opens the door, his blue workshirt tucked into belted jeans, his skin the textured brown of cigars. He looks me up and down slowly, then smiles. A friendly, appreciative smile, not a creepy one. "Well, well, well," he says. "What can I do for you?"

I introduce myself and show my press pass. "Irene Shorter said you could help."

The smile fades. "Mmm. Well, you best come on in, then." We move into a quietly furnished living room, all browns and beiges. He says nothing about his friend, his loss, his sadness, but as I lower myself into the suede armchair he offers, it's all suddenly there in the air between us like a tangible thing, taboo, and I can't mention Joe Shorter's name.

I pull the sheaf of papers from my handbag and spread them on his clean coffee table. "These are bills of sale from Mrs. Claiborne to various buyers. They were given to a reporter not long before the hit-and-run. Now that same reporter has been murdered. I need to know why."

He pulls a pair of reading glasses from his breast pocket, slides them on, and picks up the receipts. He pores over each sheet. Finally he sets them down one by one, side by side on the table.

"Here's your problem." He leans and taps the sale prices, one after another. "These horses ain't worth that much."

"What do you mean?"

"They're all good horses, sure. And these sales look legal enough. But look here." He taps one. "This filly's out of Almayer's Folly, by Son of Spider Legs. Good bloodlines, but nothing to write home about, and she's only six months old at time of sale. Untested. No way she's worth seventy grand. That's just ridiculous. Only a fool or a Yankee would pay that." He taps another one. "Now here you got a colt, two years old. I've seen this one run. He's got heart, but the stride just ain't there, and it ain't never going to be there. Short in the leg." He slides his finger to another receipt. "Now here we're talking. A filly by Nevermind out of Watch Me, two years old. Nothing but speed in her blood. A beauty. But three hundred thousand?" He shakes his head, takes his glasses off and folds them away. "What you've got here is some serious inflation, girl."

I'm scribbling in my notebook, nodding. "Go on."

"And I'll tell you something else. These buyers? I never heard tell of any of them, and if I ain't heard of them, they ain't in the business." He laughs a little hissing laugh. "That Miz Claiborne's quite a horse trader. She must have seen them people coming."

20

I'm speeding across the Causeway over Lake Pontchartrain, *ka-chunk ka-chunk,* leaning over to tuck the bills of sale into the glove box of my Pontiac, eager to get back to my *Times-Picayune* office and track down the identities of the buyers—they're clearly somehow the key—when my phone rings.

"So are you coming to get me?" Marisol's voice is tinny and impatient. "Or what?"

I glance at the clock on the dash. 3:45. *Shit.*

"I'm so sorry, *mi'ja. Lo siento.* I'm on my way."

"Well, *ándale,*" she says flatly. "I'm sitting here by myself. And some guys are staring at me."

I floor it, pissing off drivers and risking tickets all the way to Metairie.

When I pull up in the school parking lot at Grace King, Marisol is sitting on the bright steps. Alone, thank God. There's no one else in sight. My gut twists with guilt.

She gets in, slams the door, drops her backpack on the floor, and folds her arms. "You forgot me."

"No, *mi'ja*. I was just up on the other side of the lake, working. I got hung up in an interview."

"You *forgot* me," she says again, her eyebrows arched in perfect righteous teenage condemnation.

I burst out laughing. "Okay, yes, you're right. I forgot you. *Sí sí sí*, I forgot, but it doesn't mean anything except that I'm a flake when I'm working. I just get all caught up."

She sighs, her lips pressed together.

"Hey, you're the one who wanted to stay with me, remember? I never said I'd be any good at this full-time stuff."

A tiny twitch happens at the corner of her mouth. *"Verdad."*

"So all right, then. Let's get you home."

I ask my usual questions, and Marisol grudgingly describes her homework situation. Prodded, she sighs and explains one thing she learned in each of her classes today. Then she launches into the continuing, incomprehensible saga of alliances, betrayals, treachery, and realliances among her friends. The details form an intricate, endless, and unfollowable string of *Then she said*, and I'm relieved when at last we pull under the overhanging green branches of oak trees on St. Charles and get to the security gate of Soline's parking lot. I park, Marisol gathers up her things, I grab my laptop in its case, and we head to the building, where I swipe the security card again. The skid of our shoe soles on the marble steps sounds cool and echoey in the high broad stairwell. All I want to do is get inside, open my laptop, and track those buyers. Daylight spills down on us from clerestory windows as we climb.

I unlock and open the door, then stop. Behind me, Marisol gasps.

Soline's pretty apartment is destroyed. The sofas are sliced open, their stuffing spilled out like feathery guts. Pictures have been pulled from the walls, their backs cut open. Drawers from the dining room buffet lie upturned on the floor, silverware scattered everywhere.

"Wait," I say, putting out a hand. "We shouldn't go in. We shouldn't touch anything." Though I already know there won't be a traceable print anywhere.

I pull the door shut and walk back to the staircase. Sit down. Pull Marisol down beside me. Think.

I've been robbed twice before in New Orleans, but Soline's apartment has security of a different order, and this looks more like a search, a raid. Not thievery. This job is professional and almost certainly the work of the same person who searched Dr. Taffner's house and Cory Brink's apartment. It looks violent: a warning.

I feel Marisol shift quietly next to me, and I take the cell phone out of my bag. First, the police. Even if I don't think they'll track the perpetrator down, there needs to be a record, a paper trail, a pattern to point to.

But what if it's the police themselves, warning me off the bad shoot case? I close my eyes.

Marisol's voice is small beside me. "Are you okay?"

I turn and make myself smile at her. "I'm fine, honey. Just fine." I dial 911 and describe the break-in to the female dispatcher, whose bored voice makes no bones about the fact that she's unimpressed with my trivial uptown concerns when folks are getting shot. "We'll send somebody out," she says, and hangs up.

Then I call Detective Winterson. Straight to voice mail. Again. "This is Nola Céspedes, the *Times-Picayune* reporter who's still waiting for you to return my call. Just thought you'd be interested to know that my home has been ransacked." I pause. "Or maybe you already know." I hang up. Fuck him.

Then Soline, who picks up on the second ring. "Hey, Nola girl! What's up?" Her bright voice fills me with guilt.

It hurts to tell her.

"Oh, *no*," she says. "Are you all right?"

"I'll replace everything. It's my fault. They were targeting me."

"We can talk about that later," she says. "You're all right, though? You're safe?"

"Yeah. We weren't home."

There's a pause. "We?"

"You know Marisol. She's been staying with me just these past couple of nights." I glance over at her; she's watching me intently. "Just a little break from home."

"Oh, no problem." I can hear the half smile in Soline's voice. "Just thought maybe you were shacking up on the sly."

My laugh is weak. As if.

"Listen," she says, "I'm glad you called. I've been wanting to come over and get my blender anyway. Rob's blender broke, and we've been missing our daiquiris."

"Sure." Her words sink in. "Hey, does that mean y'all are doing okay?"

I can hear her smile through the phone. "I broke down and asked him about the perfume. He introduced me to the little old lady who makes his red beans and cornbread now. She's a hugger, and she wears Miss Cherie." She laughs. "I'm a crazy fool. But the good part is, he said he'd cut back on his hours and spend more evenings at home."

"Oh, Soline. That's great."

"Yeah, it is. So is tonight okay for me to come by? It'll give me a chance to see the damage myself."

"Yeah, of course." I think of what I've got to do next. Marisol's not safe here anymore. "How about after nine? Is that too late?"

She chuckles. "You're talking to the wife of a nightclub owner, my dear. Nothing's too late." We ring off.

I lay my hand on Marisol's warm knee. "You doing okay?"

She nods.

"Atta girl." I take a deep breath. "Mari, you can't stay here anymore. It's not safe. You can see that, can't you?"

Her eyes fill with wariness, but she nods.

"Okay, then."

Marisol needs to go home, but if things with her family are tense, something needs to happen, some loosening of the rules. With my busted-up pidgin Spanish, I'm the last one to play family mediator.

I dial my mom.

After a couple of bored cops have taken my statement, walked through Soline's trashed place, dusted enough objects to reasonably claim that there are no prints, and left, I grab a clean apple for each of us and drive Marisol to my mother's apartment.

Mi mamá comes out in a little flowered dress with a white handbag, *todo* cute, waving good-bye behind her to Ledia. Then the three of us head north in the Pontiac to Metairie, Marisol straining the backseat's seat belt to lean up on the shoulder of my mother's seat in the front, soaking in every moment of her attention. She adores my mother, who's asking her softball questions about school and her siblings, trying to get a feel for the situation at home without spooking Marisol. I understand why. When you're poor, you're used to caseworkers asking too many questions, and if you love your family, you learn fast to keep your mouth shut about what goes on at home. You don't know what definitions and criteria social workers will apply, and you've seen kids dragged screaming from their mother's arms because of a few mistakes, while other kids—kids actually being neglected and abused—are left to languish year after year because no one can prove it. It's enough to make a kid paranoid. And Marisol's smart. So my mother's being careful as she asks her questions.

Traffic's thick. The glare's so bright I'm squinting behind my sunglasses. It's just after five o'clock when we pull up at Marisol's apartment complex, and her father's just climbing down from the back of a pickup, which drives off. The other guys stare back at us from amid tools and equipment as it disappears.

When Mr. Cruz sees us, his nod is gruff, and he heads toward his front door without a word. Marisol, sullen at the whole turn of events, looks down at the sidewalk. But as soon as my mother starts to speak, he brightens and turns. Cuban Spanish is noticeably different from Mexican Spanish, and the oddities are enough to pique his curiosity. He waves us into the apartment, asking her where she's from.

Marta, his wife, has her hands full in the kitchen, but she rushes out when she sees Marisol. She hugs her, steps back, and holds her face, turning it from side to side, inspecting her with eyes full of anxiety and relief. The whole apartment smells delicious, like *frijoles* and *carne asada*, and Marta immediately insists that we stay, eat, talk.

We squeeze in together around a table hardly big enough for the family, under a print of the Virgin of Guadalupe and a photo of green mountains, the calendar pages beneath it neatly clipped away. After a rapid conversation I can barely follow about my mother's origins in Oriente province and their own backstory in Veracruz, the ice is broken.

While the children silently, rapidly eat, pinching rice and beans and meat into their warm corn tortillas, my mother eases into a new topic: the difficulty of raising children in *El Norte*. Both elder Cruzes are vocal on that score. The clash of values. The way girls here dress and act so wild. No respect for elders. I sit quietly, and Marisol pouts down at her tortilla soup, but my mother just listens, nodding, interjecting, *"Ay, sí sí sí,"* and *"Verdad"* from time to time, letting them get it all out: the frustration, the confusion, the underlying fear.

She's brilliant at this, patient, a natural. In another world, she would have gone into family counseling instead of working for minimum wage all her life.

When Mr. and Mrs. Cruz finally sit, spent, his big work-roughened hand lies gently over her small one. The little kids are sitting remarkably quiet and still, watching everything. Amapola, a sweet-faced child of five, asks if they can get down from the table, and Mr. Cruz nods. They each take their plates to the sink as they go.

Now my mother begins to work her magic, explaining what teenagers in America like and need, gesturing at me repeatedly as an example of American-style success and describing the wisdom of letting go a little, loosening the reins. Once she's gotten them to concede that yes, they'd like more of a future for Marisol than domestic work, my mother's job is nearly done. She gestures at her chest, and I can follow her Spanish well enough to know she's talking about her own long years of cleaning houses and, most recently, working in daycares. She holds out her hands, and it hurts to see the knotted bulges at her knuckles. She reaches over and picks up my hand, and its smoothness shames me. I hear her say *Tulane,* the *Times-Picayune.* I've never Lysoled the toilets of strangers. What I feel is guilt, like I'm standing on my mother's small, bowed shoulders. But the warmth in her brown eyes is pride, and the Cruzes are nodding. It's what they want for Marisol, too.

Then they've got to ease back, my mother says gently. They can't expect Marisol to stay inside every afternoon and evening, playing little mama to the small children, cleaning the apartment, doing everyone's laundry.

Señora Cruz looks anxiously up at her husband, gives a small shake of her head.

She's a girl, says Señor Cruz. She can stay home and help her mother. It's what girls do. It's what they're for.

No, says my mother. Not here. Not in *El Norte.* Marisol needs quiet time to do her homework if she's going to keep her grades up and get into college, and she needs some time with her friends to have fun and feel like a normal girl.

My mother turns to Marisol, and her tone becomes gentler still. *You see how hard your mamá and papá work,* she's telling her. Marisol nods, guilty and reluctant. *And you know how much they love you.* My mother waves at the small apartment, and I remember our own, even tinier and dingier, back in the Desire Projects. *They need your help. Maybe an hour or two a day, helping with the dishes, the babies.* By pulling together, all together like *una familia,* she tells her, they can be happy and find success. Love. Respect. My mother takes Marisol's hands in hers and holds them for emphasis, like she's trying to stream her message directly into the young girl's skin. Maybe she is.

Marisol nods.

Marta's eyes are wet, and all the stubborn hardness has melted from her husband's face.

My mother, *la familia* whisperer.

When we rise to go, there are hugs all around, and she gives them her phone number. *Call me,* she urges. *Call me if you ever need anything.* She looks especially long into Marta's eyes, immigrant to immigrant, mother to mother. *Or if you ever just want to talk.*

We leave and drive away, and in the car I thank her, and she's briefly giddy because she's done God's work. Exhausted, I steer the Pontiac south through the deep dusk toward Mid-City and the apartment she shares with Ledia. Her glow doesn't last. After a few minutes she launches into what's been chewing at her all this time.

"Now *dígame todo* about this break-in," she says. "That apartment of your friend is like, *cómo se dice,* like Fort Knox. So what's going on?"

I hear the fear and worry—just a different brand of the Cruzes'—under her stern tone, so I try to reassure her. I lie that it's a simple break-in, that some thief guessed a place as nice as Soline's would contain some choice valuables. I tell her nothing about the stories I'm tracking down, the murders, the black SUV on a dark street. Confiding has never been my strong suit, and the afterimage of her tired hands burns in my mind like an accusation. No way will I add to her burdens.

When she's reassured, we drive quietly through the dark streets, our windows up, our doors locked.

Finally I ask her something that's been on my mind. Something I've asked before.

"*Mamá,*" I say.

"*Sí, mi'ja.*"

"Do you think you'd feel comfortable now telling me the name of my father?"

She turns to stare at me. I glance over. Her dark eyes are full of anxiety.

"Why, *mi'ja*? What do you need his name for? Do you want to look for him?"

"No, I'm not going to look for him." Not right now, anyway. "I don't know. I'm just curious."

"He was a mistake. An accident. He did us no good. You don't need to go looking for him like they do on *Oprah*. You don't need to have him break *tu corazón*."

"But he's my father."

"*Sí*, for all the good it did you."

"I have the right to know."

She clears her throat. "And I have the right to protect you from your own foolishness. I'm still your mother."

If she can be stubborn, so can I. "I can get the information." I can just request a copy of my birth certificate from the State of Louisiana. My mother hid the original somewhere. I've never seen it. Maybe it's in a safe deposit box. Maybe she swallowed the key.

"Then get it," she says, folding her arms. "You will be a dis-obedient daughter."

"*Mamá*—"

"I'm telling you it will do you no good to know his name. I'm telling you to leave it alone."

I sigh and steer the car through the quiet streets. "Okay," I say finally. "I'm sorry. You know best."

"*Sí*," she says, drawing the word out across four beats, molli-fied. "*Claro*."

Pulling up next to the curb at her apartment, where Ledia will be waiting inside, I listen to her litany of cautions before she lets me hug her good-bye.

She clings, pinching my cheek, looking into my eyes. But only for a minute. Not like she used to. She's got someone at home now, someone who loves her and is waiting.

I idle the engine, making sure she gets in safe. The door closes behind her. A light goes on in the living room, and the curtain pulls aside. Through the window, my mother waves, and Ledia joins her, waving, too.

21

I head home to Soline's as worn out as I've ever been. My hands on the steering wheel feel loose and vague. Less than twenty-four hours ago, someone tried to run me down. Waking up early, shooting, driving all over the north shore, the interviews, the shock of the break-in, and group therapy at Marisol's apartment have left my whole body weary. I pull onto St. Charles, its long dark corridor of pavement quietly lit. Expensive. Discreet.

I brake, hold my keycard up to the scanner, watch the wide steel gate slide back, and steer the car inside to a space in the parking lot. When I get out, I'm bone-tired. I grab my laptop case and handbag. When did they grow so heavy? My legs feel almost drunk with weariness as I cross the courtyard. What was it that I was going to do? Right: track down the identities of the horse-buyers. That's the key.

If I can make it into the building. I walk on rubbery legs. Everything is slow, hallucinatory, quietly alive: the splashing waters of the fountain, the tall green stalks of oleander swaying in the night breeze, the freshly rinsed pavestones shining in the glow of discreet security spotlights. I let myself into the building with a sigh. Each stair is a small trial as I climb upward, a test of will. It's only nine-thirty, and I'm ready for sleep.

Finally, I turn the key. Stepping into the darkness, I grope for the little lamp on the console, and the room flashes into warm, bright relief. I see again the horrible mess.

And then a bomb explodes at the base of my skull, and I'm falling forward, and everything goes black.

When I come to, my eyes open slowly, and the back of my head throbs like an open wound. Only a tiny lamp casts a weak glow from the sideboard, and the room is swathed in dark shadows. I'm upright, tied to one of Soline's dining chairs, and my laptop is open on her dining table. Some dumbfuck all in black—black gloves, black balaclava, hoody, pants, shoes—is bent over it, tapping away.

Rage jerks through me, and I rock in the chair. Dumb Fuck looks up, turns to me. "What's your password?" says the voice, an unrecognizable growl. The flesh behind the balaclava is pale, but the eyes are a depthless, glittering black.

"Fuck yourself." Thank God I'm smarter than Dr. Taffner. My laptop has more security than Citibank.

The black gloved hand moves swiftly back, and my head snaps to the side.

Through the ringing in my ears, I hear the voice. "Password."

"Eat me, you stupid shit."

The glove smacks me again. Harder. Warm liquid crawls down my jaw. A strange sweetness floats in the air. Maybe it's nausea. Maybe it's a stroke—no, that's the smell of burning. Burnt hair.

Maybe I'm having my own special brand of stress-induced stroke, custom-scented for my pleasure. "Fuck you," I gasp. I sit there, panting, waiting for my vision to clear.

There's a patience in the stance of the black-clad legs, an ease with which the black arms hang, the gloved fingers loosely curled. This could go on all night, the figure's calm pose seems to say. And it's only going to get rougher.

"Tell me the password." No one has black irises, and no pupils open wide enough to swallow every hint of color, no matter how jacked up someone is. Contacts? My own vision blurs. The dark figure doubles and triples in front of me, its legs wide apart in a *V*.

I spit blood onto the polished wood floor. "You're so smart, you figure it out."

The next blow cracks the world open. Everything goes black for one second, two seconds, three. I sit, my breath ragged in my own ears, willing it all to come back: Soline's lovely ruined room, the sofa's stuffing spilling out, the white rugs, the tall windows with aqua silk draping like waterfalls. I concentrate, willing the pain away, praying the world back into existence. Slowly, the murk around me resolves into objects, their clear edges a blessing.

I feel unreasonably happy, grateful, alive.

Fuck this. "Who are you? Doucet?" If only my Olympus were on inside my handbag. "What do you want?"

The figure is silent, the black eyes staring at me. "One more chance. What's the password?"

A sudden rush of gratitude: it strikes me that Marisol—my height, my size, my coloring—is safely gone. She wasn't here alone, wasn't mistaken for me.

It gives me strength.

"I know you're with the senator," I say. "Or with NOPD. One or the other. I know one of them took out Jude Taffner, and I know the senator took out Joe Shorter. I know the buyers paid too much for those horses." What I don't know yet is why. "I know the NOPD killed Jonas Applewhite for no good god-damn reason."

At my words, the black-clad figure gains an extra level of stillness. Arrested, thinking. Then reaches back with one hand. Everything's in slow motion. When the hand comes back, it's holding a silver handgun. I can't tell what kind. Silver, long-barreled.

No, not long-barreled. Silver, with a silencer already spun on.

A weird laugh happens. My laugh. I'm laughing. I was never supposed to leave alive. I was supposed to divulge the password, let my laptop be cracked, my threat assessed. Then I was sup-posed to die like a good girl in Soline's pretty condo, another tragic victim of the city's murder rate. Just another B&E gone wrong.

"You stupid, stupid fuck," I say through lips already slow with thickening. I look into the hard black eyes and lie with everything I've got. "Do you think the DA's office doesn't al-ready know it all? Do you think the cops aren't on their way right now? Do you think you can just clean this out of exis-tence?"

There's a long silence as the black eyes stare at me. Then the gloved hand flicks the safety off.

A small silver *O* with a black cave at its heart.

I liked twenty-eight. I liked my life. The edges of my vision go dark, which people say happens before you faint. This is fear. This is good-bye.

The silver *O* shifts. Dumb Fuck has stiffened. Keys are rattling at the condo's door.

Soline, here for her blender.

"Soline, no!" I yell, and the silver gun lifts high and comes smashing down at my left eye.

Backgammon is an ancient game, perhaps the oldest board game in the world. Game boards and markers from 3000 BC have been dug up in Shahr-e Sūkhté, Iran's Burnt City from the Bronze Age.

Chess, a relative newcomer, dates from only six hundred years after Christ. Its different pieces originate in military divisions: infantry, cavalry, and so on.

Backgammon is simpler, its pieces all the same, its rules deceptively easy. When Bento's hand, reaching for dice, grazes my wrist, I always wonder if the game was invented by lovers all those thousands of years ago. We anticipate each other's moves, our eyes teasing and challenging over the board as we play against each other.

But really, in backgammon, you play against yourself. Against time, against chance. You roll with the roll you get.

When I startle awake, I'm on something soft, and I'm not tied. I open my right eye. A red stain's swelling beneath my face on the white linen upholstery of Soline's sofa. Her cool hand is on my arm, her voice murmuring something sweet and calming.

"Shit." I struggle to sit up. "Aw, shit, Soline. I'm so sorry." My words are thick and slurred.

"Oh, Nola." Her arms go around me and tighten. We sit there for a moment, listening to our breath go in and out. "I'm so glad you woke up," she says. "You had me so scared."

I pull back and try to grin. "So your couch is pretty much fucked."

She laughs softly. "I don't know who you've been fooling with, Nola Céspedes, but you sure pissed them off."

It hurts my head to nod. "The police—"

"They're on their way. I called them."

"How long have I been out?"

"Not ten minutes. I heard you yell, I came in, and some guy just about knocked me down trying to get past. Flew down the stairs like Batman." Her smile is rueful, and she rubs her palm back and forth on my arm. "Tell you what, it's some crazy shit you see up in this city."

If she'd arrived half an hour later, Soline would have found my bulleted corpse sagging in her fancy French chair, Dumb Fuck long gone.

"I'm lucky," I say.

"Yes, you are, girl." She slips an arm around my shoulders. "We are." We sit there together, waiting for the police.

Real friends don't tell you when you look like shit. After the cops left, when Fabi and Calinda arrived at Soline's apartment, it was almost midnight, and although Fabi gasped, neither of them said a word about the battered face I hadn't yet seen. All the adrenaline of fear and anger had drained away, and I felt hungry and exhausted, a deflated doll. Calinda, practically psychic as usual, had brought Chinese carry-out, and I wolfed down General Tso's chicken while Soline told and retold the story. Her gentle hands had cleaned me up after the police had taken photos, but everything felt swollen and painful. It hurt to chew, but I was too hungry not to.

"You're lucky you don't need stitches," Calinda says, inspecting me. A butterfly bandage from Soline's well-stocked bathroom is holding the split skin above my left eyebrow, and my lower lip feels like a sore balloon.

Talking about pain, despite what Shiduri Collins insists, doesn't always help.

"So what do we know about the assailant?" I say. I take a long swallow of Diet Coke. "Pale skin. Right handed." I think of that vicious backhand and take another drink, sucking down the cold energy. "Not much."

"Strong." Soline rubs her shoulder where she'd been knocked against a wall.

"Well, you can't stay here anymore," says Fabi. "You're coming home with one of us." She pulls out her cell phone. "And I'm calling Bento."

"Oh, no," I say. "No way." This is not how I want him to see me.

She starts to dial anyway, and I reach over and grab the phone out of her hand.

"Seriously," I say. "You call him, I will kill you." I nod at the carnage of ruined upholstery around us. "And I think I've done about enough damage to my friends' places. I'm going to find a hotel."

"Oh, *hell,* no," says Calinda, and Soline waves the notion away with a dismissive little spiral of her wrist.

"Look," I say, "somebody wants me, and they've obviously got reach. I'm not bringing this to your door."

"Um, duh?" says Calinda, laying a hand on my arm. "It's already *at* our door." Fabi and Soline nod.

Hot sudden tears fill my eyes. Two hours ago, I was mentally kissing my life good-bye. Now their kindness hits me in a rush. They're here.

A hotel would be hard to afford, and the thought of being alone in a strange place, hoping no one has tailed me, scares me a little. "All right, then." I shrug, and smile with the half of my mouth that works. "Who wants trouble?"

Fabi decides she does, and I nod. We all know that she's just finished redecorating her guest room and has been dying to try it out. We've seen the pretty twin bed, the little lamp and nightstand, everything cloaked in subtle shades of rose and gray. Her apartment in the Quarter has a crack alarm system, too, courtesy of her anxious parents. On short notice, it's probably my best bet.

"Let me just pack an overnight bag for you," says Soline. "We can come back and take care of the rest of your stuff once all of this is over. And I'm hiring cleaners tomorrow."

I protest. I can clean this up myself.

She puts her hand on mine. "I'm a businesswoman, not a saint. I've still got my homeowner's insurance."

"What I want," says Calinda, "is for you to e-mail me everything you've got on both of these cases."

I nod.

"Now," she says, and waits.

I get to my feet. The room heaves and spins a little as I cross to my laptop, left open on the dining table, and bend to type in my password: *Demajagua*, the plantation in Cuba where my mother grew up, where her parents worked themselves to early graves, where—if library books are to be believed—big sugar cauldrons still stand out on green lawns by the sea.

My laptop springs to life, and I type.

"I'm going to pack up those things," says Soline. "And then get my damn blender, for crying out loud."

Wednesday

22

I wake at dawn between soft sheets the color of doves. A peaked roof slants over me in a small, sweet room. Sitting up in Fabi's narrow guest bed, I feel like a well-to-do schoolgirl—a well-to-do schoolgirl who's had her face thumped. I press my fingertips to my forehead, my lips, my jaw. Everything aches.

When I pad across the room in my T-shirt and boxers and step out onto the little balcony, I can see the morning bustle of the Vieux Carré below in all directions. The day smells fresh. The morning air is cool. I count three black SUVs parked along the street. The city's rotten with them. One is empty, and two have windows tinted too dark to see inside. For all I know, they could hold black-ops teams.

I sigh. This isn't Russia, or Mexico. Here, reporters are just supposed to be broke and cynical, not killed for what they might write.

I lock the balcony door behind me when I go in. Downstairs, I find Fabi in the kitchen, already dressed to teach in a crisp pink blouse, a charcoal-gray pencil skirt, and vegan gray pumps made out of some new-age leather substitute. She's swallowing a protein drink.

"Morning, *querida*." She smiles.

I open the fridge. "Guess there's no bacon and eggs."

She purses her lips and scowls at me. "I've got to run. Make yourself at home."

I pour myself some coffee from the little stainless-steel machine on her counter. "What's on the syllabus for today?"

"Islam. Mecca. The differences between Sunnis and Shiites."

"The times, they are a-changin'. You got half-and-half?"

She puts a carton of coconut creamer on the counter in front of me and taps it with a perfect pink nail. "You'll love this. No trans or saturated fats."

"Like I said."

Fabi ignores me. "Take care of yourself today, will you? Try not to get yourself killed." She gathers up her handbag and keys and leans in. Her kiss falls on my cheek like the brush of a petal. "The extra key's right here," she says, tapping it on the counter, "and you remember the security code?"

I repeat it. "Got it. Set the alarm when I leave."

"No, set it when *I* leave. I don't want someone breaking in here to get you. And then set it again when you leave."

"No one followed us last night." Twice, I'd made her drive a box—three right turns around a block—to prove it. "I'll be fine."

Her hand goes to her hip as her eyebrows lift. She waves at my face. "Oh, you're a walking ad for fine, all right."

"Would you just go to work already?"

I lock up after her, set the alarm, and pull my laptop out of its case. Fabi, of course, has wireless, so I set up at her kitchen table with my coffee, some bizarre kind of flax cereal that looks like rabbit pellets and tastes like dust, and the bills of sale from Senator Claiborne's wife.

One by one, I google the buyers' names. With the help of LinkedIn, Facebook, and the human impulse to regurgitate every moment of our lives onto the Internet, I learn that they're all wealthy professionals. Of the seven, only two own homes in New Orleans, but Mark Elbin has a condominium about—I check GoogleMaps—oh, six blocks' walk from here.

On OpenSecrets.org, I look up campaign contributions for each of them. All donated the maximum six thousand dollars per person to Obama's 2008 campaign. All donated the maximum amount to each of the Democratic candidates' campaigns for the Senate, the House, and governor. Most of their money was wasted. Louisiana's not an easy place to be a liberal— especially not once you get outside New Orleans, which plenty of Louisianans and other folks across the South regard as our own personal Sin City, as much for the presence of political progressives as for the strippers and hookers on Bourbon Street. Feminists, gays, environmentalists, people who think taxes pay for good things like roads and schools: all of us cluster here in Babylon. Mark Elbin qualifies. On Twitter, he follows the Sierra Club, the Nature Conservancy, and the Environmental Defense Fund. His tweets are about endangered species and solar power.

I check, and none of the horse buyers donated to Senator Claiborne's last campaign, which obviously didn't affect his win. He's known for thousand-dollar-a-plate luncheons, golf-outing fund-raisers, and big-game shooting junkets with conservative donors. He doesn't need progressive dollars to run his campaign.

Yet, here are these bills of sale that total hundreds of thousands of dollars for horses that, according to Monroe Baker, are

worth far less. Padding the prices makes the Democratic donations invisible. And it's his wife's name, not the senator's, that
appears on the documents.

Once he's in office again, these Democratic donors will expect a payoff in his voting record. But what?

I finish the rabbit pellets, wash my bowl, and pour a second
cup of coffee, which I carry into the shower with me and set on
the gray marble ledge. After I'm done, I stare into the mirror,
my curls wrapped in a fluffy towel the size of Jackson Square.
Fabi's shelf of shiny black Chanel tubes and pots and compacts
tempts me, but I make the best of my battered face with my own
Maybelline, slip on my clothes, set the alarm, and head out.

Surprise is the element I want, so I walk the six blocks without
calling ahead. The building is beautiful and old, a soft, distinguished gray with a discreet brass plaque. A security camera
stares at me, so when I push the buzzer, I tilt the left side of my
face away and block the view of my swollen mouth with my
press pass.

"Yes?" A woman's voice.

I introduce myself. "I'm doing a story for the *Times-Picayune*
on supporters of environmentalist causes. Is Mark Elbin in?"
He's a partner at a swanky law firm in the CBD.

There's a pause. "No. But I'm his wife. We *both* support the
environment."

"Would you be willing to talk with me about it?"

There's relief in her tone. "Oh, definitely!" There's a buzz, and
the door clicks open. She must get tired of being taken for just a
wife, must relish the chance to have a voice. I take the stairs up
to the third floor and knock at the only door on the landing.

It opens. Mrs. Elbin is a brunette in her late thirties with taut, pale cheekbones you could crack an egg on. At eight in the morning, home alone, she's dressed in slim black trousers, a sleeveless silk blouse that cost more than my rent, and small, tasteful square-cut diamonds at her ears. Her black leather flats look Italian.

When she sees my bruised face, she blanches, and her smile falters for a millisecond. Self-conscious, I touch the new butterfly bandage over my eye but say nothing.

"Come in," she finally says. She wants to be heard.

The living room is what you'd expect: twelve-foot ceilings, chalky white walls, wood floors, antiques everywhere. A big abstract painting in baby-shit green hangs over the fireplace. It's ugly, so it must be important.

"Sit down, sit down," she says. "Would you like something to drink? I have some oolong, some red bush, some Lapsang Souchong—"

"I'm good." I sit in a velvet chair the color of saffron and pull out my Olympus. "So, Mrs. Elbin—"

"Call me Britt." Her wide smile's quick, eager.

"Britt. Can you talk about the environmental issues that matter most to you and your husband?"

I let her ramble for a while into the recorder about land conservation, climate change, species protection. She designed her own major, it turns out, in environmental studies back at a college called Oberlin, which she says like I should know the name. Terry Tempest Williams she ain't, but she seems to know her stuff.

I break in. "Louisiana's sitting on a lot of oil in the Gulf, which could help end our reliance on foreign oil. What are your thoughts on drilling?"

"Oh, goodness, that's the last thing we should do." She looks offended and horrified. There's also a shade of condescension in her tone, as if only someone truly dim could ask such a question. "We should be pouring all our resources into clean energy. Clean energy, green energy," she adds. She must like the rhyme. People do. "Wind, solar, biofuel. We really need to transition away from oil. The sooner, the better."

I nod, trying to look earnest. "You and your husband have a lovely home." I gesture at the room.

"Oh, thank you." She smiles.

"You seem to enjoy a very nice lifestyle."

"Oh, yes." She glances down in that self-deprecating way rich liberal people have. "We're very fortunate."

"And I'm guessing you support some of these environmental causes?"

"Oh, yes." She reels off various organizations, from the Nature Conservancy on down to a local group that helps homeowners Xeriscape their yards. I listen, nodding.

When she's comfortable and I've heard enough, I break in. "Do you own horses?"

She's startled. If her perfect brow could furrow, it would.

"Why, yes, we do. Though I don't see what—"

"About how many?"

"How many horses? Seven. No, eight. At our farm in Opelousas. But I really don't see—"

"Thoroughbreds?"

"Well, yes, but—"

"Do you race these horses? Show them?"

"Oh, no." She smiles. "They're just for pleasure. Just to hack around on."

"Then why"—I pull a bill of sale from my handbag—"would

your husband pay . . . let's see here . . . a hundred and forty thousand dollars for an untried colt?"

Her head twitches to the side for a moment, almost imperceptibly. A flinch. Her smile shrinks down to a small, thin line. "I'm not sure what this has to do with our support for the environment."

The clock ticks on her marble mantel as we look at each other across the air of her well-furnished room.

"Neither am I," I say.

Her voice is quiet. "I'm calling my husband."

"You do that." I rise and gather my things. At her door, I turn back. "You tell him Nola Céspedes at the *Times-Picayune* wants to talk to him."

I walk the six blocks to my Pontiac, whistling.

23

The clouds are low and thick with the threat of rain when I head north across the lake, the *ka-chunk ka-chunk* of my tires like a lulling drumbeat beneath me. I'm on my way to the senator's mansion. I pull out my phone, narrowly miss rear-ending a red Toyota 4Runner, and dial Evie Wilson.

"Hey, *chica*," I say. On both sides of me, Lake Pontchartrain shines like gray metal.

"What'd you find out?" she says immediately, and I can't keep from laughing.

"Well, hello to you, too."

"Girl, I'm warning you. Do not keep me in suspense."

I laugh again. "He's good," I say. "He's clean." Calinda e-mailed me the report this morning. "You can go to Tahiti with him. You can put all your valuables in his safe."

"Oh, thank you, Lord," she says, an audible sigh rushing out of her. "Thank you, Jesus. Oh, Lord. I'm going on a date. I'm going on a *date*. Nola, girl, you have just done your good deed of the year. Seriously. You have any bad karma, it's gone."

We both laugh. The lake speeds past beneath me.

"Oh, my God," she says suddenly. "Omigod omigod omigod. Oh, no."

"Evie? You okay? What is it?"

It comes out like a wail. "What am I going to wear?"

I laugh again.

"Girl, I got to go," she says. "I have seriously got to go."

On dry land again, I pull off on the shoulder of Copal Street and dig my little silver Olympus from my handbag. It's small and light, but tucking its metal angles between my bra and sternum is still uncomfortable. I wedge it into a position that lets me reach its on-off button.

I get back on the road. Four minutes later, I'm at the senator's horse farm, flashing my press pass and biggest smile at the guy in the guard booth, who, *gracias a Dios,* remembers me from last time and opens the gate without calling it in.

I park on the pavestones in front of the mansion, reach down my blouse to press the recorder on, grab my handbag, and slam the Pontiac's door with perhaps a little too much force.

Showdown.

At the top of the steps, I press the doorbell. Twice. Three times. I stare out over the pastures. A brown horse canters slowly across the green.

Finally, a Latina—in a shapeless tan dress with a little white apron, Lord help us—opens the door.

"Necesito el senator, por favor," I say. *"Es urgente. Importante."*

She shakes her head. "Busy."

"Lo siento," I say with what I hope is kindness, slipping past her and taking the stairs two at a time, fast. I hear her little rubber-soled maid's shoes pattering below me.

The door to the senator's office is open, and he's standing at his desk, his head bowed over a sheaf of blueprints. Two other old guys in expensive suits stand with him, staring down at the plans. Next to the American flag hanging limp from its pole in the corner, the handsome Latino guy stands, legs wide, arms crossed. Mindi Manning is stationed at her small desk on the edge of the room, her fingers arrested above her laptop, staring at me.

When I enter, the senator glances up. "Get rid of her," he says, his voice unruffled, then lowers his eyes again to the blueprints.

The guy takes a step forward. Mindi Manning gets to her feet.

"Like you did Jude Taffner?" I say. "Like Joe Shorter? Cory Brink?"

The senator straightens and looks at me. He holds up a hand to Mindi Manning and the muscle, who stop like two well-trained dogs.

"Gentlemen," he says to the suits, "forgive the intrusion. Why don't we continue this in a few minutes?"

They look at him, at me, and then let Mindi Manning usher them off through another door. She comes back and shuts it behind her.

The senator remains standing behind his broad desk. His blue eyes are cold. "What exactly is your concern, young lady?"

"You've accepted inflated payments from Democrats for your wife's horses. It's their under-the-table way of guaranteeing your future support if you win again in 2010. Joe Shorter knew something was wrong, but he didn't know what. So after Jude Taffner came here with her student and got your mandatory stable tour"—I glance at Mindi Manning—"he contacted her, the only reporter he knew. He could tell she knew horses. He could see she'd know something was wrong. He took her seven bills of sale. You had him murdered, and then Jude, and then her student."

"I have no knowledge of this." The senator's hands gather the blueprints into a neat roll and slide them into a tube. "Joe Shorter died in an accident. Very unfortunate. Lainie thought the world of him."

"Joe Shorter was run down by a black SUV with no plates. Same kind of vehicle that tried to hit me two nights ago, right after I was here."

Senator Claiborne considers me for a moment, his face expressionless, then gives the charming chuckle he's known for. "Have you given much thought to writing fiction, Miss—" He glances at Mindi Manning.

"Céspedes," she says.

"Miss Céspedes. Because your heated little story seems farfetched."

"My story's airtight," I lie, "and it'll run on tomorrow's front page."

His voice grows very quiet. "Young lady, do you know the penalties for libel?"

"As a matter of fact, I do. Jude Taffner was a good teacher." And as I say it, I realize it's true. She was no kindly mentor, no Tomás Guillory. She didn't take a personal interest in us, and she didn't encourage our dreams. She was a lousy mother and deluded herself about a boy. Her unrevised prose tilted toward the purple. But about reporting, she was rigorous and precise. She knew the rules, and she drilled us until we knew them, too. She made us into good journalists. The shape of her unwritten obituary suddenly materializes in my mind. I can write it for Luke Jourdan. Write it for real. "And I know the penalties for murder, which are what you should be worrying about right now."

He snorts as only a handsome Southern patrician can. "The death of Joe Shorter was an extremely regrettable accident."

"And Judith Taffner? Her murder in Audubon Park?"

"A terrible coincidence," he says. "A tragedy."

"Her student, Cory Brink? Come on, Senator."

A furrow flashes dark between his eyebrows, then smooths away. "Look, young lady, I don't know who you're talking about. I believe I remember a young man who came here with the reporter, but I see many, many people in the course of a week. Many important people. If the boy died, that's a terrible coincidence. But I can't be held responsible for the murder rate in New Orleans."

"And what about three hundred thousand dollars for a two-year-old filly? I've got a trainer who'll swear she's not worth it."

"The price of a horse is subjective. It depends on what a buyer will pay, on the desires of the market." His smile is laced with condescension; he's on comfortable ground. "The law of supply and demand. As any conservative would grasp."

"Look," I say. "I've got all the evidence and corroboration I need. I can run the piece tomorrow. But I don't have to. If you give me a reason not to."

His laugh is light and angry, a cocktail-party laugh turned bitter. "Is that your clumsy attempt at blackmail? Is that what reporters do nowadays? Because I can tell you right now, you'll get—"

"No. I don't want your money. I don't want anything you've got. But if I could just understand why you did it. If you just had a good reason." I can feel the Olympus's red light winking hungrily against my heart.

He looks at me for an eternity, his face immobile. If his mind is running calculations, assessing risks, it doesn't show.

Seconds tick by. In my peripheral vision, his two minions shift their weight.

Finally he speaks, and his tone is different. Simpler, more honest. He looks at me like I'm a person, not an obstacle to be outmaneuvered. The charm is back. The warmth he radiated when we first met, back when he thought I was on his side. But there's something more, too. A strange, humble look in his eyes. A look of surrender. He opens his hands and leans on the desk in front of him.

"You're in the media," he says. "So I take it you're a liberal?"

"Pretty much, yeah."

He nods. "Then you'll understand. Look," he says. He sighs and massages the knobbed knuckles of one hand with the other. I think of my mother's arthritis—she's roughly his age. Could his hands possibly hurt like hers do? "Global warming is real," he says. "It's caused by humans. By our cars' emissions, our airplanes, our power plants, our cattle ranches—a host of things." He draws in a deep breath. "But my constituents, the people who vote for me, don't believe that. Hell, half of them don't believe in evolution."

I glance at Mindi Manning, her cool eyes, her set jaw. I think of the trailer she came from, its framed Bible verses. I realize how fierce a repudiation of her past this all is, a slap in her father's red face.

"For thirty years now," Senator Claiborne continues, "the bulk of my campaign funding has come from oil companies, and the people who get rich when oil companies get rich. Without those contributions, I don't win in 2010. I'm out. I'm over." He waves his hand around the room. "All this—gone."

I glance at his two aides. Cognitive dissonance jangles in the eyes of the Latino guy. He was not in on this plan.

Mindi Manning's face, though, is flat, unfazed, the face of a good little robot—either because she knew all this already, or because she's disciplined her features to stay neutral under any circumstances, and I wonder when that happened. At boot camp? In Afghanistan or Iraq? Or much earlier, around the dinner table in that sad blue mobile home?

"Okay," I say. "So you can't afford to alienate your base. But—"

"Look. There are some House Democrats in Washington who've been developing pretty solid legislation that would ban drilling in the Gulf. If I'm reelected, I can support that bill when it comes to the Senate. With my credibility as a senior member—as a longtime Republican with a solid conservative voting record, and as a local Louisianan with real, vested interests in the issue—I can make a strong case on the floor. My vote can lead the way."

"But if you don't get reelected . . ."

"Then it won't happen. You know how things work in Washington now." His laugh is short. "Bipartisanship is a dream from the past. If a Louisiana Democrat pushes for anti-drilling laws, no Republicans will follow. It's unlikely that any Republican challenger who wins my seat would support an anti-drilling bill."

I can't believe he's saying it out loud. It's what we all suspect, what we know deep down. What no one in politics will name.

He passes his hand over his eyes, pinches the bridge of his nose. "Look, I'm conservative. But I'm a father, a grandfather. I want my grandkids to have the same Louisiana I had. Same water, same land—same climate, for God's sake." His voice swerves into ragged, pained anger for a moment, then rights it-self. "I want them to have a future."

"And the money from Louisiana Democrats? The horses?"

His smile is small. "It's not much, but it's a promise of more to come. Much more. It sweetens the deal. It signifies loyalty. When the support from my traditional donors dries up, they'll be there."

"So your wife knows about this."

"Lainie knows nothing. Lainie trusts me."

"Does she know you had her stable manager killed?"

The snap comes back to his blue eyes. "I told you. Joe Shorter's death was an accident."

"Come on, Senator. Shorter, Taffner, Cory Brink? Now me? That's quite a body count. Not to mention the breaking and entering of three residences."

He shakes his head, and his eyes are stern. "I'm telling you, I have no idea how any of these incidents happened. Listen. I'm a civil servant, a gentleman. I have a history in this state." His voice rings with pride. "I don't kill people."

I nod. "Okay, sure. But you know someone who does. Someone cleaned up your mess."

The left side of his mouth lifts faintly, and his eyes are amused. "You watch too many movies, young lady."

We all hold our positions, motionless.

Silence is a journalist's weapon. I know how to keep mine. Seconds tick by.

Then the senator speaks. "If there's one thing my party understands, it's the necessity of sacrifice."

"You know how to sacrifice other people, you mean."

"Young lady, I don't think you grasp—"

"Are you saying that the deaths of these three individuals was a necessary sacrifice to stop oil exploration in the Gulf?" Unseen between my breasts, the Olympus is steadily blinking its tiny red light.

"Not exploration. The environmental damage caused by production and consumption, and by the likelihood of drilling accidents."

"So three people had to die?"

"Those deaths were accidents. Coincidences," he says sharply. "But read the climate change reports. Millions are going to die. The future's not pretty. If I could have prevented that, and I failed to act, how would history judge me?"

The room is quiet.

"Go on," I say.

"Listen, the average citizen votes from his wallet," he says, "and the recession is deepening. Your Obama won't fix it. Nobody can. My friends in the oil industry are counting on pocketbook politics to erode any environmental concerns the general population might have. And they're right. We've seen it time and again." He clears his throat. "But I'm a leader. It's my job to think long-term."

I wait. I wait for him to say that if long-term vision includes sacrificing a few foot soldiers, then that's the tough decision he's willing to make. But he's silent. Either he's too smart to go that far, or he really didn't order any hits. Someone else decided to kill Joe Shorter, Jude Taffner, and Cory Brink.

Frost I'm not, and the senator's no Nixon. This is probably as good as I'm going to get.

"So now what?" I ask.

His smile looks pained. "That's up to you, Miss Céspedes. Do you bury this story and let history proceed? Or do you run it, and ruin everything, and waste those lives that have been lost?"

"I believe in your cause," I say. "I do." My breath comes full and slow into my lungs.

Would it be better, all things considered, to let events unfold? To let the senator do the right thing? Breaking the story won't bring anyone back, and it could damn the future of the Gulf.

But I can't know what will happen tomorrow or next week or next month. No one can. We can only act on what we see in front of us. I'm in the hot thick of it, now, and I have to decide. All the pieces are moving fast.

I breathe in and out and in, willing my mind to stillness, emptiness, the focus of the shooting range. I wait, listening. Blood thumps in my ears. And suddenly from within myself I hear a line, a touchstone since college. A line from Graham Greene's *The Quiet American*. A line Jude Taffner used to quote when our stories got too passionate or personal.

"'The job of a reporter,'" I say, "'is to expose and record.' Period."

"I see." The senator's smile doesn't reach his eyes. "Then we are in your hands, Miss Céspedes." His gaze flicks to Mindi Manning and the guy. "I believe you can find your own way out," he says to me, "having found your way in so well."

Pro forma, I thank him for his time and head down the corridor. The marble stairs click under my sandals' heels. By the time I hit the foyer, I'm already framing the story in my head. Through the glass wall that faces Pontchartrain, I see heavy gray clouds about to break.

My hand is on the doorknob when I think of the horses. I step outside. I may not be safe—not until the story runs—but the senator's goons, whoever they are, are unlikely to touch me here, right on his property, his showpiece, with the house and grounds full of staff. Dark alleys and empty parks are more their style.

I've decided I like horses. I like the gloss of them, the way they run. I like their hard muscles that are silky to the touch, and I like the way their eyes are soft and dark but still wild. I like the way they seem free even when they're running in a fenced field.

The stable's only a short walk away. I head toward the open door, my heels spiking down into the green sod. The clouds overhead are low and dark and fat.

Rain starts spattering down on the metal roof as I enter the barn. The door at the far end is a wide square of light, open to the lake. Horses whicker in alarm or greeting, and good smells of leather and horseflesh fill my nose.

I walk down the corridor, sinking silently into the clean, thick mat of sawdust, and stop by a stall where one dark horse is sticking his head out, tossing it up and down on his muscled neck.

"Hey, buddy," I say, reaching out a tentative hand to stroke his forehead. I read the little brass name-plaque. Okay, her forehead. A filly, Martian Girl. I stroke her soft cheek, and she calms. Breath blows out her nose. Her eyelids slide down, her long black lashes with a curl any girl would crave. Her chest shudders with a noise like pleasure as I scratch her long face. I rake my fingers through her forelock. "Hey, girl."

It's peaceful here, and the rain hits harder on the roof. A wet breeze blows in the open doorway and rushes the whole length of the corridor. A good, clean smell. If only things were simple like this. Animal. Natural. Horses hate violence; it upsets them. They won't willingly step on a living creature, unless it's a snake. Peaceful beasts. I lean my face against Martian Girl's velvet nose, and she lets me leave it there. I close my eyes. Maybe life in the hot city reporting crazed crimes is not really my dream. Maybe I could lead a simpler, kinder existence. Become a stable girl.

But I laugh at my own fantasy and open my eyes. One day shoveling shit and I'd give notice.

Not that we don't shovel shit at the *Picayune* on occasion.

I give Martian Girl a final scratch and turn to watch the rain falling in dark sheets onto Pontchartrain. The open doorway facing the lake has darkened with the storm, and the wind that blows through the stable is cool. A sense of ease fills me as the horses whicker and shuffle in their stalls. The rain beats down like a violent benediction.

A quick, soft noise sounds at my back, and before I can turn, a solid wall of muscle hits me from behind.

An arm locks around my throat, cutting my wind abruptly off. No air. My wind clots in my throat.

This is the move that took Jude Taffner down. I know this move. Saw it in the Ninth. It's effective. I've got maybe thirty seconds before the world goes black. Think. Calm.

The arm tightens against my windpipe. Time slows. My legs flail. A horse whinnies. Jude Taffner's hair snakes out in the water.

The seconds are ticking away, but my hand is free, and I grope inside my purse for the Beretta. My hand fumbles across my notebook, my keys.

My strength slips, and something sweeps my legs from under me. Together we hit the soft ground. The impact jars my purse, and objects shift under my hand. The Olympus grinds into my chest. Martian Girl rears and plunges, snorting, her shod hoofs ringing on the walls of her stall.

I'm kicking backward and making contact, but the grip on my throat doesn't slacken. The edges of the world begin to blur, and hatred fills me.

Then cold metal slides into my hand like a jolt of grace.

Flip off the safety, find the trigger. Aim low, hope for the best. There's no trembling. My wrist is steady when I squeeze.

And the crack explodes in the corridor of the stable, and horses rear and snort and whinny in their stalls.

The vise grip falls away from my throat. I gasp, sucking in air. The sweet smell of Chanel No. 5 fills my mouth. The scent in my apartment that night, when I was too addled to place it.

I stumble to my feet, the gun still tight in my hand. But Mindi Manning's no threat now. She lies clutching her thigh as red blood seeps between her fingers, looking up with hard blue eyes.

"Sorry, sweetheart," I say. I pull out my cell and call 911. There's a damn hole through my best leather handbag.

Mindi Manning, her pupils widening now with shock and pain and fear, bleeds onto the curled pink flakes of sawdust.

Bleeds a little too much, maybe. I sigh and pull the scarf from around my neck. How many accessories am I going to destroy? I squat beside her and twist the scarf into a tourniquet around her upper thigh and tie it off tight.

There's a shout, and the Latino guy and the guard from the booth appear in the open doorway, brought by the sound of the gunshot. Maids in their tan and white uniforms come running, their hair ruined by rain, their hands to their mouths as they stare.

The senator materializes, framed in the open doorway, but he keeps his distance. He's on his cell phone already—to his lawyer, probably. Damage control.

I'm crouched down close to Mindi Manning. I think of the

blue trailer she came from, the parents she never sees. Her lips are trembling.

"You're going to be all right," I say, and something grateful happens in her eyes. I kneel next to her in the sawdust and take her bloody hand in mine and squeeze it. It feels just like a regular hand. Warm, smooth.

The same hand that smacked me hard in Soline's apartment. That knifed Cory Brink. That throttled my journalism professor until she died. That steered an SUV straight at a man walking toward his wife with their dinner in a sack, and didn't stop.

Poor little killing machine. "And then you're going to prison," I say.

Her eyes shut.

"Contacts?" I ask.

A weak wrinkle appears on her brow, and her eyes open.

"Did you wear contacts when you came to my apartment? Black contacts?"

Her pupils widen, telling me all I need to know, and then shrink again to black dots in their little disks of blue. "Fuck you," she whispers.

"Thought so."

Her lids close, and we wait like that until the sirens wail and the cops arrive and the damp-haired EMTs pour in with their stretcher and oxygen and carry her away.

The Olympus still winks invisibly at the center of my chest like a tiny flashing garnet near my heart. As the cops are cuffing me, I turn to the Latino guy.

"You know," I say, before they lead me out, "it would be really nice if you told me your name."

His lips part, and he does.

Saturday

24

Rain pours down hard on the boards above us as I sip my iced coffee, listening to Calinda.

Mindi Manning had been raped in Afghanistan, not once but three times, by fellow Marines.

Or so she now claimed. Over there in the heat and sand and chaos, rape kits and empathetic commanding officers were hard to come by.

She'd also been having an affair with Senator Claiborne for the last seven months. Apparently, living in the staff quarters of the senator's mansion was convenient in more ways than one.

To chalk up her murders of Joe Shorter, Jude Taffner, and Cory Brink to post-traumatic stress disorder and a sad case of misplaced loyalty to the senator was perhaps a shade too simple. But that's how the defense attorney was going to pitch it to the jury, according to Calinda, who'd come to see me, full of scuttlebutt from the DA's.

I remember the senator's charm. I can see how Mindi would have fallen for him. That warmth. Those blue eyes radiant with approval.

Senator Claiborne won't get off scot-free. He'll lose his political reputation and a long and lucrative career. There may not be anything direct to pin on him for the murders, just a lot of pillow talk with Mindi Manning about troublesome individuals, followed by gifts—her watch, other jewelry—that happened to show up as love tokens when the individuals disappeared. Or so she claims. He can deny it all. He said, she said.

Maybe all that the general public will remember is his smiling declaration on TV about how he's decided to spend more time with his family rather than run for reelection next year. Maybe they'll remember his wife standing next to him, smiling, or the B-roll footage of his grandchildren romping on that wide terrace by the lake. But now everyone knows about the horses and the promises, because that's the story we ran on the front page of the *Picayune*. The GOP will make sure he's never elected again.

But Senator Claiborne will still have his galloping Thoroughbreds, his money, and his lake view. Mindi Manning, who reached into his life to create the coincidences he needed, will pay with her freedom. For three murders, she'll do a lot of time. Life without, maybe. She might get old in prison—become a husk in an orange jumpsuit, just a different version of her mother's flowered dress.

It hardly seems fair. Senator Claiborne, rich and comfortable, born with the proverbial silver spoon, just assumed that things would fall into place according to his plans, his needs. And they mostly did. Mindi Manning, born into a poor, strict, and possibly violent home, had to grapple her own way up. The military that fought abroad for oil is the same military whose men raped and then ignored her. If she's to be believed.

Maybe all she wanted was someone who'd pay attention—who'd give her, at last, the approval she craved.

I wonder about daughters and fathers, about substitute fathers. How much fathering does a girl need? How much is benevolence, and when does it warp into control? I think of Luke Jourdan, his arm warm and easy around Chloe, hoisting her onto his hip. I think of Marisol and Señor Cruz: his intensifying rules, her frustration and yearning for escape. I think of Mindi Manning and the angry, Bible-quoting father inside that trailer, the commanding officers in the Marines yelling their abuse, and the senator, who needed to have things done, things she knew how to do. With his calm, firm voice, his air of ease, and his radiant eyes, he must have seemed like a dream to Mindi Manning. Everything rolled into one: a cause, a lover, a paycheck, a father who finally praised her.

I wonder if Joe Shorter, crossing that road, was every Marine who ever gave her shit. I wonder if Cory Brink's entitled gaze reminded her of a rapist's. The troubling way she marked Jude Taffner's body—as if it had been raped, as if it were a religious murder—was really a map to Mindi Manning's own pain.

Father figures. I never thought I'd missed one. I'd always been grateful for my mother's unalloyed love, for the lack of division and drama in our little apartment in the projects. She loved me and only me. There was no man she had to please.

Now I wonder if I'm missing something, something essential. How much of my difficulty with men, with commitment, with Bento, stems not just from the rape, as Shiduri Collins believes, but also from having no father in my life?

Calinda and I are sitting outside at Fair Grinds, drinking our iced coffees and listening to the heavy rain. Our hair and shoulders are damp from our last dash up the stairs to Uri's apartment, arms full of hangers and clothes, as thunder rolled and the rain broke. Upstairs in my old bedroom sit stacked cardboard boxes and my suitcase. Calinda spent her Saturday helping me lug it all back over. Uri's brown dog Roux had sniffed everything, licking my hands, his tail thumping against the boxes.

What Uri hadn't wanted to discuss when we met at The Columns—what he'd told me later, after the Manning shooting, when I'd called with all my news, including the break-in at Soline's—was that Brian, who found Uri "too distracting," had moved out. After spending a couple of nights in Soline's apartment alone, jolting awake from dreams of being tied and beaten, I was grateful for Uri's offer to move back home. With the help of a real-estate stager, Soline will use the payout from her homeowner's insurance to refurbish her condo and put it on the market again.

Calinda's talking about the senator's liability and the fate of Mindi Manning, about Jonas Applewhite and Detective Winterson and the sluggish way that justice crawls.

Detective Winterson had called me on Wednesday night. I'd been curled up on Soline's bed, pressing my still swollen lip, rubbing the sore places on my wrists where the cuffs had been, trying not to think about what the apartment looked like. When the phone rang, I started. Jumpy.

"I pulled the file on the Applewhite case," Winterson said. "Talked to Cinelli and Doucet. Separately."

"And?"

"Yeah. Discrepancies in their stories. I should have caught it at the time. I was new then. Dumb."

"And now?"

"Still dumb, not so new." His heavy sigh sailed through the line. "I've put Internal Affairs on it."

Score. "Is this on the record?"

His tone was gruff. "It's going to be, now or later. What the hell. Go ahead."

"Thank you," I said. "Thank you so much."

"Hmmph." He clicked off without saying good-bye.

High in my chest, I felt the little pinball ping of happiness. Lights, bells. The triumph of a win that makes a difference. What I saw in my mind's eye was Mahonia Applewhite, crisp in a new frock from Sinegal, her pocketbook clutched tightly against her side like a battlement, heading into the courtroom.

When I first started the Taffner case and started to put the pieces together, I thought I'd find conspiracies. A cover-up at NOPD that went all the way to the top. A political web of intrigue at the senator's mansion. Instead, I found broken people, moving in selfish desperation, fueled by fear and need. Not the satisfying patterns of a well-designed Machiavellian plot. Something sadder, more human, and more real.

Both of the stories I'd inherited from Jude Taffner had shown me again the recklessness of power, its brutality, its dirty urge to indulge its desires and then cover the evidence. To bury its bodies like a cat buries shit. And they would have stayed buried, too, if Jude hadn't dug them up. Both stories remind me again of just why I became a journalist.

Yet across the country, newspapers are laying off their reporters, and universities are eviscerating their J-schools. The economy, they all say: something's got to go. But journalism? The watchdog of the people? If things don't turn around, it'll end up as a lapdog. Who will expose and record?

How small our legacies can be. Jude Taffner left a couple of unfinished stories, perhaps a few hundred students who'd recall her with varying degrees of appreciation, and a vacant tenure-track position at Tulane. A pretty little shotgun house, a betrayed husband, a child with hair like dark honey.

Each of us: so small. A few ripples, then gone.

I sip my iced coffee and nod at Calinda, who's still talking about the Claiborne case.

But behind my eye contact, I'm thinking about Bento, and couples, about apology and forgiveness, about running away and not looking back.

There's a new number in my cell phone, and the senator's handsome aide wants to meet for coffee. He wants to talk. It could be a great interview, a scoop, an in-depth look behind the scenes.

Or it could be something more.

When he called me, I was quiet. All the things I couldn't say rushed through my mind in a blur of heat.

Coffee would be lovely. Coffee in a warm and low-lit place at dusk would be lovely. Coffee with you would be lovely. You would be lovely. The warmth, the liquid, the lips, the brown, the cream. The blue-black night lowering down around us would be lovely. Us inside warm and talking and pressing the warm rims to our mouths. All of it lovely.

I barely knew the guy, and I was going all Molly Bloom on him. The power of fantasy, I guess. If I'm not careful, I'll end up like Jude Taffner, self-deceived into a love affair with a man who doesn't exist.

What I'd said on the phone was *Maybe.* What I'd said was I'd call back. I'm trying to find a middle path between desire and what Shiduri Collins says health is.

Inside Fair Grinds, Richard and Juliet are bustling behind the counter, talking while they work. A married couple, the owners of the coffee shop. After Katrina, this building was one of the few in New Orleans with gas and electricity. Richard and Juliet let people come here to bathe, talk, cry. They gave away hot coffee and ice.

She smiles up at him, her hand easy on his arm. He says something. His hand grazes her shoulder.

I think of Bento's long brown fingers in the half-light as they shift stone disks around the backgammon board. I think of my own hand, reaching out to make a move.

There's circumstance, and then there's what you do with it.

What to do. How to live.

The truth is, I don't want a double life. I don't want to be Jude Taffner, a workaholic, going through the motions, confiding my desires to a computer. Cheating to get what I need—which, in her case, turned out to be only an illusion after all. I don't want to end up hurting Bento, lying to him like she lied to Luke Jourdan.

A double life's not what I want. But just one life—just one man . . .

Maybe I'm a product of my environment. This whole town runs on desire, on excess, on getting way too much of what's not good for you. The Blakean path to wisdom: *Sooner murder an infant in its cradle than nurse unacted desires.* Around here, no one nurses unacted desires. We act. We lose ourselves in music, in bourbon, in the moment. Desire is the engine that drives us.

Richard and Juliet are still talking, gesturing, their smiles easy and warm as they whisk around behind the counter. A good couple's love can become a shelter, not just for themselves. It can expand to care for even strangers.

Is that what Bento and I could become? A good couple? A shelter?

But Calinda's legal monologue is dwindling to a halt, and I pull my eyes back to hers.

"Nola," she says suddenly, breaking off in mid-sentence, and I'm afraid she can tell I was drifting. I look at her, ready to apologize.

But a veil falls away from her face, the scrim of work and chat and professional concerns. Her hands fumble out across the table toward me. I reach and grasp them with both of mine. Her grip is tight, clutching.

Something's happening, and I don't know what.

"Nola," she says again. She takes a breath like you take a gulp of water. Her eyes, big and dark, meet mine. A tremor shakes her lips. "I'm pregnant," she says.

The rain pours down above us. I hold her hands tight.

I need to be excited for her. I need to push my lips into the smile she's waiting for. She's on the cusp of the most momentous change of her life. It's time to tell her that I believe in her, that I'll be there for her. Because I do, and I will.

But my throat is locked. My heart is spinning and falling inside me. I know what it's like to be a fatherless child in this city. What it means, what it does.

I look into her eyes. She's waiting.

"Oh, Calinda." My voice sounds warm and full, and I hope she can't hear the trembling in it. My lips find a curve. "Now, that's news."

Gratitude

For reading

My husband, James; my agent, Mitchell S. Waters; my editor, Margaret Sutherland Brown; and copyeditor Helen Chin. You made this a better book.

For your research

Lawrence N. Powell, author of *The Accidental City: Improvising New Orleans*; Nathaniel Rich, author of "Jungleland: The Lower Ninth Ward in New Orleans Gives New Meaning to 'Urban Growth'" in *The New York Times Magazine*; Dennis C. Rousey, author of *Policing the Southern City: New Orleans, 1805–1889*; and again, Ned Sublette, author of *The World That Made New Orleans: From Spanish Silver to Congo Square*

For the line about gripping privilege like a baseball bat

Stephanie Elizondo Griest

For your enthusiasm, interest, and support

My wonderful colleagues at the University of Nebraska–Lincoln and all my dear friends, especially the Colemans, Emily Levine, Reza Zaidi, and the usual crew: Alexis and Marco Abel, Emily Hammerl and Roland Végső, Jeannette Eileen Jones and Alex Vazansky, and Julia Keown and Simon Wood

For your love

My family—especially my sweet son, Grey, and lovely Amara. You inspire me.